What transpires when you blend Jane Austen's memorable characters with Sarah Price's distinctive Amish voice? A classic retelling of *Sense and Sensibility* is born—a truly captivating but heartbreaking tale of two sisters who learn the hard way that the road to love is sometimes incredibly rocky and that appearances can often be painfully deceptive. Sarah Price has splendidly brought my favorite Jane Austen tale back to life—a modern-day masterpiece for sure and certain!

—DIANA FLOWERS
SENIOR REVIEWER, *OVERCOMING WITH GOD* BLOG

If you think you already know the story line and every twist and turn in *Sense and Sensibility*, guess again! Sarah Price expertly weaves biblical truths throughout the text—something lacking (gasp!) from Jane Austen's original work! I was amazed that I found myself flipping through the pages as if I had never read *Sense and Sensibility*. Brilliantly executed, Sarah Price!

—SUSAN FERRELL
BLOGGER

# SENSE and SENSIBILITY

# SENSE *and* SENSIBILITY

THE
AMISH CLASSICS
SERIES

# SARAH PRICE

ReALMs

Most CHARISMA HOUSE BOOK GROUP products are available at special quantity discounts for bulk purchase for sales promotions, premiums, fund-raising, and educational needs. For details, write Charisma House Book Group, 600 Rinehart Road, Lake Mary, Florida 32746, or telephone (407) 333-0600.

SENSE AND SENSIBILITY by Sarah Price
Published by Realms
Charisma Media/Charisma House Book Group
600 Rinehart Road
Lake Mary, Florida 32746
www.charismahouse.com

Cover design by Justin Evans

Visit the author's website at www.sarahpriceauthor.com.

Library of Congress Cataloging-in-Publication Data:
Names: Price, Sarah, 1969- author. | Austen, Jane, 1775-1817. Sense and
    sensibility.
Title: Sense and sensibility / Sarah Price.
Description: First edition. | Lake Mary, Florida : Realms, [2016] | Series:
    Amish classics ; Book 4

Identifiers: LCCN 2015045839| ISBN 9781629986593
(softcover) | ISBN
   9781629986609 (ebook)
Subjects: LCSH: Amish--Pennsylvania--Lancaster County--
Fiction. | Austen,
   Jane, 1775-1817--Parodies, imitations, etc. | GSAFD:
Christian fiction. |
   Love stories.
Classification: LCC PS3616.R5275 S43 2016 | DDC
813/.6--dc23
LC record available at http://lccn.loc.gov/2015045839

16 17 18 19 20 — 98765432
Printed in the United States of America

*Trust in the LORD with all your heart, and lean not on your own understanding; in all your ways acknowledge Him, and He will direct your paths.*
—PROVERBS 3:5–6, MEV

*This book is dedicated to my two children, Alexander and Catherine, for tolerating my endless hours of isolation in my office. In many ways they are very similar to Eleanor and Mary Ann. Like the Detweiler sisters, my two children are so similar in many ways while different at the same time. Alex's serious and subdued nature topped with a dry wit is countered by Cat's vivacious appetite for adventure. They balance my life and keep me grounded with their sense and sensibility. No mother could love her children more than I love these two amazing young people.*

# ❦ A Note About Vocabulary ❦

THE AMISH SPEAK Pennsylvania Dutch (also called Amish German or Amish Dutch). This is a verbal language with variations in spelling among communities throughout the United States. In some regions, a grandfather is *grossdaadi*, while in other regions he is known as *grossdawdi*.

In addition, words such as *mayhaps*, the use of the word *then* at the end of sentences, and, my favorite, *for sure and certain*, are not necessarily from the Pennsylvania Dutch language/dialect but are unique to the Amish.

The use of these words comes from my own experience living among the Amish in Lancaster County, Pennsylvania.

# ❦ *Foreword* ❦

THE IDEA FOR this series was a long time in coming. I started to read quite early in life, and my taste for books transcended the typical chunky books that preschoolers are made to read. I confess that my first love was Laura Ingalls Wilder's books, which I devoured practically on a daily basis. To say I was a bookworm would be putting it mildly. Children would take bets on whether I could finish a book in a day, a challenge I won easily on most days.

So my transition to classic literature came at an early age, with my favorites being Jane Austen, Charlotte Brontë, Emily Brontë, Charles Dickens, Thomas Hardy, and especially Victor Hugo. Christmas was fairly predictable in my house. Just one leather-bound book always made it the "bestest Christmas ever."

In writing Amish Christian romances, something I have been doing for twenty-five years, I have always tried to explore new angles to the stories. I base most of my stories on my own experiences, having lived on Amish farms and in Amish homes over the years. I have come to know these amazingly strong and devout people in a way that I am constantly pinching myself as to why I have been able to do so. I must confess that, on more than one occasion, I have heard the same from them: "We aren't quite sure what it is, Sarah, but...there's something deeply special about you."

Besides adoring my Amish friends and "family," I also adore my readers. Many of you know I spend countless hours using social media to individually connect with as many readers as I can. I found some of my "bestest friends" online, and despite living in Virginia or Hawaii or Nebraska or Australia, they are as dear to me as the ones who live two miles down the road.

Well, something clicked when I combined my love of literature with my adoration of my readers and respect of the Amish. I hope that by my creating this literary triad, my readers will experience the Amish in a new way—that they will experience authentic Amish culture and religion based on my experiences of having lived among the Amish and my exposure to the masterpieces of literary greats from years past.

It's amazing to think that a love of God and passion for reading can be combined in such a manner as to touch so many people. I hope that you, too, are touched, and I truly welcome your e-mail messages, letters, and postings.

Blessings,
Sarah Price
sarah@sarahpriceauthor.com
http://www.sarahpriceauthor.com
http://www.facebook.com/fansofsarahprice
Twitter/Pinterest: @SarahPriceAuthr
Instagram: @SarahPriceAuthor

# ❧ *Prologue* ❧

WITH THE HEAVY green shades pulled down to cover the windows, a darkness shrouded the room like a thick and faded woolen blanket. A thin streak of June sunlight, pierced through a small tear in one of the shades and cast a beam of light on the edge of the ageless pine dresser against one wall. The smell of sickness and death permeated the room, adding to the gloomy atmosphere and announcing that the end was inexorably approaching.

A man sat in a ladder-back chair by the bed. His weathered face and somber demeanor added years to his biological age. He was dressed in a plain white wrinkled shirt haphazardly tucked into black trousers held up by old leather suspenders. The room was warm and beads of sweat dotted his forehead. With the back of his hand he wiped at them and sighed.

For a moment it appeared as if his father's breath slowed, so much so that his chest stopped rising and falling. The son leaned over to listen to the labored breathing of his ailing father, who slept in the bed with his head propped up by two pillows.

A look of concern crossed the son's face, his eyebrows knit together as he watched his father and waited. When nothing happened, the chest remaining still for too long, the son bent down and the edge of his graying beard brushed against his father's face, prompting a reaction from the older man. His father gasped for air, and the son sat back in the chair and sighed softly.

Tapping his fingers against the arms of the chair, the son looked away from the bed. His eyes, dark brown in color, scanned the room. The bare walls held nothing of interest to look at: no mirror, pictures, or even a calendar. Even the small square nightstand by the bed was almost empty, the only items gracing it being an unlit kerosene lantern and a tattered black Bible.

"John?"

The man in the chair sat upright. "I'm here, *Daed*," he said softly as he reached out his hand to lightly touch his father's arm. "Right here."

His father moistened his dry, cracked lips before trying to open his eyes. His eyelids appeared heavy, and he struggled to lift them. "Where are you, John?" He raised a shaky hand and reached in the direction of his son.

The chair creaked as John leaned even closer, his weight shifting on the seat. His father reached out for him, unaware of the hand on his shoulder. As John positioned himself over his father, he took ahold of his hand with both of his, grasping it tightly so that his father could feel his touch.

"I'm going home, John." The words came out in a raspy, strained voice.

John glanced away from his father. "Don't say such things, *Daed*."

"*Nee*, 'tis true. God's calling me home." This time his voice sounded more forceful.

He had always seemed fierce and strong, much different from the shell of a man who lay dying in the bedroom that he had shared with not one wife, but two. John, however, only remembered the second. "Rest, *Daed*. You need your strength."

"For what? The journey to heaven?" The obvious reality of the situation could not be denied by father or by son. The end was near, and denying it was futile. What should have been a solemn moment, a moment to share the end of his earthly life and ask his son for prayer, suddenly changed. As if realizing something, the father tried to smile. "Just think, John, I'll see your *maem* again. And my *bruder, ja?*"

Shifting his weight, the intensity of his father's words feeling heavy on his shoulders, John cleared his throat. He didn't like this responsibility of sitting bedside in what everyone presumed was the last day his father would spend with them. But his father had requested that he, as the only son, sit with him for a while. Uncertain what else to say, John merely repeated what he had said before.

"You need to sleep, *Daed*."

"What I need to do, John, is speak to you," his father managed to say in a determined voice. "I may be leaving soon. But you"—he squeezed John's hand with a surprising amount of intensity and tried to maintain his grip as he continued speaking—"you, John, will be left behind to tend to things."

At this announcement John froze in the chair and stared at his father. "What do you mean, *Daed*?"

"This place…this farm. It's yours. It has been in the Detweiler family for generations." He paused and moistened his lips. John reached for the half-filled glass of water on the nightstand to hand to his father, who took it with trembling hands. A few sips seemed to quench his thirst, and he handed the glass back to his son. "But on one condition." He pulled John closer so that his son had no choice but to lean over him and look into his face. "You must promise to do one thing for me. One thing is all that I ask of you for inheriting this farm and all that I have."

John frowned. "*Ja*, of course, *Daed*. Anything."

The old man shut his eyes and this time successfully smiled, his dry lips closing as he did so. "*Gut*, that's what I wanted to hear."

Silence.

When his father made no attempt to continue the discussion, John remained seated. He knew his father was far more contemplative than the rest of the family. It was a trait that had been long admired by the men and women in the *g'may*. When two preachers died within six years of each other, his father had been nominated to accept the position if the lot fell to him. Neither time did his father select the Bible with the white slip of paper in it, the paper that would have been the deciding factor, that would have made him a preacher for the rest of his life. Yet the nominations by his fellow Amish men and women spoke of their high regard for his discipline and righteousness.

Unfortunately, as hard as he tried to emulate his father, John never quite seemed to succeed.

On the other side of the first-floor bedroom door, while he waited for his father to speak about the one promise he wanted from him, John heard someone walking across the kitchen floor. There was a brief pause, as if the person stopped just outside the room to listen, the light from the hallway casting a shadow under the door.

John cleared his throat, hoping the noise would keep whoever was out there from interrupting this private meeting with his father. He suspected that his father had requested him to sit there for this very purpose: to discuss his final wishes. It was a discussion John dreaded but could not deny, for he knew it was important, and he sensed that, most likely, it would be their last.

"John, as my only living son, you inherit everything," his father went on. "But I ask that you take care of my *fraa* and *dochders*."

Straightening his back, John frowned. His...half sisters?

His father opened his eyes and stared at him. "Provide for them so they live comfortably. All of them." He coughed, a racking noise that came from deep within his chest. After a few seconds, he settled back into the pillow, taking deep breaths as if trying to find the energy to continue speaking. "All my money has gone into this farm, John. My savings...it isn't enough for them to live on." His eyes widened and he stared directly at his son. "Do you hear me, John?"

"*Ja, ja,* I hear you, *Daed*." He wasn't certain of how he was supposed to respond. "Of course I'll provide for them. That's what family does."

He didn't miss his father's slightly raised eyebrow.

"I mean, they are my family too," John added, stumbling over his words. "They'll never want for anything. I promise."

The older man, content with his son's pledge at last, shut his eyes one more time and released his son's hand. He spoke no further words as, exhausted from just that short exchange, he fell into a restless sleep, his legs twitching under the white sheets and one of his hands trembling just a touch as it rested on the mattress by his side.

John sat back and watched his father take what appeared to be his last sleep. The labored breathing caused his chest to rise and fall, a continuous movement until he struggled to catch his breath. Each time he hesitated, his son leaned forward, wondering if that breath would be his father's last. As routine set in, John settled down for what promised to be a long afternoon, his mind wandering away from his father and into the lush fields that spread out as far as the eye could see, just beyond the outer wall of that very room.

# ❧ *Chapter One* ❧

JOHN WAITED FOR Fanny to help little Henry step down from the buggy, his son clambering over the folded front seat and stumbling out the open door. His wife didn't catch the child in time, and the four-year-old fell to the ground, rolling onto his back so that dust covered his black pants and white shirt.

"My goodness, Henry!" Fanny shrieked. Grabbing his arm, she yanked him to his feet and began to swat at his clothes in a swift, furious fashion. "What were you thinking, child? Now you are a complete mess."

"He's fine, Fanny," John said in a calm voice.

His wife glared at him, her dark, calculating eyes piercing. "I imagine that's easy for you to say. You won't be the one washing his white shirt, nor will you be the one mending holes in his pants." Returning her attention to the child, she reprimanded him again. "You must be more careful, Henry. And patient! I was standing right here to help you!"

The small boy, his chubby cheeks red and his pudgy hands fighting her swats, looked around at the farm. "*Grossdaadi's* farm is yucky."

Fanny took a step back, keeping a firm hold on Henry's hand, and followed her son's gaze. Those dark eyes scanned the barn and fencing with a critical eye. "*Ja, vell,* this is home now." Her tone spoke of her disapproval just as much as her downturned mouth and wrinkled forehead. "And I reckon it's better than that horrid house we were living in!"

Rolling his eyes, John clicked his tongue and slapped the reins on the horse's back, urging the horse to move ahead and toward the barn so he could unhitch the horse. As the buggy lurched forward, Fanny jumped back, dragging Henry with her.

From the porch, two young women sat on a bench, a wooden crate of corn between them. Both wore black dresses and white, heart-shaped prayer *kapps* that covered most of their brown hair, neatly groomed and pulled back into small buns at the napes of their necks. The older of the two glanced at her sister and noticed the look of disdain in her blue eyes.

"Now, now, Mary Ann," she said softly. "Best be getting used to this."

"Oh, Eleanor!" The younger sister reached down for another ear of corn and tugged at the husk. "*Daed* isn't even passed two weeks yet! Have they no compassion?"

"*Vell*, it is their farm now."

Mary Ann ripped at the corn husk. "Two weeks, Eleanor," she hissed under the breath. "Poor *Maem*!"

Eleanor understood what her sister meant, but she also had enough sense to know that there was nothing they could do about it. Their half brother, John, had warned them that Fanny was intent on moving into the farmhouse right away, even though the *grossdaadihaus* stood open and available to them. Their mother had accepted John's implied request that they move, knowing that she was at the mercy of her stepson and his wife. Besides, with it now being mid-July, the growing season was well under way, and they needed

John's help with the farm. After their father passed away, neighbors had pitched in to help with chores, but that could not continue indefinitely.

So for the past two weeks, the small family of four had focused their grief on cleaning the smaller *grossdaadihaus* and moving their mother's belongings into it. In many ways Eleanor had recognized that the distraction (and anger) seemed to help everyone focus their attention on what they now had left rather than on what they had just lost. But the distraction was over, and now, as Eleanor and Mary Ann sat on the porch watching the buggy's occupants look around, they realized that a new reality had just arrived at the farm.

Both of the women watched as Fanny began walking toward the gardens, a disapproving expression on her face and a bored, distracted look on her son's. Her words carried in the still air, although Eleanor was not beyond suspecting they were spoken just a little louder than necessary for the benefit of anyone who could hear.

"These weeds! Just horrid!" Fanny said to Henry, who wasn't paying the least bit of attention. "And the fencing! Why, a simple paint job would suffice in making at least this part look far nicer!" She shook her head and clicked her tongue as if in great despair.

Mary Ann threw the husked ear of corn into the crate and stood up, turning rapidly to disappear through the screen door into the house.

Alone, Eleanor sighed. Such a time, she thought to herself. How would all of them, especially *Maem*, get through this awkward and stressful transition?

"Hello there, Eleanor!"

John approached the porch at last, an awkward smile on his face. Eleanor could tell he was uneasy by the way he kept touching his beard and averting his eyes. Even though they had grown up together, for their father had remarried shortly after the death of John's mother, they had never had a close bond.

The oldest (and only) son in the family, John always felt a touch of possessiveness over what should rightfully be his. As a child, if any of his sisters received attention from their father, John would make a fuss and rage, his jealous temper tantrums shocking everyone else in the family. As the girls grew and matured, John remained a rebellious child at heart. Feeling sorry for his young son's loss of his own mother, their father catered to John's whims rather than discipline him. Their mother seemed helpless over how to handle her stepson, who answered most of her attempts to both nurture and regulate him with, "You're not my real mother."

Eleanor knew she hadn't been the only one to breathe a sigh of relief when, seven years ago, he had married Fanny and moved off the farm. The *grossdaadihaus* would have been the logical place for John to bring his new bride. Fanny, however, would not hear of living in such cramped quarters, preferring, instead, to remain at her own family farm.

John's departure from the family farm, at the insistence of his wife, had created a void Eleanor had been forced to help fill. Still, the thought of having to listen to Fanny complain about every little thing, from the condition of the house to the smell of the dairy barn, made Eleanor and even Mary Ann willing to step up and help out. So instead of helping on the very farm he was set to inherit, John spent those seven years living with his in-laws and working alongside his father-in-law.

The irony was not lost on anyone that the moment their father passed away—the catalyst for the farm to change hands—Fanny insisted on moving to what she had previously considered inferior accommodations. Of course she had insisted on living in the farmhouse rather than the *grossdaadihaus*.

"Good day, John," Eleanor said in as pleasant a voice as she could muster. "Have you your things, then?"

John glanced over his shoulder toward his wife and son. "*Nee, schwester.* Fanny's hired a company to move them. I reckon they'll be here later this afternoon."

"John!" Fanny called out his name as she approached the porch. "You simply must hire someone to paint that fence around the garden. I'll not be having folks judge me on its appearance!"

"The fence is fine," John muttered, still avoiding Eleanor's steady, emotionless stare.

Clearing her throat, Eleanor forced a smile and looked at her sister-in-law. "I'm sure Maggie could tend to the fence, Fanny. The weather is just right for it."

As if seeing Eleanor for the first time, Fanny's dark eyes narrowed. Her face bore no other expression and her lips never moved to greet her sister-in-law. Instead a moment's silence lingered between them until little Henry lifted one foot and scratched the back of his leg, losing his balance and bumping into his mother's leg. Abruptly, Fanny lifted him back to his feet. "Careful," she warned her son.

He ignored her.

"Perhaps," Eleanor said, "you would like to come inside. *Maem* prepared some fresh meadow tea and sugar cookies for your arrival." She said the last part directly to Henry, a smile still on her face. "I don't suppose anyone here would like sugar cookies?"

"Me! Me!" He jumped up and down excitedly.

"It's not even ten o'clock!" Fanny snapped. "You know there are no sweets until at least the afternoon."

"Just this once, Fanny," John said. "It's been a long morning."

Fanny protested no further, but her arched eyebrow and stern look at her husband spoke of her disapproval.

As they walked into the house, Eleanor gave herself a few moments for her eyes to adjust to the dim light in the room. Fanny took no time to huff and walk over to the shades. With a quick snap of her wrist, she raised each one so that light beamed into the large kitchen and gathering room.

"The heat—" Eleanor started to say.

"Oh, Eleanor," Fanny interrupted. "I prefer bright light, not living like a little mole in the ground! Surely the sun cannot warm this room so much!"

Eleanor bit her lower lip, knowing there was no need for any additional attempts to persuade Fanny. Her sister-in-law's headstrong ways and determination to prove everyone else wrong, or even beneath her, was renowned among Eleanor's family. Instead, she changed the subject. "*Maem* and Maggie have moved into the *grossdaadihaus*. Mary Ann and I are still upstairs, and Henry's room is prepared for him." She watched as Fanny studied the kitchen area. "And we made certain to clean the kitchen extra well."

"*Danke.*" The single word of gratitude from Fanny surprised Eleanor.

"I'll let you get settled, then," Eleanor said, moving toward the side door of the house. "The lemonade's in the refrigerator, and the cookies, under that covered plate." She didn't wait for a response. Quietly, she slipped through the door and crossed the small walkway that connected the *grossdaadihaus* to the main house. For the first time since her mother had moved into the smaller residence with Maggie, she felt a wave of relief instead of resentment. The practicality of moving next door suddenly made a world of sense to her. If only there were enough room for her and Mary Ann! But a *grossdaadihaus* was not meant to be a house for an entire family to reside, just young couples starting their lives together or elderly couples enjoying their twilight years. Only now it would house *Maem* and her youngest daughter, Maggie.

Leaving the main house was hard enough on her mother. While *Maem* had not expected one of her daughters to inherit it, she certainly had not expected her husband to pass so suddenly. Now a widow at only forty-four, *Maem* was also at the mercy of her deceased husband's son from a first marriage. Eleanor knew her mother struggled to remain calm and pleasant while, in the privacy of the kitchen, she had confessed to feeling devastated by this unforeseen change in her situation. But only to Eleanor, her oldest daughter.

Now, in the kitchen of the *grossdaadihaus*, Mary Ann stood at the counter, her arm draped around *Maem*'s shoulders. Eleanor joined them and followed her mother's gaze out the small window, watching as John began dragging several suitcases from the back of the buggy. He disappeared from view, and Eleanor thought that was probably for the best.

"Now, *Maem*," she began. "This is just the way things are."

*Maem* turned away from the window and twisted the white handkerchief in her hand. As Eleanor looked at her, she realized how much her mother had aged in just two weeks. Her hair looked grayer and the wrinkles by the corners of her eyes appeared deeper. So much had happened, with *Daed* falling ill so unexpectedly and then passing away.

To add John and Fanny throwing them out of their home was almost more than a person could bear, Eleanor thought.

"Oh, Eleanor," Mary Ann cried out. "How can even you possibly try to make sense out of this? Why, any decent person would have waited longer."

*Maem* glanced at Mary Ann as she reached over to pat her hand. "Now, now, Mary Ann. Your sister is correct." She returned her tired eyes to Eleanor. "Remember Job encountered far worse trials in his life. *Daed*'s passing, while unfortunate—to say the least—is part of God's plan. We dare not question it, but accept."

"Oh fiddle-faddle!" Mary Ann stepped away from her mother and sister. She spun around, the skirt of her black dress billowing out as she turned. "There is nothing about Fanny's behavior that can be accepted by even the most holy of people!"

"Mary Ann!"

Ignoring her mother's rebuke, Mary Ann continued. "She's about the most self-serving person I have met! And I'm including *Englischers* in that statement! Everything revolves around that little Henry. If she pops one more sweet into his mouth, he may well explode, although she pretends to regulate his sugar intake. Pure hogwash!"

Despite her best attempt to remain stoic, Eleanor failed to hide her smile at Mary Ann's last comment. It was true that little Henry was more than cherubically chubby. He was downright obese from all of the sweets Fanny permitted him to eat, regardless of whether or not she made him wait until the afternoon before having them. "Mary Ann," Eleanor finally said, hoping she sounded more disapproving than she felt over her sister's remark. After all, as the eldest of the three sisters, it was Eleanor's job to act the role model.

Mary Ann waved her hand at Eleanor. "I saw you smile. You know it's true!"

"True or not, there are just some things we should keep to ourselves," Eleanor said, her voice soft and even. "I reckon that would be one of them."

"The true part or the keeping to ourselves part?" Mary Ann asked the question with such a straight face that Eleanor found herself, once again, resisting the urge to smile.

The back door to the kitchen, over near the sitting area, opened and twelve-year-old Maggie slipped inside, the screen door slamming shut behind her. Her hair had fallen from her bun and hung in wisps down her back. With her dirty feet and bare legs, she looked more a tomboy than a future Amish woman.

"Oh, that dreadful Fanny!" she said, her dark eyes blazing.

"Now, dear child," *Maem* said softly. "She is your sister-in-law and the mistress of this house now."

"More like an outlaw than an in-law," Maggie quipped.

Ignoring Maggie's sassy remark, Mary Ann and Eleanor directed their attention to their youngest sister. Between climbing trees and hiding under tables to read verboten books, Maggie seemed to hear the most interesting discussions that she was always more than willing to share with the rest of the family.

"Tell us, dear *schwester*," Eleanor said. "What have you learned?"

"*Vell*," Maggie started, enjoying the attention of her family. She took her time, dramatically drawing out her story. "Seems that Fanny invited her *bruder*, Edwin, to come stay for a while."

"Edwin? To come here?" *Maem* exclaimed, clearly surprised by this news. She began twisting her handkerchief

9

again. "I wonder why. I was under the impression that he's to inherit his own farm on the other side of Route 100. Why should he come stay here?"

Maggie reached behind her mother's back and took two cookies from an open plastic container. She took one bite before she continued talking, bits of crumbs falling from her mouth. "To help John make this farm more efficient." She enunciated the word *efficient*, using the mocking tone of Fanny. "I always thought *Daed* did a right *gut* job, don't you think?"

Mary Ann shook her head, a scowl wrinkling her otherwise porcelain-smooth skin. "Such rubbish! They haven't been here an hour yet and they are changing how things operate? Doesn't seem much to improve on. You feed the animals, milk the cows, clean the manure, and then head out to the fields. Such an addled-brain woman she is!"

This time, *Maem* did not let her comment slide. "Really, Mary Ann. You know there is a lot more involved in operating a dairy farm. I reckon it's rather nice that Edwin is sacrificing his time to help his brother-in-law learn the business."

Maggie wrinkled up her nose. "The worst part is that he's to take my room. Fanny says it's inappropriate for him to stay with Eleanor and Mary Ann on the other side of the house."

Eleanor glanced up and met her mother's eyes. Neither spoke what they thought, about their disapproval of uprooting a child from her bedroom not once but twice, as Maggie had already moved to make way for little Henry.

"*Ja, vell*, I shan't like him," Maggie said with complete defiance. "Especially if he's anything like that mean old *schwester* of his!" She walked over to the kitchen counter and grabbed a red apple from the fruit bowl. "Maybe I'll just sleep in my tree house!" Without waiting for a response, she tossed the apple in the air, caught it, and hurried out the door.

The three other women remained silent for a few long moments, as if digesting Maggie's news. Eleanor knew how Maggie felt; she too wished she could just climb a tree and disappear from Fanny's presence. However, doing so was not an option for a twenty-year-old young woman. Nor would it make the situation go away.

Mary Ann was the first to speak. She turned to her mother, hand on her hip, and sighed. "Really, *Maem*. Must we tolerate this? Now Maggie is to be displaced? Again? It's bad enough that she had to give up her room for little Henry! What honorable and righteous woman would do such a thing?"

Before *Maem* could respond, Eleanor placed her hand on Mary Ann's arm. "We are fortunate enough to have John's help with the farm. At least now you can return to the garden center."

Prior to their father's illness, Mary Ann worked outside of the house, her income a welcome addition to the household. Gardening had always been Mary Ann's passion. She knew all of the flowers and spent her spare time poring over seed catalogs and books about flora and fauna. When springtime began to bud, Mary Ann spent her free evenings in the gardens, creating such beautiful flower beds that, at one point, *Maem* worried that one of their neighbors might complain to the church district's bishop. The last thing that either of her parents wanted was to appear proud and vain. However, the members of the *g'may* had a surprisingly different reaction: instead of complaining, they often sought out Mary Ann's advice on how to duplicate her efforts.

Working for the garden center in Manheim had been a natural, and easily predictable, next step for her.

Since their father fell ill, however, she had been forced to leave her job in order to help with the farm chores. It was a decision made by the entire family, but one that left Eleanor feeling as if she had failed her sister by being incapable of managing the farm without her assistance. While Mary Ann never once complained, Eleanor knew that her sister felt a longing to help people design flower beds.

"Oh, I don't know about that," Mary Ann said, a hint of caution in her voice. "Dare I leave you and *Maem* alone with Fanny? Especially with people still visiting to pay their respects?"

"It will begin to taper off," *Maem* said, the corners of her mouth downturned at the reminder of her husband's passing. "Life must go on."

Eleanor nodded. "We'll handle Fanny, *schwester*. You should leave a message for the garden folks this evening. The sooner you contact them, the sooner you can start working there again."

With nothing left to argue, Mary Ann hurried outside, most likely to use the phone in the barn to call the garden center. Eleanor crossed the room toward the kitchen area and fetched her mother a glass of fresh meadow tea. When she handed it to *Maem*, she smiled. "Everything happens for a reason, *ja*. God's plans are not always our own."

Her mother merely nodded once, and with little conviction, as she accepted the glass of tea and returned to what she had previously been doing: nothing.

# ❧ *Chapter Two* ❧

I DARE SAY, JOHN, giving them money on top of everything else? Haven't you done enough for your stepmother and her *dochders*?" Fanny's voice carried through the partitioned wall of the kitchen and into the great room that separated the main house from the *grossdaadihaus*. It was a large room, mostly devoid of furniture, used only on worship Sundays, quiltings, and special events. The hardwood floors shone from being polished because most recently it had been used for a funeral.

But today Eleanor had wandered into the room to collect a guest book that resided on the built-in bookshelves in the back. She remembered that she had placed it there after her father's casket had been removed from the room by four men and put into the back of a special buggy used to carry the deceased on their final earthly journey to the cemetery. As the men and women slowly departed from the room, Eleanor noticed the guest book on a pine bench. She hadn't wanted anyone to misplace it, so despite her despair over losing her father, she took advantage of the moment to place it on the middle shelf.

Earlier that day, however, her mother remembered the guest book and remarked that she wanted to send notes of gratitude to the four hundred people who attended her husband's viewing and funeral. With so many notes to write, she knew she should get started right away.

Without missing a beat, Eleanor got up from the sofa where she had been crocheting a lap blanket and hurried to fetch the guest book. She opened the door that connected the *grossdaadihaus* to the main house by way of the large gathering room. Without any lights and with the shades drawn, the room was dark. But after twenty years of living in the house, she knew exactly where to walk in order to reach the bookshelves.

That was when she overheard Fanny talking with John.

At first, when she heard Fanny complaining, Eleanor almost didn't pay attention. Fanny and complaints went hand in hand. Just ten days had passed since John, Fanny, and little Henry moved into the house. Ten very long days, Eleanor thought. During that time Fanny made her disapproval of the farm more than clear to everyone and anyone who stopped by. Visitors who came to offer their condolences to *Maem* needed to pass by the main house before getting to the smaller *grossdaadihaus* located in the rear of the building. At times Eleanor had wondered if Fanny stood at the window, waiting for someone to arrive so that she could burst through the screen door to greet them and pull them into her kitchen. Many of them never even made it back to see *Maem*; by the time Fanny was done talking to them, they needed to return home and attend to evening chores.

On more than one occasion Eleanor opted to rescue a visitor. She cringed when she entered what used to be her mother's kitchen. It wasn't just seeing Fanny sitting on *Maem*'s favorite chair. No, it was subjecting her ears to Fanny's harsh criticism about the condition of the farm her husband had inherited. The more Fanny complained, the more Eleanor realized that Fanny's negative comments reflected poorly on Fanny rather than on her and Mary Ann's feeble attempts at managing the farm when their father took ill.

According to Fanny the fence needed mending, the hay cutter needed sharpening, and the population of cats living in the barn needed culling. But when Fanny began criticizing the gardens, Eleanor would politely interrupt and direct the visitor through the large gathering room so that neither she nor the guest would have to listen to any more of Fanny's long list of grievances.

After all, gardening was Mary Ann's forte.

Eleanor seemed to be the main conduit between her mother and Fanny. *Maem* felt intimidated by Fanny's steady stream of protests about the wrongs done to her by having to move to the farm. Maggie refused to go over there, opting to remain with her mother or stay outside in her tree house. And as for Mary Ann, her inability to deal with the idiosyncrasies of Fanny made everyone unanimously agree that she could not interact with Fanny unless it was under the most controlled of situations.

Now, however, as Eleanor overheard Fanny talking with John and realized that her mother and sisters were the focus of the discussion, it was all she could do to remain silent. Truly Fanny tested her each and every day she lived on the farm.

"Your *daed* may have *said* you should take care of your family, but are half sisters really family? I mean, you barely *know* them!" She stressed the word *know*, drawing it out as if it was the worst of words for his situation. "Besides, they'll marry, if they're fortunate, and move off to live with their husbands' families."

"*Ja, vell*, at least Eleanor and Mary Ann both took their kneeling vows last autumn," John said.

"Exactly. They are ready to get married and will do so sooner rather than later, I hope. Let them be someone else's burden to carry."

Eleanor straightened her back and stared at the door that separated her from Fanny's kitchen. She couldn't help but wonder if she had just heard correctly. Had Fanny just insinuated that she and her sisters were not truly his kin? That family should not take care of each other? That once married—if married!—the connection between the family would be severed? The enormity of such a claim spoke volumes about Fanny's character, something that wasn't really in question by her or her sisters. Eleanor waited patiently for her older brother—half brother, she reminded herself—to defend his sisters.

"Fanny, I merely wanted to invest some money for them. We have, after all, saved enough over the past seven years from living with your parents." It sounded as if John might have been reading a paper, *The Budget* most likely, for the crumpling of paper filtered through the thin wall. "And there wasn't much left for them. After all, *Daed* used his savings to upgrade the dairy equipment before he fell ill. We are, after all, the beneficiaries of that investment."

Eleanor waited for Fanny's response. It was true that *Daed* had not known of his illness when he depleted most of his savings to fix the cooling system and to purchase a new diesel-powered milking system. When he had taken ill and the prognosis determined to not be in his favor, Eleanor had learned of the financial straits that faced them.

Everything was gone.

*Daed* was a very successful farmer. Between the dairy cows and crops, *Daed* worked hard and prospered because of it. Learning that *Daed* had not planned for their future shocked Eleanor. It was only with the greatest of reluctance that she spoke to her mother. Between the two of them they knew they needed to scrape together some savings. While they could not replenish what was lost, they managed to save enough for *Maem* to live on for the rest of her life, that was for sure and certain.

The only problem was that she still had three daughters to take care of.

"Beneficiaries?" Fanny set down a plate on the counter, the banging loud and sharp. "Really, John! We'll be working from sunup to sundown just to milk that herd of cows and tend to the crops! While investing some money for them is quite thoughtful and kind—I can think of no other *bruder* who would do such a thing!—the real question is what can we *afford*? Heavens to Betsy, I do not wish for you to leave me in such a situation as your *daed* left them!"

"Perhaps just a small investment, Fanny," John said, his voice sounding exasperated with the discussion. "A small amount of money to help until the girls marry." He sounded pleased with his solution. "That should be sufficient, *ja*?"

"Providing them with the *grossdaadihaus* is more than sufficient, don't you think? I mean, it's not like they need money for running a farm," Fanny scoffed. "That responsibility has landed squarely on your shoulders, if I might say so myself."

"Hmmm."

"And what would giving them money actually do?" Fanny gave a light laugh.

Eleanor did not need to see her sister-in-law. She could envision Fanny's expression, her brown eyes partially shut and her lips pressed together. Since her upper lip was so thin, it would barely be visible. And her chin would be tilted in the air as she spoke in a haughty manner.

"Truly, John, too much money placed in *their* hands and you could have a real *situation*." The way she said the word *situation* made it quite clear to Eleanor that Fanny meant it in a negative way. "As it is, they have so few needs anyway. They only have to pay for food, and certainly they have enough for that. A surplus of money is going to lead to a sense of worldliness that will never attract the attention of any suitors!"

After a brief hesitation, John cleared his throat. "You do have a point there, Fanny."

Eleanor caught her breath. If anyone was worldly, it was Fanny. She was already discussing repainting the house and barn, even though neither needed much more than a touch-up here and there. And she wanted to change the clothesline so that it could be seen from the road, not hidden behind the house. Eleanor suspected she knew why; Amish women liked to secretly compete with each other, trying to be the first person to hang out their laundry on wash days. Some even went so far as to hang out dirty clothes, just so that any passing-by Amish women would admire her work ethic.

*Without doubt,* Eleanor thought, *Fanny is a dirty-laundry hanger, for sure and certain.*

Unaware of Eleanor's eavesdropping, Fanny continued, sounding inspired by her husband's words of agreement when she added, "And it isn't as if your stepmother has any experience handling money. It would be disastrous. Mismanaged money would surely create unnecessary stress in their lives, and that means just one more thing that you'd have to handle."

Eleanor felt the heat rise to her cheeks. While it was true that *Maem* had never handled money, Eleanor knew that her mother was anything but ignorant. Hadn't she been a teacher at the Narvon schoolhouse when she met their father? A smart woman who knew what it meant to work from before sunrise until well after sunset, *Maem* did not shirk at responsibility either. She had always been beside *Daed*, whether it was milking the cows or working in the fields.

"I never did look at it that way," John said.

"And anything you give to them takes away from our little Henry." Clearly Fanny was on a roll now. Her passion for her son outweighed any compassion for others. "What about future sons? We'll have to buy them a farm too, *ja*? If you give money to your stepmother and her *dochders*, why, we'll have nothing left for our boys!"

"Farms *are* expensive..."

Eleanor could listen no more. With her heart beating rapidly and her cheeks burning, she grabbed the guest book from the bookshelf and hurried back to the door that led to the *grossdaadihaus*. She knew she could never tell *Maem* about that conversation; her mother would be horrified at the greed and selfishness expressed by John and his wife. And Mary Ann already had nothing kind to say about Fanny; telling her sister would just add fuel to the fire. No, this was a secret Eleanor must keep to ensure that peace reigned in her small family.

Facing John and Fanny was hard enough as it was. Now, however, Eleanor knew she'd have to work extra hard to hide her true feelings.

# ❧ *Chapter Three* ❧

ELEANOR RAISED HER hand to her brow and wiped away the beads of sweat. Her navy blue dress clung to her body, and she knew that she had perspiration marks under her arms and down her back. It was unseasonably hot, even for late July. The air in the dairy barn didn't move, even with the windows opened as wide as possible. The stench of manure seemed extra pungent because of the humidity. And while she didn't mind the odor so much, the heavy air felt oppressive.

The long row of cows, their heads dipped down to eat the hay in their metal mangers, waited patiently to be milked. Twice a day, once at four in the morning and once at four in the evening. The chore did not take very long with two people doing it. However, after the morning milking, the cows were let out to pasture and the long, concrete aisles needed to be cleaned of manure and dirty hay. Once the barn chores were completed, something else always needed attention, such as the garden (although Mary Ann tended to both the vegetable and flower gardens), laundry, cooking, canning, cleaning...The list of things to do never seemed to end.

It was a long day's work for anyone. And the added heat made the day that much more unbearable. She was glad that it was almost evening. Once the chores were finished, she could enjoy supper with her mother and sisters before retiring to her shared bedroom on John and Fanny's side of the house. Hopefully she could get through the main room and up the stairs without having to exchange niceties with Fanny. Running into Fanny was something she did not look forward to, so she and Mary Ann often tried to figure out when she would be putting little Henry to bed so that they could scurry upstairs and into their room to avoid seeing their sister-in-law.

In the evening hours, after the sun set, the second floor of the main house seemed to cool down. With a cool breeze blowing through the open window, Eleanor found it much easier to sleep at night. *That* was something she looked forward to. But for now, she needed a break from the heat.

"Let me go fetch some water, John," she called out. "I'll be right back."

Without waiting for an answer, she walked around a cow and headed toward the door that led outside. She wasn't certain why it wasn't propped open, so she took an extra minute to find a large rock to place on the ground and hold the door in place. A little extra breeze might help cool down the dairy.

"Hello there!" a voice said from behind her.

Startled, Eleanor spun around and placed an open palm on her chest. "You scared me!"

A young man stood before her, his blue eyes seeming to dance as he stared at her, smiling. "I can see that." He removed his straw hat and held it before his chest, his curly brown hair flopping over his forehead. He was a handsome man in a plain sort of way. Taller than many other Amish men, he appeared willowy. His clothes were perfectly pressed and there was not one blemish on his white shirt. However, she noticed dust on his boots.

Without appearing too forward, the man glanced down at her dress and then her bare feet before he lifted his eyes back to her face. "Hot in the dairy barn, *ja*?"

Too aware of her appearance, including her dirty dress, her messy hair, and the sweat stains under her arms, Eleanor looked away. "Quite," she responded softly.

"A sign of a hard worker is one who works without complaint," the man said. "God favors those who toil while others play."

*A strange thing to say,* she thought, and stole another look at him, wondering if he was being judgmental or sincere. When he smiled, the one corner of his mouth lifting just a touch higher than the other, she saw nothing but admiration in his expression.

"And you are...?"

He held out his hand so that she could shake it. "Edwin Fisher, at your service."

Eleanor couldn't help but notice that his grip on her hand was strong and his skin calloused, an indication that he too was a hard worker, and from the dark color of his skin, she suspected he spent many days working in the fields.

"Edwin Fisher?" she repeated. "You're Fanny's *bruder*, then?"

"*Ja*, that would be me." He withdrew his hand and slid his hat back on his head. "One of them, anyway." He paused. "The eldest one."

"We've met before?" She couldn't recall meeting him at John and Fanny's wedding. Surely she would have remembered such a striking man, even if the wedding was almost seven years ago.

He seemed to ponder her question, taking time to think before responding. "*Mayhaps*," he said. "But you were a bit younger at the time." Again he smiled, his teeth perfectly even and white. "If I do recall properly, you were a bit busy tending to your youngest *schwester*, Maggie." He touched his finger to his lips as if trying to remember something. "Seems like she was quite the handful, if I recall properly."

"Oh!" She felt her cheeks burn. Of course he had been at the wedding! Seven years ago, at thirteen years of age, why would she have noticed a man anyway? Embarrassed that she had even asked such a question, Eleanor looked down at the rock she had just placed by the barn door. "*Ja, vell*, I reckon not much has changed in that category, I fear. Maggie is still quite the handful."

"Ah," he said. "True character never changes, so I should not be surprised."

Eleanor didn't respond. She wasn't certain whether his words reflected personal philosophy from a critical perspective versus a favorable one. When she detected no malice in his words, just a quiet shyness surrounding his observation, she couldn't help but wonder if he truly was Fanny's *bruder*. The contrast between the two personalities was so remarkable that, as she led Edwin to the main house, Eleanor pondered the mystery of how two people born in the same house and raised by the same parents could be so different.

Eleanor suspected that having Edwin around the farm for a few weeks would be far more pleasant than they'd anticipated.

"Why, Edwin!" Fanny was seated on the blue sofa in the sitting area of the great kitchen. She was patching up a tear in little Henry's black pants. When she saw her brother, however, she immediately set down her sewing and hurried to properly greet her brother. "We expected you several days ago, Edwin," she said, a stern look in her eye. "You might have called to let John know you'd be delayed."

"And it is so nice to see you, too, *schwester*," he replied.

Eleanor quietly excused herself and hurried over to the *grossdaadihaus* to alert her mother and Mary Ann of Edwin Fisher's arrival.

"Different from Fanny? Why, that is enough that I should love him right away, then!" *Maem* said shortly.

Eleanor smiled. The last straw between *Maem* and Fanny had been over the family china. Fanny had claimed it far too fancy for *Maem* to have, and since John was bequeathed the farm, that meant he should have the china too. True to her nature, *Maem* did not argue but merely shut down, focused on her mending, and never discussed the subject again. But Eleanor knew that Fanny's selfishness was taxing *Maem*'s nerves.

"I'm quite sure we will like him well enough when we get to know him better," Eleanor responded.

"Like him? That seems a far inferior sentiment, Eleanor, for a man that you say appears to be everything Fanny is not," *Maem* commented wryly.

Later that evening *Maem* and Eleanor discussed whether they should visit the main house to meet him, especially when it became clear that Fanny was not in a hurry to make the effort to provide proper introductions. Maggie, however, refused to join them, choosing to stay in her tree house, for she vowed to live there rather than give up her bedroom to this strange newcomer. And Mary Ann remained resolute in her determination that anyone related to Fanny must have inherited the same self-centered manner. She, therefore, refused to extend herself to the guest.

"Taking a little girl's bedroom," Mary Ann quipped, slamming the silverware drawer so that the spoons, knives, and forks rattled inside the plastic organizer. "What depths of depravity will Fanny go to next? And this Edwin cannot possibly be such a kind man, Eleanor, if he agreed to such an arrangement!"

Eleanor tried to smile. "It's just a bedroom, and it certainly would not be proper for a grown man to sleep with a four-year-old."

But Mary Ann would not ameliorate her poor opinion of Edwin Fisher. An affront had been made against her sister, which, by her logic, was just one more insult to the family. Of course Edwin had nothing to do with the decisions about sleeping arrangements, a fact that Eleanor hesitated to mention for fear of yet again encountering Mary Ann's wrath about Fanny Detweiler.

So when Fanny brought Edwin over to introduce him to the family, Eleanor felt some personal satisfaction. While she too was not a big fan of Fanny, it pleased her to see that her sister-in-law could demonstrate a modest amount of civility.

Maggie, true to her threats, had remained hidden in her tree house from the moment Edwin arrived and refused to descend the ladder even for meals. However, the rest of the small family greeted Edwin with polite smiles.

He was a tall man with narrow shoulders and a thick shock of dark brown hair cut in a traditional Amish style: straight across the forehead and longer over the ears. His face mirrored his body: long and thin. As Eleanor studied him, she could see he was unusual in appearance, and not necessarily in a bad way. His large blue eyes took in the surroundings of the small *grossdaadihaus* without the appearance of disdain

25

or judgment. When he responded in kind to their smiles, his mouth did not spread across his face; instead, just one corner lifted, almost as if he had a tic. For a moment Eleanor wondered if he was nervous to meet them.

"It's very nice to meet you," *Maem* said, extending her hand to shake his. "Quite kind of you to come help John."

Edwin shook her hand and nodded his head politely. "I am rather pleased to assist John," he said, speaking in a proper manner, with the words clipped just a touch at the end. Inwardly Eleanor groaned. Her illusion of Edwin being nervous dissipated. The proud manner of speech would undoubtedly fuel Mary Ann's aversion to Edwin and be the topic of the day at the supper table. "And my *bruder*, Roy, is quite capable of assisting at my parents' farm while I am away."

Eleanor thought she heard a noise of indignation from Mary Ann. When she looked at her sister, Mary Ann merely lifted an eyebrow at her as if to tell her, *I told you so.* And then Mary Ann spoke, her tone sharp and clearly disapproving as she addressed Edwin directly: "Your room is the first room at the top of the stairs."

Edwin looked at her for a long moment, blinking his eyes as if not understanding what Mary Ann said. Finally, he turned to *Maem*. "Ah, *ja*," he said, stumbling over his words. "Fanny had mentioned that I was to stay here." He looked at *Maem* and dipped his head. "With you." Then he returned his attention to Mary Ann. "But, you see...about that..." He lifted a finger in the air and shook it as if making a point. "I do believe that a mistake has been made in those sleeping arrangements."

His words must have shocked Fanny, for all pretense of propriety forgotten, she let her mouth open as she cried out, "A mistake? There is no mistake!"

*Maem* looked from Fanny to Edwin. Eleanor wished she knew what to say so that she could help her mother. But this was clearly a battle between Edwin and Fanny.

"*Danke*, though, for the offer," he said, returning his attention to *Maem*. "While I appreciate the gesture, I believe an oversight has been made. It seems that particular upstairs bedroom is already occupied by another member of your household." He turned and gave a stern look to Fanny. "No one shall be displaced on my behalf. I am, after all, just a visitor to the Detweiler farm. I'll be just as comfortable on a simple cot down in the basement."

"The basement? A cot?" Fanny rolled her eyes and shook her head. "Where you get these fanciful ideas, Edwin, I shall never know!" She didn't wait for a response before she tossed her hands into the air, clearly disgusted with Edwin's proclamation as well as his rebuke. "And to miss the breeze and the view from that window! It is your loss, Edwin. I shall hear none of it when the damp from the basement makes your joints ache in the morning!"

Edwin glanced at Eleanor, a mischievous gleam in his eyes, and winked at her. "Indeed," was his simple reply to Fanny.

That evening, despite Eleanor's previous hopes that she might enjoy a quiet supper with her mother and sisters, she found herself seated next to Edwin at Fanny's kitchen table— or, rather, the family table that Eleanor had sat around for her entire life until Fanny claimed it as part of John's inheritance. Maggie sat on the other side of him while *Maem*, Mary Ann, and little Henry sat across from them. Fanny made a great display of the meal, preparing a freshly killed chicken (which Eleanor had cleaned for her!) with wonderful vegetables from Mary Ann's garden.

Edwin seemed overwhelmed at the attention bestowed on him by his overbearing sister. Yet his manners were refined enough that Eleanor suspected she was the only one to notice how his knee jiggled under the table whenever Fanny spoke.

"Edwin's set to inherit the family farm, you know," she said, her eyes glancing past Eleanor as if she were invisible and not even there. Instead, her gaze rested on Edwin. "Six generations of Fishers! Why, we can trace our ancestors right back to Christian Fisher himself!"

Eleanor feigned interest, especially since half of the Amish in Lancaster County could make the same claim. "Oh, really? How interesting!"

Fanny smiled at Eleanor's comment, mistaking the blandness of her remark to be envy. "Indeed! How many Amish families can do that? I mean, he practically started this entire settlement back in the 1700s!" She laughed, delighted with herself. "Every Amish home has his book. Our great-great-great grandfather."

Edwin leaned toward his sister. "I'm sure there are a few more greats thrown in there, Fanny."

But Fanny ignored his comment. "Why, if Amish had royalty, the Fishers would be it!"

Across the table, Mary Ann's mouth opened as if to speak out against Fanny's prideful remark, but *Maem* nudged her before she could say what they were all probably thinking.

"Ah," Edwin said, setting down his fork. "But we do have royalty, my dear *schwester*."

Surprised that he would side with Fanny on this, Eleanor looked at him.

"Only He sits on the throne of heaven in a kingdom reserved for the righteous who let others praise them, rather than sing their own glories from their own mouths." Without looking at his sister, he reached out, picked up his water glass, and lifted it to his lips. "And even then, the sincerity of humility in humanity is often displayed for the lowest of the low instead of the highest of the high."

Mary Ann coughed into her hand, and Eleanor shot her a look to behave. Fanny, however, had caught the double meaning of his words. With a huff, she resumed eating, and that was the end of any conversation of the direct descendants of Christian Fisher being royalty, in this world or the next.

And with that, Eleanor knew that while she didn't believe in love at first sight, she did believe that she esteemed Edwin Fisher enough to consider a friendship with him, despite her feelings toward his sister.

# ❦ *Chapter Four* ❦

M Y WORD!" MARY Ann unpinned her prayer *kapp* and carefully set it on the small dresser, letting the two thin strings dangle over the edge. There was a mirror on the wall, and as she began to pull out the bobby pins that held her hair into the bun at the nape of her neck, she stared into the reflection, watching Eleanor. "What a dreadfully long evening it was!"

"You say that every evening!" Eleanor laughed lightly.

Mary Ann made a light puffing noise in indignation. "It seems every night we are forced to visit with Fanny now that her *bruder* is here. And that makes for dreadfully long evenings!"

Eleanor was already changed and sitting in bed, the white sheet pulled up to her chest. With the windows open a cool night breeze finally kept the humidity at bay. It was a welcome relief after the past week of hot, sticky nights. It seemed that Edwin's arrival had brought the poor weather. While Eleanor loved the summer months, she had a hard time sleeping during the hot spells. In fact, she was beginning to think that Edwin had chosen wisely when he claimed that a cot in the cool basement was just as suitable as a bedroom.

"Dreadful? I can't imagine why you'd say that," Eleanor said, her eyes avoiding Mary Ann's, even though she felt the intensity of her sister's stare in the mirror. She could tell when her sister was going to go into a tirade. Clearly this was one of those times. So instead of feeding into Mary Ann's drama, Eleanor tried to focus on the Bible in her hands, even though she was too tired to actually read. "I thought the evening was rather enjoyable." Indeed, she'd enjoyed getting to know Edwin over the last week, even though it meant spending more time in the company of Fanny and Henry.

"Really?" Mary Ann practically spun around as she spat out the word in complete surprise. With one hand on her hip, Mary Ann glowered at her. "Enjoyable? The conversation at supper could not have been more dull. Fanny is the only woman I know who can say something and nothing at the same time! And that child of hers is spoilt! Why, he behaves like a complete ruffian! Nephew or not, his constant habit of not listening, interrupting the adults, and stumbling about is enough to grate on anyone's nerves!"

"He *is* a bit of a handful," Eleanor admitted.

"And Fanny making such a fuss over him." As she talked, Mary Ann unwound her hair from the twisted bun and let it fall down over her shoulder. She ran her fingers through it, working out any knots before she picked up the brush. Like that of all three of the Detweiler sisters, her hair was long and chestnut brown with a touch of sun-kissed highlights in the front. Since they, like other Amish women, never cut their hair, it hung down to her waist. However, unlike Eleanor's and Maggie's, Mary Ann's hair hung in loose waves. When she shook her head, it flowed down her back against the white of her nightgown. "She tells Henry not to do something, and lo, he does it! I reckon we shouldn't be surprised, for there is no discipline in that household. None whatsoever!"

Eleanor tried not to smile as Mary Ann slammed her hairbrush onto the dresser and turned around, her hands on her hips. "There is a little discipline," Eleanor said lightly.

"Oh *ja*! From Fanny to John, that's for sure and certain!"

Unable to contain herself, Eleanor covered her mouth as she gave a soft laugh.

"It's true!" Mary Ann moved to the bed and crawled in next to Eleanor, sitting with her back to the headboard. "If only she'd discipline Henry in the same manner, perhaps he'd be more pleasurable to be around. Did you see him at the table playing with his food? Fanny asked him three times to stop, but he just ignored her! Why, *Daed* would have taken us outside behind the barn if we did such a thing to *Maem*! What ails that brother of ours?"

"Half brother," Eleanor added wryly.

Despite having exhausted that particular topic, Mary Ann was not finished with her criticism of the evening. She braided her hair so that it hung over her shoulder as she continued. "And after supper, why, Edwin's reading of *Martyr's Mirror* was so lacking passion and feeling. I don't think I could have listened to much more. Does he have no feelings that he can read that book with such reserve?"

Eleanor laughed, putting her finger into the Bible to hold her place as she shut it. "Oh, Mary Ann! Not everyone reads as passionately as you do! You cannot hold him to your standards, now, can you?"

"Cannot or should not?"

"Both," Eleanor said.

"Seriously, Eleanor?" Shaking her head, Mary Ann expressed her displeasure. "*Martyr's Mirror*? How could anyone not feel admiration and ardor for the suffering of our ancestors? How much they sacrificed for our freedom to worship! It is our duty and honor to read their stories with as much enlightenment and emotion as possible." She pressed her lips together disapprovingly. "Your Edwin's reading made it seem so...ordinary!"

"He's not *my* Edwin, and you embarrassed him," Eleanor said softly. She could still see him in her memory, glancing up at her when Mary Ann interrupted him during his reading. "Making him repeat lines and try to sound more excited. More heartfelt and emotional. His patience with your criticisms, and the fact that he even wanted to read out loud when no one else volunteered, should speak enough for his fine character, *ja*? No one else read, nor would they, after you scared them with your tireless instructions on how to properly read *Martyr's Mirror* to honor our ancestors."

"Fine character?" This time Mary Ann rolled her eyes. "Is that all you can see in him, then? Fine character?"

Eleanor paused to contemplate her sister's questions for a moment. What exactly did Mary Ann want her to see? Or, more importantly, what did she want her to say?

Ever since his arrival a week ago, Edwin had been nothing less than helpful and pleasant to everyone on the farm, especially the Detweiler women. Always respectful, he deferred the authority of the farm to *Maem*, asking for her permission when he felt it was needed, a fact that infuriated Fanny, who took to pointing out that the farm belonged to her and John, not *Maem* anymore. One day Eleanor overheard him chastising Fanny for saying such a thing. He reminded his sister that *Maem* and her daughters had just lost the most important man in their lives and now their world was upended.

She felt a bittersweet fondness for his protection: glad to have it but wishing it wasn't needed.

Even Maggie liked him, especially when she had learned that she need not give up her room to accommodate his visit. Several times Eleanor had seen Edwin climbing up the ladder to sit in the tree house with Maggie. When Eleanor inquired as to what they discussed, the answer was always the same: animals. Maggie's love of animals was well matched with Edwin's knowledge of them.

While *Maem* tried to find excuses not to join John and his family for supper, Edwin always found *Maem*'s door open for him to visit for coffee and dessert afterward. He was admittedly reserved and quiet, offering his opinion only when asked, but Eleanor found nothing inappropriate about that. In fact, when *Maem* inquired about his future, a question that shocked Eleanor and delighted Mary Ann, he managed to smile and reply with a soft "God's plan for my future is yet to be seen, isn't it, now?"

Both Mary Ann and *Maem* were visibly disappointed in his response while Eleanor secretly cheered. Good for him, she had thought, to not get swept into a web of speculation about something he could not control. Only God could determine their futures. Both Eleanor and, she suspected, Edwin knew that her mother was inquiring for the sole purpose of finding out what his intentions were in regard to Eleanor. After just one week his favor toward Eleanor was apparent, even if he did remain properly aloof and formal when it came to expressing any interest in her.

Eleanor would have expected nothing less from such a man. His disposition was, indeed, impeccably Amish in nature, and she respected that.

Of course Eleanor would not share such private thoughts with her sister. So, instead, she responded with a more vague answer. "A man of fine character is the foundation of all other virtuous traits, *ja*? Without the one, you cannot invite others...at least not those of a godly nature. And frankly I've had numerous opportunities to work alongside him, both in the dairy and in the pasture. I find him to be rather interesting. He's certainly well versed in Scripture, and that's quite admirable."

Mary Ann stared at her. "Scripture? Have you nothing else to talk about with him?"

"Is there anything more important than Scripture?" Eleanor countered with an air of reproach.

"Oh, Eleanor!" Mary Ann shook her head, clearly disapproving of her sister's comment. "You know what I mean. What do you know about Edwin? His likes? His passions? His hopes for the future? Do you know any of these things?"

"*Nee, schwester*, I do not. But I do know that I am"—she hesitated, then admitted—"rather fond of him." Deep down, however, Eleanor did know what her sister meant. But she wasn't comfortable telling Mary Ann how Edwin's quiet manners and insightful thoughts made her feel. No Amish woman would dare to confide, even in her sister, that a man's very presence made her heart quicken and her senses tingle. And she certainly wasn't going to mention the private conversations she shared with Edwin in the early morning hours while milking the cows, long before the rest of the household awoke.

Courtship among the Amish community was not as open as Mary Ann obviously desired. In fact, as far as Eleanor knew, most Amish courtships were kept private until the time came to marry. While she sensed that Edwin shared her opinions and emotions, she did not feel confident in expressing this thought aloud. He had made no attempts to take their friendly relationship a step further, such as asking her to ride in his buggy or seeking out her company without others around. To speculate about his intentions would be far too painful if she learned that he was, indeed, just a kind, friendly man.

With an overly dramatic sigh Mary Ann turned to confront her sister. "I've noticed how much attention he pays to you, Eleanor. And I dare say that you don't seem to mind it, although I hope that he too can sense your fondness for him. I'd feel much more accepting of a match between the two of you if I felt that there was something stronger than only reciting Scripture to bind your heart to him."

Eleanor watched as Mary Ann picked restlessly at her braid. She was a pretty girl; Eleanor would not deny that. But she had read one too many romance novels when she was younger, sneaking them from the local library without *Maem* and *Daed* knowing about her thirst for love stories. Ever since she turned sixteen and began attending the youth gatherings, Mary Ann seemed quite the authority on courtship, even though she refused the two young men who offered to drive her home from the singings.

"If he pays any attention to me at all, Mary Ann," Eleanor finally responded, "it is because he is polite and kind. There is no courtship or 'match' between the two of us."

Pulling her knees to her chin, Mary Ann turned and smiled at her sister. "Oh, but I'm sure that a match is there, Eleanor. At least a delay in you recognizing it means that I can enjoy more time with you before he whisks you away to that Fisher farm down in Narvon." She lightly pushed

Eleanor's shoulder. "I hate the idea of you moving so far away!"

At this, Eleanor gave a soft laugh. "I can assure you that you are mistaken, Mary Ann. I am not moving anywhere with anyone, even if I do have high regard for Edwin Fisher."

"Aha!" Mary Ann leaned over her sister, her long braid brushing against Eleanor's shoulder. She pushed her face into Eleanor's, her blue eyes searching her sister's. She smiled mischievously, as if she had caught Eleanor in a trap. "I knew it! From fondness to high regard! Why, Eleanor, if we keep talking about this, *mayhaps* you'll actually admit that you care for him!"

But Eleanor would disclose nothing further and turned onto her side. "Tomorrow's a long day, Mary Ann," she said, hoping that her cheeks did not display her true emotions. "Outen the lantern and go to sleep."

"Perhaps I too shall have a high regard and fondness for Edwin Fisher," Mary Ann said lightly, "when I get to call him *bruder!*"

Eleanor lifted her head from the pillow and gave her a sharp look. The last thing she wanted was for anyone to cause gossip that would embarrass both her and Edwin. "That's enough, Mary Ann. The light!"

Even after Mary Ann huffed and blew out the small lantern, Eleanor stared into the darkness and wondered at her sister's words. She could not deny that she felt a fondness for Edwin. He was everything that Fanny was not: kind, thoughtful, compassionate, and selfless. A match, however, seemed unlikely. After all Edwin Fisher was to inherit a large farm that had been in the family for generations. While he needed a wife who could help him, the practical reality of the situation was that he would find that wife in his own *g'may*, likely a young woman familiar with large-scale farming. In fact, because courtships were kept secret, Eleanor suspected that he might already be courting someone who fit that very description.

All the more reason, then, to be sensible and guard her heart. So why did she fear that her fondness and high regard might soon cross over into territory infinitely more dangerous?

## ❧ *Chapter Five* ❧

"C OME WALK WITH me," Edwin said softly.

Startled, Eleanor looked up and saw him hovering over her shoulder. She hadn't heard him approach her. For a Sunday afternoon in mid-August the weather was perfect for sitting on the porch with her Bible on her lap. She had just been reading Psalms and pondering a particular verse. When she heard his voice in her ear, she briefly wondered to whom he spoke. When she realized that no one else was nearby, she started. "A walk?"

He smiled and reached for her Bible, gently taking it from her hands. After carefully marking her place with the red ribbon that hung from the book's spine, he closed it and set it on the small plastic table next to her chair. "*Ja*, a walk. When two people stand next to each other and their legs move them forward, at which point they can exchange a bit of dialogue and camaraderie? You are familiar with this, *ja*?"

She laughed at his joke and stood up. When he reached out for her elbow to assist her down the porch steps, his gentle touch on her arm made her feel light-headed. She had never been touched by a man, and the fact that her flesh warmed beneath his hand made her remember the conversation she had with Mary Ann just a week ago in the privacy of their bedroom.

While Eleanor continued to silently harbor her high regard for and fondness of Edwin, she also recognized a new feeling, one that seemed to swell up and fill her with an overall sensation of warmth whenever she saw him. She kept her expectations low and her public relationship with him as innocent as possible. The last thing she wanted was to speculate over his friendship or have people gossip about her, especially if she was mistaken in regard to the extent of his attachment to her.

Earlier that day they had attended worship service at the Lapps' farm just down the lane. As usual Eleanor had walked to the service with Mary Ann and Maggie. *Maem* stayed home, her allergies getting the worst of her. Eleanor suspected that allergies had nothing to do with her mother's absence since she had never before demonstrated an allergy to summer's ragweed. Still, she understood why her mother didn't want to attend, so she hadn't made a fuss. After all, like the rest of them, her mother was still mourning for the loss of her husband. No one would dare question why she had remained home instead of attending service.

Worship services were held every two weeks, and the location always rotated. This Sunday the service had been held in the large workshop over the Lapps' barn, where the cool morning breeze quickly changed to thick humidity. As the three-hour sermon continued, Eleanor felt as if her dress clung to her body, and she knew that beads of sweat formed on the back of her neck and knees. Fortunately the post-service fellowship had been moved outdoors so that everyone could benefit from the shade of the large oak trees and the cool breeze from the brook that cut through the nearby pasture.

She hadn't been able to talk with Edwin either before or after the service. She knew that he had ridden along in the back of John and Fanny's buggy, little Henry seated on his lap. When the buggy passed the three Detweiler women who were walking along the side of the road, Henry had stood on the backseat of his parents' buggy, leaning on Edwin's shoulder and waving out the open window, his hand already sticky from eating something pink that morning.

During the worship service at the Lapps' farm, Eleanor focused on the hymns and the sermons, not on the men who sat on the right side of the barn. They were all dressed the same: black trousers, white shirts, and black vests. The bland sea of black on the right side was balanced by the black dresses worn by the women on the left. The only splashes of color were the dresses that the unbaptized children wore. Once or twice, she let her eyes wander and caught sight of Edwin sitting against the far wall and facing the center of the room. With so many people at the worship service, and seated between them, Eleanor could hardly see him beyond the side of his face which was turned toward the man preaching in the center of the room, pacing back and forth between the men's side of the room and the women's side.

As usual the worship service was broken into three parts: singing, preaching, and praying. Three hymns were sung, two sermons were preached, and one long prayer was prayed. Occasionally the unbaptized members would be excused at the end so that an announcement could be made that impacted the church district. Today was not one of those days.

Eleanor enjoyed both the sermons and the singing. She had listened attentively to the preachers as they spoke about the dangers of worldliness, and she participated energetically with the *g'may* when they sang. For Eleanor the three hours spent at worship were a time to meditate and clear her mind while reflecting on God, not to fall asleep or watch other people, although she knew that Mary Ann was prone to nodding off while Maggie often fidgeted.

Once the service ended Eleanor had been far too busy helping the other women with serving food and replenishing drinks to think about Edwin. The men tended to keep to themselves, sitting at their own tables, and when the meal was over, they disappeared outside to catch up on the latest community news. The women, however, served food, cleaned dishes, and when all of the members had eaten, spent their time visiting with each other. By then most of the younger men had already left, either to socialize with their own friends or to take a much-needed nap at home.

Though Eleanor had not seen Edwin much during the service, now he stood by her side, protectively holding her elbow much longer than need be as he walked slowly beside her down the dirt path that ran between the cornfields.

"A right *gut* service today, *ja?*" he asked, a nonchalant tone in his voice. She wondered if he was quizzing her or just making idle conversation.

"*Ja*, it was," she responded. And she meant it.

"'Blessed is everyone who fears the LORD; who walks in His ways. For you shall eat the fruit of the labor of your hands; you will be happy, and it shall be well with you. Your wife shall be as a fruitful vine in your house, your children like olive shoots around about your table,'" he quoted from Scripture.

Eleanor delayed her response, uncertain what, exactly, to say. While she had paid attention to the sermon, she certainly had not memorized any particular passage. Instead, she had focused strictly on the message: follow God's Word. The verse Edwin had recited to her summed up everything the preacher said. How had she missed the most important aspect of the worship service? The very key to happiness as God intended for His people?

Edwin must have sensed her conflicting emotions, so he spoke for her. "I feel that is the secret to life, Eleanor. Don't you?"

"The secret?" She paused as if thinking about that word in the context in which he used it. "Is there truly such a thing as a secret to life, then?"

He nodded his head, his black hat, worn only on Sundays and for other special events, bobbing so that he reached up to steady it. "The Bible gives us such explicit instructions. I wonder that more folks do not follow them. It is the owner's manual for living during our short stay here on earth."

She took a few steps, pondering his words. "I reckon you have a point, Edwin. If we fear the Lord and follow His ways, the Bible tells us we shall never want for food or happiness."

"Exactly!" He seemed pleased with her, walking a bit farther by her side and staring ahead of them.

She wondered what he was thinking, for his mind was clearly in a whirl. He was a deep thinker, one of the things she found admirable about him. While he thought deeply, he spoke only when he felt it was important. Some Amish men spoke frequently to maintain the appearance of being a deep thinker. The reaction from those listening was often the reverse of what they wanted.

"Of course," she said, careful to speak slowly so she did not appear too proud, "what one person considers as 'walking in His ways' is not always the same as another. If a person is not happy and well, is it because they do not fear and walk with God? Who determines whether the Amish way is the right way or whether the Mennonite way should be followed? Or perhaps even the Lutheran, Jewish, or Catholic way?" She shuddered at that idea. "If each group believes that God spoke to them, which way of thinking and living is the right way? I cannot imagine God could choose between people based on one or two rules that differ among religions, especially if, in their hearts, the people sincerely worship him."

Edwin smiled, a reaction that startled her. She hadn't meant to be humorous or mocking and certainly hoped he did not take her question in such a manner. When she heard his next words, she felt immediate relief.

"I expected no less from you, Eleanor. Your ability to ask the very questions that linger in my mind make me believe you have stepped inside my head!"

"Oh now, I would never do such a thing as invade your thoughts, especially if they reside only in your head. I would give you much more privacy than that," she quipped, to which he laughed. "But I do wonder why the wife is by the sides of the house and the children around the table. I don't think I would like to be outside looking in at the rest of my family."

This evoked more laughter from Edwin. But he did not comment on her observation. Instead, they walked in silence once more, but the quiet held a new aura of understanding, respect, and even intimacy, a change that Eleanor was not opposed to welcoming.

# ❧ Chapter Six ❧

Dear Cousin,

We were saddened to learn of Henry's passing but rejoice that he is now with God in a better place. Remember Ecclesiastes: "A good name is better than precious ointment, and the day of death than the day of birth."

Frankly, while we were disheartened to learn that you were removed from the family home so suddenly, it did not come as a surprise. There are righteous people and then there are others.

Your husband was a very righteous man and helped many people during his lifetime. In fact, he once helped my own father-in-law who was, I believe, a distant cousin of his own. I should like to repay your husband's kindness by offering you the very life-right that has been taken away from you by your stepson, John. There is a cottage on our property, modest in size but large enough to accommodate you and your dochders. It has not been occupied for a while and will need some work. But remember that "in all labor there is profit." I believe that you and your dochders should benefit greatly from starting a new life in a new location. Besides, my mother-in-law and my fraa are quite certain that your company on our farm will add greatly to their daily joy.

Please correspond soon regarding the cottage so that I can know to have it cleared from debris and rubbish.

Your cousin,
Jacob

Eleanor set down the letter and raised her eyes to stare at her mother. "I'm not quite certain I understand this, *Maem*." She had known that her mother suffered with the arrival of Fanny, but she hadn't realized how much until this moment. "You wrote to your cousin and told him you wish to move?"

*Maem* nodded her head emphatically. "*Ja*, I did."

"Whatever for?" Eleanor frowned and glanced at the small, tight writing on the letter. "We do not even know this man." She reached for the envelope and flipped it over so that she could read the return address. "And to Quarryville? That's so far away!"

*Maem* stood up and walked to the kitchen counter. She stood there for a moment, her back facing Eleanor, and stared at nothing. At last she took a deep breath and turned around. "Eleanor," she said, "these past weeks have been simply awful. I'm a stranger in my own home, an unwanted guest at best. This is a time of great change and sorrow, and I need my family around me. I cannot stand to have my *dochders* separated...and miserable."

Her mother had finally spoken what everyone else certainly thought. The move from the main farmhouse to the smaller *grossdaadihaus* had been as traumatic as Eleanor had expected.

To begin with, only Maggie could move to the small *grossdaadihaus* house with their mother, for there were only two bedrooms, and the one was too small for more than a single bed. That meant that Eleanor and Mary Ann needed to remain in the main house, living alongside Fanny, John, and little Henry. The family was, indeed, separated. If that wasn't terrible enough, Fanny continued to do everything in her power to ensure that Eleanor, Mary Ann, and their mother knew how unwelcome they were, even if, on the surface, no one could fault her manners.

And that made everyone miserable.

Why John and Fanny had not occupied the *grossdaadihaus*, the two bedrooms certainly more than enough room for their small family of three, was the unspoken question that lingered in the air. To displace *Maem* and her daughters so soon after their father's death seemed callous and cruel. But no one would dare to complain, even though Eleanor suspected that more than a few people in the *g'may* had gossiped that Fanny had forced out the Detweiler women. Regardless of what people thought or said, there was little recourse, for the farm was, after all, John's rightful inheritance, and as such, they had the right to live there, even if it meant the insensitive removal of its previous residents.

"We aren't truly separated, *Maem*," Eleanor reassured her. "It's only in the evenings that Mary Ann and I return to their side of the house. And we are just fine sharing a room. As for Maggie, I'm sure she is much more comfortable with you than over at the other side of the *haus*."

Clearly *Maem* was not finished expressing her feelings, for she went on, ignoring Eleanor's reasoning. "And then there is that Fanny! Why, she is just too much! She complains over everything about the farm. She might have delayed her move if she thought so poorly of the place." *Maem* paused and let her shoulders droop. "Your *daed* worked so hard on this farm. All of her complaints are simply an insult to his memory!"

Eleanor wished there was something she could say to make her mother feel better. The truth was that she felt the same about Fanny. Earlier that very day Fanny had made a fuss over the antiquated style of the downstairs bathroom.

She insisted that John find someone to replace the toilet and sink, claiming that there was no amount of scrubbing that would remove the stains on the porcelain. At the time Eleanor wished she could point out that the stains were from the well water and not poor cleaning on the part of her mother. However, Edwin had spoken up and addressed the matter, telling his sister that an old porcelain sink, stained or not, certainly did its job as well as a new one and with 100 percent less the cost.

"I'm sure that she wishes John provided a more contemporary home," Eleanor conceded. "But that isn't a reason to move, *Maem*. This is, after all, our home."

"Is it, Eleanor?" *Maem* gave her a look that indicated she felt otherwise.

It was true that Fanny was taking over the farm. She had even ripped up some of Mary Ann's perennial gardens since to her mind their colorful display seemed far too prideful. When Mary Ann returned from work, she almost cried upon seeing the destruction. Many of the plants had been collected throughout the years from friends and family, both near and far.

Another blatant affront to the family was when Maggie's climbing tree had been cut down. Fanny claimed it blocked her view from the kitchen window. But Eleanor suspected that Fanny feared little Henry would try to imitate Maggie and climb the tree. If he fell and was injured, Fanny would be inconvenienced, as it would be her responsibility to tend to his needs.

*Maem* sighed. "It's bad enough that we've been displaced from our home, but I know for a fact that your *daed* requested for John to take care of us. It was his last wish before he died."

Eleanor tried to remain stoic. The memory of Fanny complaining to John still lingered in her mind. She knew better than to share that information, so rather than respond to her mother's heartbreaking confession, she chose to remain calm and say nothing.

Her mother did not need any fodder to continue. She appeared to have enough to complain about without Eleanor adding more fuel to the fire. "As it is now," she continued, "we are living like paupers and working like slaves. For what? The right to live in our home? Separated from each other? And what do you think will happen when Edwin leaves? You'll be back to working like a man in the dairy and fields, and what kind of life is that for you? And Mary Ann? She'll have to cut back her hours at the garden center, for sure and certain, especially when Maggie returns to school. I can't do all of the gardening and chores by myself."

Eleanor could argue nothing on behalf of Fanny. While she knew there were two sides to every story, in this case, Fanny had left no room for compassion. Still, Eleanor couldn't make sense of her mother's comments. To leave the *grossdaadihaus* to move somewhere else would certainly mean more expenses for the family. There was something else amiss.

"Please tell me what is truly bothering you, *Maem*," Eleanor coaxed softly. "It's better to air it all now than to let it fester like an uncleaned wound, *ja?*"

*Maem* stood up from the table and began to pace the kitchen floor, wringing her hands before her. Whatever was bothering her, Eleanor suspected it had been building for quite some time. "You know your *daed* did not leave his estate properly prepared. He told me that John was to give me some money and instructed me on how to live off the interest. Fanny must have learned about it, for John has not held true to his promise to your *daed* on his deathbed. She probably thinks having us live here in the *grossdaadihaus* is more than enough."

Holding her breath, Eleanor waited for her mother to continue rather than comment on what was already spoken.

"And truth be told, Eleanor, I just cannot take one more second in her company. I know I should love my neighbor, and I pray myself to sleep that I can find it in my heart to do so. The airs that she puts on! It's a wonder the bishop hasn't caught wind of it and spoken with John. I'm sure that will be coming soon."

The door opened, and on glancing over her shoulder, Eleanor saw her sisters approach them. Both of their cheeks glistened and Maggie was out of breath. From the glow on their faces Eleanor knew they must have been out walking, something Mary Ann often wanted to do, almost always dragging Maggie alongside her.

"Such serious faces!" Mary Ann said as she walked to the kitchen sink carrying a basket of tomatoes from her garden. She set it on the counter and walked over to the sink to pour herself a glass of water. "I hope nothing has happened."

Eleanor sighed. "*Maem* wants us to move."

Mary Ann gasped, and Maggie jumped in the air, cheering at the news.

"Maggie, calm down," *Maem* said, a gentle reprimand to remind her youngest daughter that she was not only indoors but behaving like a hooligan.

Mary Ann laughed. "Oh, *Maem*! Don't stop her! If I wasn't almost eighteen, I'd jump and cheer too!"

"And you'd be scolded just the same!" But *Maem*'s eyes glowed, most likely from the enthusiasm displayed by both daughters.

Maggie reached out for Mary Ann's cup and refilled it with water for herself. When she finished, she dropped the cup into the sink and skipped over to the table. "Where shall we live, then? Shall we move to Indiana? Or what about Colorado? Doesn't that sound so exciting?"

"With that Troyer fellow's settlement?" Mary Ann made a face. "There's only thirty or so families there, Maggie. And *The Budget* stories make it sound rather dull. Hardly any visitors and certainly not a lot of suitors... or friends, in your case... to pick from."

"Colorado! Whatever would make you think of that?" Eleanor smiled as Maggie slid onto the chair beside her.

A simple shrug was the only response. But Eleanor knew the root cause of Maggie's suggestion. She loved studying geography, often drawing her own maps of the farms in their neighborhood. When school was in session, she often asked to borrow the teacher's atlas and had even requested permission to bring it home over their summer break. She loved to listen to Mary Ann or *Maem* read *The Budget* newspaper and then find on the maps the different Amish communities mentioned there.

Colorado seemed exotic and exciting to the twelve-year-old. But Eleanor agreed with Mary Ann. Without a farm or vocation, they would have few options for making a living there, and since everything was spread out, it would most likely be rather dull.

"You're going to have to hitch your horse a bit closer to home, Maggie," Eleanor said. "*Maem*'s cousin has a cottage that is sitting vacant on their property." She lifted the letter from the table and held it out for Mary Ann to take. "They live south of Nickel Mines."

Mary Ann hesitated, as if digesting this news, before she took the letter. "Quarryville?" Her eyes scanned the letter. "That's quite far from Manheim, almost fifty miles, ain't so?"

Maggie reached for the letter. "Where is Quarryville anyway?" She didn't bother to read it after Mary Ann handed it to her. "Will I have to go to school there?"

"*Ja*, silly goose!" Eleanor nudged her with her elbow. "You have two years left."

Groaning, Maggie flopped forward and rested her forehead atop the table.

"When are we to move, *Maem*?" Mary Ann asked.

"As soon as possible. School starts the first week of September, and it's better to start fresh," she said, her lips pressed together firmly, "and with family that genuinely wants us."

Later that evening, as both Detweiler families and Edwin sat around the picnic table enjoying a family meal together, *Maem* made the announcement. It was met with mixed reactions. Eleanor kept her eyes on her plate, her appetite having fled even before she dished food onto it. While the rest of the family enjoyed the fried chicken, corn salad, and sliced tomatoes, fresh off the vine, Eleanor had merely picked at her food, dreading the moment when her mother would share the news.

That moment was now.

Edwin dropped his fork and turned to look directly at Eleanor. "Moving? To Quarryville?"

Fanny, however, seemed rather pleased. "I think a cottage sounds quaint, don't you, John?"

"Quaint, indeed." He nodded his head and took another bite of food.

"And when will this move take place?" Edwin asked. He continued to stare at her, a concerned look in his eyes. "Autumn? Winter?"

"Sooner than that, I'm afraid," *Maem* responded. "Maggie needs to be settled in for school, and as it stands, we have imposed on your sister Fanny long enough."

At the mention of her name, Fanny glanced up, apparently not noticing the edge of sarcasm in *Maem*'s voice.

"I'm...I'm sure it's no imposition at all." He looked at his sister and gave her a stern look. "Right, Fanny?"

"I certainly would understand if they'd like to get situated before the winter months," Fanny responded. "Especially if the cottage is available now. It might not be available in a few months' time, *ja*?"

Edwin looked as crestfallen as Eleanor felt.

"You are all invited to visit us," *Maem* said, addressing both John and Fanny. Without even giving them time to respond, for they all highly doubted that either one would ever visit, *Maem* shifted in her chair to look at Edwin. "You too, Edwin. You will always have a place at our table."

He nodded his head but committed to nothing more. Instead, like Eleanor, he stared down at his plate, apparently as unhappy about this change of circumstance as she was.

# ❧ *Chapter Seven* ❧

ONCE THE DECISION was made and announced, the move itself happened quickly. Within a week most of the items that Fanny permitted them to take— for she lorded over them while they packed—were contained in just a few suitcases and boxes.

"The sewing machine table belongs here with the *haus*," she had said when Maggie started to move it toward the kitchen area.

Indignant at the claim, Mary Ann stepped forward. "How so, Fanny?"

"It belonged to John's grandmother," was the simple reply.

"She was our grandmother too!" Mary Ann retorted.

"Mary Ann," *Maem* said softly, "let it stay."

Triumphantly, Fanny walked over to the piece, a beautiful maple table with iron wheels and foot pedals. When Fanny examined it, she frowned and lifted the corner of her apron as if to wipe away a smudge left behind from Maggie's hand. "What use would you have for such a fine piece of furniture anyway?" Fanny said, her eyes still on the sewing stand. "You have Eleanor's regular sewing table anyway."

Clearly resentful of Fanny, Mary Ann could not resist asking, "Perhaps you'd like to keep that too, Fanny?"

Fanny's mouth opened and she glowered at her sister-in-law. "Such insolence! I certainly do not have need for two sewing tables!" Still, she had remained behind to oversee the packing, laying claim to more items than she granted permission to leave the property.

On the day of the move a Mennonite driver arrived with a pickup truck. Edwin knocked at the door of the *grossdaadihaus* to alert them to the man's arrival.

"I'll help you load up the boxes and furniture," he said when he entered the room. He looked at the small number of boxes that waited on the counter. "Is there more upstairs, then?"

Mary Ann started to say something, but suspecting that it would not be kind toward Fanny, Eleanor nudged her with her shoe.

"Just two suitcases of clothing and linens, I believe." Eleanor started to walk up the stairs to retrieve them. To her surprise Edwin offered to help her.

Once in the bedroom Eleanor felt self-conscious that she was alone with him. She hurried over to the bed (for Fanny insisted that they must buy new and leave the bed frames and mattresses behind) and started to pick up the one suitcase that contained her mother's dresses. She felt Edwin stand behind her. Turning around, she gave him a nervous smile and tried to step aside so that he could retrieve the other suitcase.

"Eleanor," he said, his eyes glancing at her and then down at the floor. "There is something I've been meaning to say to you..."

For a moment Eleanor felt a quickening of her pulse. The way that he appeared so skittish and anxious made her wonder if, *mayhaps*, he might have something on his mind besides the move. "Oh?" She set the suitcase down on the floor and stood before him, her eyes searching his face as she waited patiently for Edwin to speak up.

"I..." He hesitated and shuffled his feet. "You see..."

"Eleanor!" Mary Ann called up the stairs. "Hurry up. *Maem* needs your help with moving the kitchen table. Are you up there?"

Edwin forced a smile and stepped back. "I suppose it can wait," he mumbled as he bent over to pick up the suitcase at his feet.

Disappointed, Eleanor looked away.

Whatever it was that Edwin wanted to tell her would have to wait, just as she would, for she had no idea when she would have an opportunity to talk with him again. She listened to him carry the suitcase down the stairs before she retrieved the second bag from the bed. With one final look around the room that had, at one time, been her grandparents' and was supposed to have been her parents' when they grew older together, she hoisted the bag so that she could carry it out of the room and down the stairs, traveling the very same steps Edwin had just taken. *Two steps behind*, she thought as she dragged the bag down the stairs. *Always two steps behind.*

---

The cottage in Quarryville was smaller than Eleanor antici-pated. Made of old gray stone and dating back to the late 1700s, it had low ceilings, and the small windows let in little light. The narrow porch ran the length of the house, while a simple split-rail fence separated the house from the road. But with its three bedrooms, two upstairs and one downstairs, there was at least room for all of them to sleep comfortably.

The living area was just one large room, with a walk-in fireplace on the north side and a narrow wooden staircase along the south wall, as well as the entry to the downstairs bedroom. Along the side where the morning sun would rise were two windows and a door. When opened, the door barely missed brushing against the bottom step. The windows and their wide sills were covered in layers of dirt and bird droppings, but they were large and welcomed sunshine into the room.

Eleanor wandered over to the kitchen area, stepping over leaves and sticks that must have blown into the cottage from a door left open. If cousin Jacob had cleared out the rubbish and debris, she could only imagine what it had looked like beforehand. Discouraged, but refusing to show it, she ran her finger along the dusty counter and the top of the wood-burning stove. Bending down, she opened one of the oven doors and noticed that, at least, had been cleaned out by the previous residents of the cottage.

The bathroom was located underneath the stairs, the door hidden in rich wainscoting. An attractive feature, Eleanor thought, and that was the only positive thought she had as she assessed their new home.

Maggie dashed up the stairs, eager to explore the three bedrooms. The sound of her shoes on the wooden floor echoed in the silence of the first floor. *Maem* stood there, her eyes wide and her cheeks pale. Mary Ann, however, wasted no time in sharing her opinion of their new residence.

"There's so many spiders!" Mary Ann complained, swiping her hand at the cobwebs in the doorway to the pantry. "And definitely mice." She pointed to one of the shelves where rodent droppings lay in abundance.

"Oh, help," *Maem* muttered under her breath. "Don't let Maggie know. Surely she'll want to capture them and keep one for a pet!"

Deciding to take charge, Eleanor hurried over to the kitchen window and unlatched and opened it. She shut her eyes as she leaned toward it, breathing in the fresh air that immediately started clearing the musty smell in the small cottage.

Maggie ran back downstairs and joined Eleanor at the window. "I reckon I'll take the small bedroom," she said, a disappointed tone in her voice.

"That's a good girl," Eleanor responded, placing her hand on her sister's shoulders. She knew how disappointed they felt, for she felt the same. But with the way that their father had left the estate, they had few options. At least here they would be free of Fanny and her constant criticisms.

"*Maem*," Eleanor said, trying to sound cheerful, "there's a lovely view here of the meadow. And I find the kitchen rather cozy, don't you, Maggie?"

"*Mayhaps* when it's fixed up." Maggie stood on her tippy toes to peer out the window. "But I do like the climbing trees that line the lane."

Eleanor smiled at her. "I noticed those too, Maggie!"

"May I go try them?"

While Eleanor would have preferred Maggie to offer her help in cleaning up their new home, she couldn't deny such an innocent request from her youngest sister who, truly, suffered the most from the move, having to adjust to a new school, new friends, and a new lifestyle. "*Mayhaps* for a spell, but then come back to help unpack, *ja?*"

Maggie needed no further encouragement before darting out the open door.

"*Ja, vell*," Eleanor said after taking a deep breath, "seems we have much to do, then."

Mary Ann stepped over an empty crate that had been left in the middle of the room and opened another window. There were no screens to keep out the bugs, and she wiped off the dusty windowsill with the edge of her apron before leaning outside. "Oh, for heaven's sake!" she cried. "Take a look at this garden!" She pointed toward the lane where Maggie was already trying to climb a tree. "That hasn't been tended for at least a hundred years! The weeds are as big as the house!"

Curious, Eleanor hurried across the room and peered over Mary Ann's shoulder. For once her sister was neither exaggerating nor being overly dramatic. Weeds had grown so high that, on entering the cottage, Eleanor had mistaken them for planted shrubbery. Vines wove through the fencing and crawled up the corner of the house, wrapping themselves around the chimney. "Oh dear."

"*Maem!*" Mary Ann turned toward her mother, her eyes large and pleading. "As awful as Fanny is, must we truly live here?"

*Maem* seemed to contemplate Mary Ann's question, her brow wrinkling and her eyes glazing over. For a moment Eleanor thought her mother might actually cry, and sensing the frustration that was bubbling to the surface, she smiled and clapped her hands together.

"Now, now, let's make the most of it!" Eleanor moved away from the window and the awful view of the overgrown garden. She assessed the large room and took a deep breath. Keeping everyone busy would help calm rattled nerves and thwart any emotional outbursts regarding the sorry state of their new living accommodations. "Let's focus on the kitchen, shall we? I'll scrub the floors, Mary Ann can wash the windows and sills, and *Maem* can focus on the shelves. We'll be unpacked and ready for supper before the sun realizes it is time to set!"

With jobs assigned, the trio of women worked, the silence broken only by the noise of water running and rags being dipped into buckets. Eleanor tried to keep her mind focused on positive thoughts, knowing that if she didn't, she too might succumb to the feelings of despair that her mother and sister felt. After all, not only had she left the only home that she had ever known, but she had also left Edwin.

Eleanor wiped the sweat from her brow and leaned back on her heels. She tried to forget his reaction when he heard they were moving to Quarryville. His face had given away his emotions, and for the first time, Eleanor realized how Mary Ann's observations, while premature, had been more accurate than she had allowed.

"I must visit then," Edwin had said to her later that evening, his head dipped so that their foreheads almost touched as they stood by the edge of the cornfield. "*Mayhaps* when I am finished here? In two weeks?"

Eleanor nodded her head but said nothing.

"*Mayhaps* sooner?"

She knew that traveling so far would mean he'd have to hire a driver and leave the farm for at least two or more hours at a crucial time during the late weeks of summer. Without Eleanor or her sisters to assist John with hay cutting and baling as well as the regular chores, Edwin's help would be even more important. Besides, at some point in time, Edwin would be needed back on his own family farm, and that was even farther away from Quarryville.

Eleanor had appreciated his offer as well as his help with packing up their few household goods that were taken to the new cottage in Quarryville. Only now, as Eleanor looked around at the pitifully few boxes that were piled by the front door, she realized that Edwin had spent much more time than was necessary when helping them. Seven boxes, two benches, one rocking chair, and a kitchen table that needed to be put together. That was the remainder of what had been their lives on the Manheim farm.

"Knock, knock!"

Eleanor started at the strange voice and immediately looked to the door. Her mother was already dusting off her apron as she walked to greet the couple that stood there, watching the three women with curious smiles on their faces.

"Cousin Jacob," *Maem* said, extending her hand to shake his.

He was a rotund man, his suspenders stretched to the max over his large, protruding stomach. His graying beard appeared wiry and unkempt, the bottom of it hiding the first two buttons on his shirt. But the smile on his face and sparkle in his eyes lessened the severity of his image. "Making yourself at home already, then?" he remarked lightly as he glanced around the room. "And from the looks of it, having quite the task ahead of you!" At this he laughed, and the portly woman beside him did too. "Have you met my mother-in-law?" He motioned to Eleanor and Mary Ann, waving them over to join them. "Widow Jennings is what we all call her."

The large-boned woman with a cherubic face laughed and swatted playfully at his arm. "*Ach*, Jacob! I detest that name!" But she offered no other to take its place.

Eleanor shook Widow Jennings's hand and glanced over at Mary Ann to do the same. Out of the corner of her eye she exchanged a look with her sister and knew without doubt that they shared the same thought. Jacob Miller and Widow Jennings appeared close enough in age to be married, and their casual banter bespoke of a friendship that seemed more than unusual. Eleanor could only imagine what Jacob's wife must be like.

After the pleasantries were exchanged, Eleanor tried to fill the odd moment of awkward silence that fell over them. "We...we cannot thank you enough for the cottage," she managed to say to Jacob, hoping that her voice did not give away her personal disappointment in the size and condition of the habitation. "It was very kind of you to offer it to us."

"*Ach*, Eleanor! You are family, *ja*? And that's what family does. Helps each other during the difficult times." He leaned over and mumbled to Widow Jennings, but loud enough for all to hear, "At least the good ones do, the ones that stop thinking of their own needs long enough to notice others!"

Again they both laughed as if sharing a wonderful private joke, a joke that Eleanor suspected had to do with her half brother and his wife, Fanny.

"Now, girls," Widow Jennings said when her laughter had faded. "We insist that you come to the *haus* for supper. Your company is mandatory at our table. And you must meet Jacob's good friend, Christian Bechtler. He'll be stopping in for some supper as well."

"I...I..." *Maem* didn't know how to respond and stumbled over her words.

"We'd be delighted," Eleanor ignored the pleading look from her sister and responded on behalf of her mother. While it would have been easy enough to plead weariness from the day's move, Eleanor also knew that they had no food for supper. Besides, it would be impolite to decline when Jacob was their benefactor.

"Just *wunderbarr!*" Widow Jennings said. She exaggerated whispering to *Maem*, "One of your two *dochders* should do right well as his *fraa!*" Once again she laughed, and Jacob joined her.

"Oh!" *Maem*'s intake of breath and quick glance in Eleanor's direction did not escape Jacob and his mother-in-law's attention.

"What's this?" Jacob said inquisitively, looking from one to the other.

Widow Jennings immediately seized the opportunity to inquire further. "Perhaps one of your *dochders* has a special friend already, *ja?*" She eyed Eleanor suspiciously and with a knowing smile on her lips.

Eleanor colored at the suggestion.

"*Vell, ja,*" *Maem* said, surprising Eleanor with her candor. "We do expect a visitor to come calling on my oldest."

"*Ach!* A wedding this autumn?" Widow Jennings looked at Jacob, her eyes wide and full of hope. "Jacob! You must start preparing!" She returned her attention to *Maem* and Eleanor, unaware that Maggie had slipped back into the room. "And who is this special friend, hmm?"

Eleanor started to shake her head to indicate that her mother had spoken too quickly on her behalf when Maggie made her presence known. "Why, you must mean—"

"Shh!" Eleanor cut her off before she could speak Edwin's name.

But it was enough information to delight Widow Jennings. "Oh, a guessing game! I do love little puzzles. Surely we will find out who this friend is. Might you give me a hint, Maggie? A letter perhaps?"

"*F!*" Maggie said, shooting a glance at Eleanor as if to say, "What harm could one letter do?"

"*F...F...*" Widow Jennings glanced at the ceiling as if pondering the possibilities. "Frederick? I don't think I know any Fredericks in the area."

Jacob held up his hand. "There was that one Frederick. The one who married the Blank girl, *ja*?"

"He's from Ohio and *married*, Jacob," Widow Jennings said, stressing the word *married*. "Clearly a married man is not our mysterious courter with the *F* name!" She paused, thinking. Then, as if an idea crossed her mind, she lit up and widened her eyes. "*Mayhaps F* is not his first name, but his family name!" Delighted with the game, she clapped her hands like a child. "Oh, I shall have much fun in asking around to see if we can discover who this mysterious friend is!" She chuckled to herself, clearly amused by the challenge. "I do so love a good mystery!"

Jacob leaned forward as if telling a great secret. "She does, I fear. My *fraa*, Leah, is just the opposite. Much too much work to do and no time for playing games. But Widow Jennings does favor a good game of trying to determine who is courting whom!"

Again, Widow Jennings playfully pushed at his arm. "Now stop, Jacob! You'll have them thinking all sorts of bad things about me! Such as I'm a gossip or bad person!"

He laughed. "You are a gossip, but surely not a bad person." Without further delay, Jacob started for the door. "We must be going. The farrier is coming, you know." He waited for Widow Jennings. "Farrier starts with *f*. I reckon it's not him, is it now?"

They both laughed as they headed toward the door, Widow Jennings pausing in the doorway to bid them good-bye one last time. "I have no doubt we shall all become fast friends! In fact, you should dine with us every evening until your *haus* is properly set up. I'll make certain to tell my *dochder*, Leah, to plan on that!" One quick glance around the room and her eyes bulged from her head. "And I see that fixing this place shall take quite some time, *ja*?"

No sooner had they left than Mary Ann turned to Eleanor and, moaning aloud, rolled her eyes in defiance. "Why did you accept their invitation, Eleanor? We've just arrived and she's quite much to deal with after such a stressful day!"

Eleanor straightened her shoulders and stared directly at her sister. "It's the right thing to do, Mary Ann. They are, after all, our hosts!"

"Of what?" Mary Ann gestured around the room mockingly. "Four walls and a roof that probably leaks when it rains? I'm surprised there aren't any snakes in here, along with the mice and spiders."

"That sounds rather ungrateful," Eleanor chided.

"At the first sign of a snake in the house I will personally move back to Manheim, Fanny or no Fanny!" *Maem*'s indignation caused Eleanor to smile, especially when Mary Ann shivered at her own mention of snakes.

Maggie lit up at the mention of a snake. "If you do find it, don't kill it, *Maem*!"

Ignoring Maggie, *Maem* sighed as she looked pointedly at Mary Ann. "Grateful we should be, for regardless of your initial impression of Jacob and his mother-in-law, they have been the only decent family members to step forward and offer us a place to live." Her eyes roamed around the room. Eleanor didn't have to wonder what her mother saw underneath the dust and cobwebs and cracked paint on the walls: hard work and a lot of it. "And I believe that ten snakes hiding in the pantry here are better than the one snake living in our former house."

To that comment neither daughter replied. They merely shook their heads at the reference to Fanny and returned their attention to the chore at hand: cleaning their new home.

# ❧ Chapter Eight ❧

THE LARGE FARMER's table was set for twelve, and one place setting remained empty. Mary Ann sat next to it, having been assigned the spot next to the end of the bench. The platter of sliced ham and the bowls of steaming vegetables, all fresh from the garden, created a pretty picture, especially with the people seated around the table.

Jacob sat at the head of the table with his wife, Leah, beside him. Widow Jennings assumed the other end of the table, and the children sat quietly in between. They ranged in age from eight to two years of age, and from the looks of Jacob's wife, another one might be on the way. Clearly the young mother, her hands full with caring for a household and four young children, had no time or energy for socializing. She had a forlorn look—dark circles under her eyes and no hint of a smile on her face. Eleanor had glanced at Mary Ann when they were introduced to Leah, and without one word being shared between them, Eleanor had known that Mary Ann immediately disliked Leah, having immediately identified that Leah was one, and only one, word: *dull*.

Unlike Jacob or his mother-in-law, the rest of his family was not as talkative, either from not having the opportunity to get a word into the conversation or by choice, Eleanor did not know. What she did know was that Jacob's wife was much younger than he, and had she been a little less morose, they might have become friends.

After they prayed silently and began eating, Widow Jennings began her lively conversation once again. She talked about the garden and the members of the church district, mentioning the names of their leaders. Eleanor learned that Christian Bechtler was one of the *g'may*'s preachers, despite being an older man who had never married.

"Such a rarity!" Widow Jennings exclaimed, her mouth full of ham. She continued to talk while she chewed the food. "Isn't it, Jacob? An unmarried man being nominated! Whoever heard of such a thing?"

Jacob took over when she paused to swallow. "*Ja*, that's true. But he is such a righteous man, so godly and submissive to the Lord. If an exception was ever made, this was the man to do it for!" He punctuated the air with his fork as he spoke.

When an unusual silence fell between the two, most likely because they were taking their next bites of food, Eleanor took the opportunity to inquire further. "And what does Christian Bechtler do?"

Waving her own fork in the air absentmindedly, Widow Jennings answered enthusiastically. "He runs a harness-making store. Quite a large one, if I might add. And rather fancy harnesses. Not just plain ones for the Amish folk, you know." Then, as if she was telling a great secret, she lowered her voice and leaned forward. "People say he has clients from all corners of the country and Europe too! Quite a successful fellow, he is! Employs quite a few of the young men in our district, bless him. But he lives alone in that large *haus* of his. And with right *gut* farmland too! No *fraa*, although there was speculation at one time..."

"He'd be a right *gut* catch for one of you girls!" Jacob interrupted, pointing his fork at Mary Ann first and then at Eleanor.

"*Ach!* Jacob! Don't forget that Eleanor is already spoken for!" Widow Jennings said teasingly. "The mysterious man with the name that begins with *F*!"

Eleanor flushed and lowered her eyes.

*Maem* did her best to change the subject so that she could alleviate her daughter's discomfort. "What happened to his intended, then?" she inquired, regarding Widow Jennings's comment about Christian Bechtler.

"*Ach*, heaven help us!" Widow Jennings pressed her hand on her heart and leaned forward. "I'm not one to gossip, but there was a young woman who caught his fancy. When he was younger, you know, of course. But she had a questionable *rumschpringe*, and Christian's parents were quite adamant that their family name not be sullied by such talk and speculation. They sent him to Ohio to apprentice at a harness-making store. When he returned, she was gone."

"How tragic!" Mary Ann exclaimed. "Gone, as in perished?"

"*Nee*," Jacob said, lowering his voice as he glanced toward the door as if expecting someone. "Gone from the Amish community. She run off, she did."

"With an *Englischer!*" Widow Jennings added in a low voice. "Christian was most devastated and spent much time trying to locate her, I'm afraid."

Mary Ann's eyes widened. "Did he ever find her?"

Leah cleared her throat and glanced toward her children, each one of them sitting quietly on the bench but listening intently to the conversation.

Jacob laughed. "Little pitchers have big ears…"

Ignoring her son-in-law—and grandchildren for that matter—Widow Jennings lifted an eyebrow as she stared at Mary Ann, who was clearly giving her undivided attention to the subject. "Of course, there is a little more to the story..."

But Widow Jennings could disclose no additional information, for the door opened and a tall man entered the room, pausing to remove his straw hat and hang it on a hook on the wall.

His dark hair framed his face, a handsome face in Eleanor's opinion, that was too obviously lacking the mustache-less beard that all married Amish men wore. Unlike most Amish men he was not very tan, most likely since, as Widow Jennings had pointed out just moments before, he worked inside, unlike the Amish men who farmed. But he had a pleasant look about him, one that spoke of high virtue and humility at the same time.

"I apologize for being late," he said politely to Widow Jennings. His deep voice commanded everyone's attention, all eyes turning to look at him. Unaware of the charismatic presence that seemed to surround him, he nodded at Jacob and his family before he glanced at the Detweilers. His eyes, so dark and flashing, seemed to linger, just for a second, on Mary Ann, especially when she slid over to permit him more room to sit next to her. "The Detweilers, *ja*? It's a pleasure to meet you. We have been looking forward to welcoming you to our community."

Only after he was seated, and said a short silent prayer, did the conversation resume.

Widow Jennings was quick to introduce him to the newcomers, pausing just briefly to add, "And we dare not neglect to mention that you should form no attachments to

Eleanor, Christian. She has a special friend." The way that she emphasized the word *special* brought a fresh blush to Eleanor's cheeks, and for just one moment, she wished she could sink into the floor.

Jacob laughed, clearly unaware of (or simply unconcerned for) Eleanor and Christian's discomfort regarding the joke told at their expense.

Christian's dark eyes darted to look at Eleanor. He forced a friendly smile. "I can assure you," he said in slow, drawn-out words with nothing but kindness behind them, "that my attachments will be made equally to all of the Detweilers, Widow Jennings. They are, after all, your family as well as new members of our church district."

His response pleased everyone at the table, and Eleanor knew, at once, that she appreciated his kind handling of Widow Jennings's crass manners.

For the rest of the meal his attention focused on discussing matters related to farming with Jacob, not on anything of particular interest to any of the women or children around the table. And when Leah excused herself to change the baby and put the youngest children to bed, Maggie and Mary Ann looked as if they too wanted to leave.

Eleanor shook her head at them, glancing at the plates as a silent indication that they could not leave until everything was cleaned and put away. In response Mary Ann rolled her eyes.

"Well, Bechtler, I don't believe I shall listen to your advice on the autumn haying," Jacob said at last. He pushed his plate forward and his chair backward, both at the same time. With good humor, he raised an eyebrow at his guest. "You are, after all, known for harness making, not crop predicting, *ja*?"

71

Widow Jennings laughed.

Christian smiled, clearly not offended by Jacob's remark. "Ah, true," he said politely. "But many a farmer comes to my shop and shares their secrets. I have the benefit of many while you, dear friend, have the benefit of only a few."

"*Ach, vell* now!" Jacob tapped his hand against the edge of the table, his eyes twinkling at the good-natured comeback. "You have me beat on that one, Bechtler! I can't argue that!" He winked at Eleanor and Mary Ann. "But I still say that, once we say the after-prayer, I'm going to bore you with more of my strategy for the back two paddocks and, even worse, ask you to walk with me to see!"

"It will be my pleasure," Christian responded. "Perhaps the young women would like to walk with us to see as well?" He looked directly at Mary Ann when he said this.

A moment's silence followed his invitation, and all eyes turned to Mary Ann. She seemed to stumble over her words, and Eleanor knew that her sister had been caught off guard. "Oh, I…" Mary Ann fidgeted on the bench, wringing her hands on her lap. "I…"

Eleanor leaned forward, placing a hand on Mary Ann's arm and speaking up on behalf of her sister. "What a kind invitation," she said. "But I do believe we shall leave the walking and hay-making talk to you two men. We should help clean up the dishes and then retire to the cottage. It has been a rather long day."

"Of course," Christian said, nodding his head at the wisdom of her words. "Perfectly understandable."

Without another word, Jacob cleared his throat and bent his head, an indication that the other people remaining at the table should do the same. Almost thirty seconds went by, each person silently praying their gratitude to God for the food they had just shared with each other, before Jacob lifted his head, and with one more obvious clearing of his throat, stood up, an indication to Christian that it was time to leave the women to their work while the men took a leisurely after-dinner stroll through the back fields.

# ✣ *Chapter Nine* ✣

I's going to rain!" Maggie whined, leaning backward as Mary Ann tried to drag her through the front door. After a long day spent first at worship and then trapped inside the house, Mary Ann insisted on taking a nice, leisurely stroll outside. She wanted to see how far back Jacob's property went and, as usual, felt drawn to the back portion with its wooded area that surely provided a haven for woodland creatures.

However, despite Mary Ann's determination not to walk alone through the old lane at the back of the farm, Maggie was equally determined not to go.

"*Nee*, it's not!" Mary Ann retorted, pushing at her younger sister.

"You always say it's not going to rain, and then it does!" Maggie's resistance included grabbing at the door frame so that Mary Ann couldn't drag her beyond the entrance.

"The sky is perfectly blue!" Mary Ann tugged at Maggie's arm.

"It's gray!" Maggie retorted, her fingers gripping the frame even harder.

"*Ja, vell*, you see gray and I see blue. Same colors, just at different points on the spectrum. Besides, I'm tired of being cooped inside!" Mary Ann refused to release Maggie's hand. "It's been a week of nothing but work, work, work."

Eleanor looked up from where she sat, reading from her daily devotional book. "And church."

Mary Ann made a face. "How could I forget? After surviving Christian Bechtler's long-winded sermon today? That's just one more reason I need to get some fresh air and walk!"

No one could argue with Mary Ann on that comment. Even Eleanor had thought Christian's sermon, while spoken with great eloquence, was a little too long, especially since there were close to two hundred people in the large gathering room at the farmhouse down the road. With poor air circulation, the temperature of the room increased quickly, causing several heads to bob up and down as people tried to stay awake. One man with a long white beard who sat toward the front of the men's section actually took to snoring, a fact that caused several of the younger children to giggle.

Mary Ann, however, had expressed her displeasure during the entire walk back to the cottage. And later on, when Christian showed up on their doorstep, his Sunday attire still impeccably clean with nary so much as one food or coffee stain, Mary Ann could hardly stay in the same room as him. The more his eyes wandered in her direction, the more Mary Ann looked away.

Finally Mary Ann prevailed on Maggie for a walk, and with them gone, the house quieted down and Eleanor could sit and rock in peace while her mother read the Bible. A breeze from the open window carried the soft songs of sparrows that were playing in the trees just beyond the cottage. The way the cottage was situated, trees and shrubbery blocked its view from the nearby street. The isolation was definitely different from the farm in Manheim, for they could not see the street nor hear passing horses and buggies.

In just over a week the house had come a long way toward slowly becoming a home. After two days of cleaning Eleanor had insisted that they repaint the main gathering room and adjoining kitchen so that it appeared less gloomy. It was so small that the four of them finished it in just one day. The difference, however, was immediately apparent. Even Jacob and Widow Jennings commented one evening on how lively the cottage felt, now that someone was taking care of it. A few other older women from the *g'may* stopped by to meet them and wish them well, and they too complimented the newcomers on the transformation in their home.

While Christian Bechtler's services might not have met Mary Ann's expectations—although Eleanor suspected that nothing Christian did would have made that conquest!—both Eleanor and her mother were quite pleased with their new church district. Now that August was almost over, Maggie would be starting school in a few days, and that would leave the older Detweilers time to interact more with the women of the *g'may*.

Eleanor was particularly anticipating the time when her mother developed a small social network so that she could attend quilting bees in the winter. Despite two months having passed since the funeral of John Detweiler, an air of sadness lingered around his widow. No matter how much *Maem* tried to hide it, Eleanor saw through her poorly acted attempts to appear happy.

So when she heard her mother sigh and close the Bible, Eleanor was not surprised on looking up from her reading to see a desolate expression on her mother's face. "Everything all right, then, *Maem*?" she asked.

Her mother looked around the room. Her eyes appeared tired. There had been far too much change in her life over the past two months. Eleanor's heart broke for her. "Oh, nothing more than missing your *daed*, I reckon," her mother said at last. Her attempt at a soft smile failed. "Everything happened so fast." She hesitated and shut her eyes. "So unexpected…"

Out of respect Eleanor remained quiet. She suspected her mother needed to share her feelings. It had been such an emotional time, but her mother had bottled up most of her sadness, holding herself together as custom and tradition dictated. After all *Daed* was with Jesus now, and while his wife and daughters missed him, they all knew that heaven was a much better place for him. Somehow, though, that knowledge did not make the pain go away.

*Maem* took a deep breath. For a moment she appeared to be silently praying, her lips moving ever so slightly. When she finally opened her eyes and met her daughter's concerned gaze, Eleanor was startled to notice the dark circles under her mother's eyes and the drawn, gaunt look of her face. It was apparent that *Maem* had lost too much weight. She'd have to make certain her mother ate better.

"I must say that your *daed* would be rather disappointed in John."

Eleanor bowed her head, too embarrassed for her half brother to respond. With nothing kind to say about his behavior, she knew that the only response to offer was silence.

Her *maem* sighed once again. "I practically raised that boy after his *maem* died. I did my best for him as if he were my own son."

The truth of the matter was that, indeed, *Maem* had raised John. His birth mother had died from a complicated pregnancy, leaving father and son alone to fend for themselves. At five years of age, John needed a new mother and Henry needed a wife. Henry waited an appropriate amount of time before he started courting again. John had just turned seven when his father finally remarried.

The greatest tragedy was that *Maem* truly doted on him. This only made his abandonment of his stepmother and half sisters even harder to forgive, never mind trying to understand it. What disturbed Eleanor the most was that, had Fanny not been so aggressive in her desire to establish a new pecking order at the farm, the families could have lived and worked on the farm in a communal manner that would have ensured John and Fanny's success as well as *Maem* and her daughters' survival.

Fanny, however, had been far too determined to establish herself as head of the Detweiler household, even if that meant displacing *Maem*.

*Maem*'s eyes roamed around the room, taking in the plain, bare walls. No calendars, no quilt samplers, no cross-stitched Bible verses adorned the wall. They didn't even have room for a display cabinet.

"This is not the life that he wanted for you girls, that's for sure and certain."

"We will make do, *Maem*," Eleanor said, trying to reassure her.

"And you...I know that you have given up the most with this move, Eleanor."

At this statement, Eleanor frowned. "What do you mean? Certainly I have given up no more and quite possibly less."

Her mother shook her head and finally managed that soft smile. "Not being near your Edwin must be quite difficult. It was my sole delay in deciding to move away from that farm.

But I trust that the affections are deep enough that we shall soon see him on our doorstep."

Before Eleanor could respond, the front door burst open. Maggie ran into the room, breathless and panic-stricken.

"Heavens to Betsy, Maggie!" Eleanor cried as both she and her mother jumped to their feet.

"Oh, *Maem*, it's Mary Ann!" Maggie tried to catch her breath. She fell against her mother, burying her head against *Maem*'s shoulder. "I told her not to cut through that back field."

Eleanor placed her hands on Maggie's shoulders and turned her around. Facing her sister, Eleanor stared directly into her eyes. "What has happened, Maggie? You must tell us."

"The horse kicked her," Maggie finally said. "Right in the knee."

She was about to ask her where Mary Ann was when she heard the sound of a man's boots on the doorstep. With her hands still on Maggie's shoulders, Eleanor looked up in surprise. Indeed an Amish man walked into the room, carrying Mary Ann in his arms. "What is this?" she asked, hurrying to the stranger's side as he crossed the small room toward the rocking chair *Maem* had just vacated. She helped him situate Mary Ann so that she sat comfortably, her leg propped up on the small ottoman.

"She's all right," the man said, kneeling before Mary Ann. He looked up at their mother and explained. "I found the two of them near the fencing along the back paddock. When I saw the horse kick her, I hurried right over and examined her knee. I don't think it's broken."

Neither *Maem* nor Eleanor spoke, both being too stunned to say anything.

"*Ach*, my manners." He stood up and extended his hand. "John Willis at your service. Most people call me Willis though. There are quite a few Johns to be confused with in the *g'may*, it seems." He glanced at Mary Ann and smiled.

Eleanor saw that Mary Ann, despite her pale cheeks and trembling hands, could not remove her eyes from Willis's face. In truth, Eleanor could not blame her sister, for Willis made a striking figure in his black pants and pale blue shirt. His tanned skin, the color of bronze from clearly having worked outside, glistened with perspiration from having carried Mary Ann such a great distance. When he looked at Mary Ann, his dark eyes seemed to flash, staring deeply into her face as if they were the only two people in the room. And Mary Ann did not turn away when he did so.

"Willis, please, won't you sit?" Eleanor said, breaking the silence in the room at last. She gestured toward one of the other two chairs in the room.

He tore his eyes away from Mary Ann long enough to stand. "*Nee*, I cannot. Cows cannot wait. But if I may, perhaps I might stop by tomorrow to see how that knee is holding up?"

"We can't thank you enough," *Maem* managed to say.

He dipped his head and took his hat from Maggie, smiling his gratitude at her. Then, with one last look at Mary Ann, he departed from the cottage.

A few seconds of silence filled the room, each one of the Detweilers staring at the door in which Willis had just departed.

"Heavens to Betsy," *Maem* whispered to herself.

"Oh, *Maem*!" Mary Ann gushed. "Did you see him?"

Eleanor turned her head and looked sharply at her sister. "Mary Ann!"

"He picked me up like I weighed nothing," she sighed, ignoring her sister. "And he was so polite, wasn't he?" This question was directed to Maggie, who sat nearby, her eyes glowing and her attention focused on Mary Ann.

"And handsome!" Maggie added dreamily. "I just know he will come calling on you, Mary Ann!"

Putting her hands on her hips, Eleanor shifted her reprimand. "Maggie!"

*Maem* collected herself and shooed Maggie out of the room, instructing her to run up to Jacob's house for Widow Jennings to help tend to Mary Ann's knee.

"I miss all of the good conversations!" Maggie mumbled as she sulked out of the room.

"Honestly, Mary Ann," Eleanor said when their youngest sister was gone from the house. "You must be more discreet."

"Oh fiddle-faddle!" She waved her hand at Eleanor dismissively. "What is there to be so discreet about? He was polite and certainly is handsome! Besides I should be able to speak freely in my own home and with my own family."

With a raised eyebrow, Eleanor gave her a warning look but said no more on the matter.

For the rest of the afternoon and well into the evening, Mary Ann seemed lost in her own thoughts, a small smile on her face as she gazed out the window. And when Widow Jennings and Jacob finally stopped by, for they had not been home when Maggie went to fetch them, it was clear that they were both more concerned about her happiness than her health.

Eleanor focused her attention on preparing their supper rather than participating in the discussion about John Willis, a man apparently known by many but of which little was known. After all, while he visited his aunt frequently, his parents' residence was in a more distant church district up near Narvon. While Eleanor could not force her sister to display more discretion in allowing others to learn of her interest in Willis, she could demonstrate a model of sense by not gossiping with the others. And pray that Mary Ann's sensibility would not be injured by her instant attachment to the young man in question.

# ❧ *Chapter Ten* ❧

O<small>N</small> M<small>ONDAY</small> <small>MORNING</small>, John Willis stopped by the cottage shortly before nine o'clock. Eleanor happened to be standing at the kitchen sink and saw him walking up the lane, his steps brisk and hurried. Eleanor glanced over her shoulder at Mary Ann, who sat in the rocking chair, nursing her knee. True to his word, he had come visiting as soon as was proper to check on her condition.

"John Willis is here," she said to the others in the room.

Mary Ann, galvanized by the announcement, sat upright and winced at the pain in her knee. "Oh! How do I look?" she asked, staring first at Eleanor and then at her mother. She smoothed back her hair and pinched at her cheeks. *Maem* hurried over and covered Mary Ann's exposed leg with a crocheted blanket and then quickly put away the sewing basket that was set out.

When he knocked at the door, *Maem* sat back in her rocking chair, setting the Bible on her lap, and Mary Ann nodded for Eleanor to answer the door.

"I've come to see the patient," Willis said cheerfully as he entered the room, a small bouquet of wildflowers in his hands. He handed them to Mary Ann as Eleanor brought over a chair for him to sit beside the sofa. "I picked them myself while I walked."

Mary Ann buried her nose in the flowers and breathed deeply. "Oh, they are from a butterfly bush! They smell simply divine." She reached out to hand them to Eleanor. "Would you...?"

Taking the flowers, Eleanor carried them to the sink and put them in a tall glass vase to set on the table. From that vantage point she watched as Willis leaned over and softly inquired further about how Mary Ann was feeling. When he reached over, hesitating for a moment before he pulled back the blanket to investigate her swollen knee, Mary Ann's expression changed from fondness to adoration.

"Ah, the swelling should be down by the day after next, I reckon," he said as he gently replaced the blanket. "Just in time for the weekend."

"What is this weekend?" Mary Ann asked coyly.

Willis smiled at her. "The day I shall take you for a ride to see the area in a safe and pleasant manner: by buggy!"

Mary Ann lit up and gave him a soft smile. "That would be right nice, Willis."

And then they began to share verses from the Bible, the Song of Solomon seeming to be the book of interest for the two of them. Eleanor rolled her eyes and busied herself at the kitchen sink, taking time to wash a bowl that was already clean. Listening to them recite songs of love was almost too much to bear for Eleanor. Given how little they knew of the man, the intimacy seemed far too inappropriate in Eleanor's opinion, something she reminded herself to mention to Mary Ann later.

Not twenty minutes had passed when, in the distance, she heard the sound of horse hooves. Peering through the small window in the kitchen, she spotted Christian Bechtler riding his horse around the bend by the evergreens and down the lane that ran alongside the split rail fence.

"Preacher Bechtler is coming," she called out over her shoulder. She dried her hands on the front of her work apron and, out of habit, quickly looked around the room. She already knew that everything was tidy and clean because *Maem* had readied the house earlier that morning in anticipation of John Willis's visit. As she looked around, her eyes fell on Mary Ann and Willis who were whispering, their heads bent forward so that their words could not be overheard by anyone else in the room.

"Did you hear me, Mary Ann?" Eleanor said, taking a step toward the front door.

Willis got up to leave, but Mary Ann waylaid him with a quick—and far too desperate in Eleanor's opinion—hand on his arm. "Must you leave so soon? Just because Christian is here doesn't mean you must go!"

He graced her with a warm smile and placed his hand over hers, a gesture that Eleanor noticed with concern but Mary Ann with delight. "But I shall return, Mary Ann. Saturday if not sooner. You will be here waiting, *ja?*"

Eleanor glanced at her mother, who, rather than finding his question inappropriate, stood watching the scene unfold with a happy expression on her face.

"*Mayhaps* tomorrow, Willis? We've had such a good visit. I cannot believe that we share so many favorite verses!"

He wasted no time to lower his voice and let his eyelids droop as he recited one last scripture from the Song of Solomon.

"My beloved speaks and says to me:
'Arise, my love, my fair one,
    and come away;
for now the winter is past,
    the rain is over and gone.
The flowers appear on the earth;
    the time of singing has come,
and the voice of the turtledove
    is heard in our land.
The fig tree puts forth its figs,
    and the vines are in blossom;
    they give forth fragrance.
Arise, my love, my fair one,
    and come away.'"

"Just *wunderbarr*," Mary Ann whispered, staring at Willis with a starry-eyed look on her face that was unmistakable even from where Eleanor stood. "You recite with such passion and confidence."

If Willis was embarrassed by her words, he didn't show it. Instead, he responded with "Two traits that are inspired from the very words of King Solomon himself!"

Mary Ann sighed.

Willis gifted Mary Ann with one last smile, just as Christian's boots echoed on the front step. He glanced toward the opened door where the newcomer's shadow darkened the room. "And with that, I regrettably must take myself away." He nodded his good-bye to her and then to the rest of her family before hurrying to the door, pausing only to lift his hat from the hook and wish Christian a fine day.

Eleanor watched Christian's reaction. He appeared perplexed at the appearance of John Willis, staring after the younger man. And when he entered the house and greeted

Mary Ann, he would have been blind to have missed the dreamy expression on her face. Eleanor suspected that his visit was not just to check on Mary Ann's knee but also to sit with Mary Ann. Accident or not, Christian had most likely intended to visit anyway.

"How is your knee today?" he asked when he could find his voice.

At first she did not respond.

"Mary Ann!" Eleanor snapped. "Preacher Bechtler has asked you a question!"

"What? Oh!" She emerged from her daydreaming and turned her attention to their new visitor. "Preacher Bechtler! How nice of you to stop by."

He held his hat before him, his hands as steady as his gaze. "I heard you had an accident yesterday and wanted to see how you fared."

"*Danke*," Mary Ann said, although her heart was clearly not full of genuine gratitude. "I'm quite fine now, although I do feel a bit sore."

When she offered nothing else to the conversation, Christian looked over his shoulder out the open door. "I had not known John Willis returned to the area," he said, his voice soft. "He was not at worship yesterday."

At this news Mary Ann brightened, and for the first time, turned an animated face toward Christian Bechtler. "You are familiar with Willis, then?"

"I am," he said slowly. "But only in a capacity in which there is very little I can share."

Eleanor noted the briefest of hesitation in Christian's selection of words, and for a moment, she wondered what, exactly, he meant.

His visit remained brief, his intention strictly to check on Mary Ann, and on finding her not only in fine health but also in a dreamy state of infatuation, there was little else to discuss. When he excused himself and wished them all well, Eleanor had to prod Mary Ann to mind her manners and say good-bye.

"Honestly, Mary Ann"—Eleanor scolded her sister as soon as Christian left to continue his business for the day—"your conduct is shameful!"

Her mouth opened and she stared at Eleanor, a flashing look in her eyes. "I have no idea what you are talking about!"

"You've only just met that Willis man. We know nothing about him, and here you are making cow eyes at just the mention of his name as if he's come calling with courtship on his mind."

Defiantly Mary Ann lifted her chin. "He did come calling. Today."

"To check on you," Eleanor responded harshly. "Out of concern. Mary Ann, you have no sense when it comes to such matters! Why, you'll develop a reputation faster than you can shake a stick if you keep this up."

"Well, I'd rather express my emotions," Mary Ann shot back, "than deny them to the point that I'm viewed as having no feelings at all!"

Eleanor gasped and raised her hand to touch her chest by her heart. To hear her sister's opinion, something that certainly reflected observations of Eleanor's relationship with Edwin, hurt. She remembered Edwin's last conversation with her, his desire to tell her something only to be interrupted by the needs of her family. What had he wanted to share with her? In her heart she suspected that he wanted to share his feelings for their special friendship. In her head she knew that the moment was gone, and with distance separating them, she would not learn the truth for quite some time. Still, for her sister to suggest that she had no feelings?

"Girls, please." *Maem* raised her hand to her forehead. "I can't handle bickering right now."

A silence fell over the room, the tension lingering long after the words had been spoken. Eleanor tried to erase Mary Ann's harsh words from her head and heart. She knew that her sister didn't mean to insult her. They were so different from each other, and while always the most steadfast of friends, it was becoming increasingly difficult to ignore those distinctions that made them unique.

While only two years older than Mary Ann, Eleanor had always been more aware of consequences to actions. Perhaps it was her birthright as the oldest daughter to look out for her younger sisters. Or maybe it was just her nature to assume the job of modeling the proper behavior that was expected of young women. Either way, of one thing Eleanor was certain: in the world of the Amish, appearances mattered. Outsiders to the Amish communities might not understand, or even see, how a group of people who chose to live plain, shunned worldliness, and practiced forgiveness in even the most harrowing situations could sit in judgment of others.

But Eleanor knew it was true, particularly when it came to courtship.

Women did not aggressively pursue men. And for the most part men did not aggressively pursue women. Courtship usually began with quiet conversations in the comfort of the buggy on a ride home from a youth gathering. The less known about any potential interest, the better. And Eleanor understood the rationale behind this. After all, should a relationship *not* develop, both parties' reputation and self-esteem would remain intact. Appearances mattered. Without this unspoken custom a young woman could find herself with questionable gossip being spread about her. Once a woman's reputation was tarnished, polishing it back to its original state was a difficult process.

After a few moments of silence, time needed for tempers to cool down, Eleanor cleared her throat. For the past several days she had been going over their financial situation. With August almost over and autumn bringing a flurry of activities, such as baptism, communion, and, most importantly, weddings, they would be expected to bring baked goods and, in some cases, gifts. And then winter would descend on them. Since Fanny had fussed about the canned goods in the pantry, declaring that the food was part of the farm and should not move with them, they had few supplies to sustain their small family. That meant they would have to spend money at the food store.

"*Maem*," Eleanor began slowly. "I reviewed the bank statement the other day."

"Oh, help!" *Maem* threw her hands in the air and shook her head.

Eleanor pointed down to the pad of paper. "We do not have enough money for firewood and food. With what little Fanny let us take from the pantry..."

Mary Ann scoffed, "Which was nothing!"

Eleanor shot her a look and continued talking. "With what little canned food we have, we will be at Jacob's mercy until next year when we can grow our own food."

At this *Maem* sighed, her shoulders dropping and her eyes taking on a look of sorrow. "If it's not one thing, it's another! First the bickering, now the finances!"

"Before you get too excited, I had an idea."

At this statement both Mary Ann and *Maem* stopped what they were doing to pay attention to Eleanor. Her acumen for business was something held in great esteem by both of them.

"As you know, we are coming into the season," Eleanor began slowly. "We'll have wedding invitations, which, especially for those in Manheim, will require hiring drivers and baking extra goods. Without a pantry to help us through the winter, we'll need to spend money at the food store, and that is just something we don't have extra of."

"Food or money?" Mary Ann quipped lightly.

"Both." Eleanor leveled her gaze at Mary Ann as if to indicate how dire the situation truly was.

"What would you have us do?" *Maem* asked. "Give up meat and fresh vegetables?"

Her sarcasm was not lost on Eleanor's ears. But she ignored it. "So I was thinking of ways that we could make ends meet until next spring. Or even longer. And I thought of something we could do to earn money."

If she had piqued their curiosity before, she now had their rapt attention.

"So many women work in the fields or go to market, but they still have so many chores at home. And that's only the Amish. The *Englischers* are often two-income families, *ja?* So they really do not have time for chores. Why don't we offer our services to sew their clothing?" It was an idea that had struck her, almost like a soft voice whispering in her ear, just a few days ago. Late at night, long after the rest of her family retired to bed, Eleanor had stayed up with a pen and paper. Under the soft glow of a small kerosene lantern (for she didn't want to waste the propane in the stronger

lantern that hung over the kitchen table), she made calcula-
tions until almost eleven o'clock at night.

"Sewing?" *Maem* seemed genuinely interested.

Nodding her head, Eleanor smiled. "I figured it out on
paper that, if we offer these services, we could certainly make
enough money for extra food," she said, looking directly at
her mother, "including beef and fresh vegetables. We'd also
have enough to buy Maggie a new winter coat. She's grown
so much taller, and we haven't any more hand-me-downs to
give her."

Mary Ann exhaled loudly. "I truly hate sewing, Eleanor."

"Probably not as much as you hate being cold and hungry."

With a dramatic hand gesture, as if waving Eleanor away,
Mary Ann dared to respond, "Hopefully I'll be married and
on my own farm in the spring. I won't have to worry about
these things anymore."

"And what a joyous day that will be for all of us," Eleanor
retorted. "In the meantime we have to be practical and think
of the upcoming months."

To her surprise *Maem* nodded her head. "I do believe that
is an idea worth pursuing, Eleanor. Proactive actions help
ward off negative consequences. I, for one, would hate to
need aid from the *g'may*. Without the farm, there are fewer
chores, which gives us time to pursue this idea."

Eleanor flushed, unaccustomed to praise. Praising others
set them apart from others. It also created inflated feelings
of superiority and increased an individual's vanity. So she
responded in the best manner she could to deflect the praise.
"I'm sure anyone would have thought of it," she replied in a
genuinely demure tone. "And Mary Ann, I know that you
hate sewing. But a little bit won't hurt you, especially if it
helps the family."

"I just wish we had a garden," her sister replied. "I hate being cooped up inside all day long."

Eleanor felt that familiar tug of sorrow for Mary Ann, knowing that it had pained her to walk away from her beautiful gardens at the Manheim farm as well as her job at the garden center.

But they all knew that such a sacrifice was needed, unless they wanted to ask the *g'may* for financial help, and that was not something anyone desired. *The Lord helps those who help themselves*, Eleanor thought as she bent her head to continue working on the garment she was sewing. And *mayhaps* Mary Ann was right. If Willis was indeed interested in courting her sister, she'd have her own gardens to tend in the spring.

# ❧ *Chapter Eleven* ❧

S EVERAL DAYS PASSED and John Willis stayed true to his word. He became a regular visitor at the Detweilers' cottage, stopping by to check on "the patient," as he took to calling her. Then, when she began to put her full weight on the knee, he would offer to hold her elbow and walk up the lane with her.

Alone.

To Eleanor's dismay John Willis hid his affections in the same manner as Mary Ann: he simply did not. His manner of speaking with her openly about subjects such as the romantic—and sometimes overtly passionate!—innuendos behind the Song of Solomon did not go unnoticed by Eleanor or *Maem*. Several times, in the heat of a discussion, the topic between the two starry-eyed duo grew so intense that Eleanor had to send Maggie from the room.

Fortunately most of his visits tended to be during the day, and Eleanor was thankful that Maggie had started school, although Maggie herself felt the complete opposite.

Now that the cottage was set up and the Detweiler women were situated in the community, they could begin their earnest effort of starting to offer sewing services. Already Widow Jennings had spread the word—in what way, Eleanor could only imagine—and several people had stopped by to inquire further. As Eleanor had predicted, many women were too busy working outside of the home and could use the assistance of an extra set of hands to help with sewing, especially with wedding season arriving soon. Young women needed new blue dresses for their upcoming marriages. The very fact that so many knew of the weddings ahead of time surprised Eleanor, who was used to the game of secrecy that surrounded courtship. Apparently the younger women of Quarryville were not held to such traditions, a point that Mary Ann used to her advantage.

"The difference is," Eleanor stated firmly, "that they are already engaged!"

"Oh fiddle-faddle!" Mary Ann said dismissively. "I shall be too, soon enough. Wait and see!"

By the time Saturday arrived, Willis had already made plans to take Mary Ann to the youth gathering on the other side of the *g'may*. While he didn't live in the church district, he knew many of the youths from spending time with his aunt and her husband throughout the years. And with the heat of summer abating now that September had come, the youth were taking advantage of the good weather to play volleyball.

While Mary Ann detested volleyball, a fact she did not share with Willis, she immediately accepted his invitation.

Shortly after Saturday's supper, a simple fare of fresh bread, pasta salad, tomatoes, and meatloaf, Mary Ann stood by the open kitchen window, her face turned to the breeze as she waited and watched for his arrival. Her fingers tapped nervously against the counter as her eyes scanned the empty road.

"Oh, Mary Ann!" Maggie gushed, spinning around in a circle near the kitchen table. "Just think of it! You'll be married by November for sure and certain!"

"Hush!" Eleanor scolded her when Mary Ann did not. "This whole courtship is far too much in the open as it is. We don't need anyone to overhear such talk!"

Maggie shrugged and looked around. "No one is here but us."

"And that's bad enough!"

But Maggie didn't care, choosing to enjoy the romantic notions that filled the house. Mary Ann seemed to live in a fog, her eyes always misted over and her lips smiling as if she had the greatest of secrets. Even *Maem* had begun secretly drafting a list of who to invite to the wedding. Whenever Eleanor was nearby, she hid it so that she avoided being chastised for putting the buggy before the horse.

Still, Eleanor felt concern for knowing so little about John Willis. Earlier in the week Jacob had stopped by, bringing a large box of freshly butchered meat: ground and chunks for stew. Mary Ann had immediately questioned him about what he knew of Willis, to which Jacob had only commented that Willis was set to inherit a nearby farm from a widowed aunt who had no surviving sons. Willis visited each August before returning to his family's farm that was north of Narvon.

Jacob's lack of information only confirmed Eleanor's suspicions that something was not quite right. However, as much as she disapproved of Mary Ann's open conduct with Willis, she could not deny that the feelings were returned in kind.

"Where is he?" Nervously, Mary Ann glanced at the clock. She wore her new dress, the light green one that she had made shortly before their father passed away. The color flattered her lightly tanned skin. "He said he'd be here by six thirty."

"It's only six fifteen, *schwester*," Eleanor said.

Mary Ann scowled.

"You don't even care for volleyball," Eleanor stated. "Being someone you are not just to please another is no different from lying."

"Oh, hush, Eleanor!" Mary Ann glared at her. "I'm trying new things. What is so wrong about that? Besides, what do you know of my likes and dislikes?"

Ignoring her sister's dirty look, Eleanor responded, "I know you dislike volleyball, and from the impatience you are displaying right now, I reckon you also dislike waiting!"

"*Maem!*" Mary Ann whined.

But *Maem* merely smiled to herself, pretending to read the Bible that lay open on her lap.

"Come, Mary Ann," Eleanor said gently, hoping her softer tone might calm down her sister. "Sit for a spell so you don't look so anxious."

But Mary Ann heard none of that, or ignored it, for she continued to stand at the window and gaze outside, her eyes searching the horizon.

A few minutes later the sound of horse hooves could be heard in the room, although the hedge of evergreen trees hid the horse and rider from view. Excited, Mary Ann hurried to the front door and stood on the stoop, a smile on her face that could not be missed. Eleanor joined her and watched as a lone man sauntered around the trees.

When Mary Ann saw that it was Christian, and not Willis, her smile disappeared and she seemed deflated of enthusiasm. "Oh, help! It's only Bechtler," she mumbled, grumbling even more when Eleanor nudged her ribs.

"Good evening, Christian!" Eleanor called out, raising her hand to wave to him.

He stopped his horse, a beautiful black Dutch harness with a striking white blaze that ran from its forehead to its nose, and nodded his greetings to the two ladies. Within seconds he dismounted from the horse, and holding the reins in one hand, he approached the house.

"Good evening to you too," he said as cheerfully as one could expect from Christian Bechtler. He turned his face toward the sky, shutting his eyes for just a moment as if enjoying the feeling of the sun on his cheeks. "God's blessed us with some fine weather this week."

"Indeed he has." Eleanor smiled at him and wished that Mary Ann would stop scanning the horizon over his shoulder. Her impertinence toward Christian was a source of never-ending discomfort for everyone in the family, especially since his interest in her was more than obvious even if it was unspoken.

Clearly Christian noticed Mary Ann's surveillance of the road, and as politely as he could, he stepped aside so that she could have a better view. His reward was a forced smile of appreciation that lacked any warmth from her. Eleanor wished that she could shake her sister for her lack of manners, especially to such a kind man as Christian Bechtler. His admiration of Mary Ann never wavered, despite her obvious dismissal of his high regard for her.

"Where is he?" she mumbled to herself.

Being an honorable and righteous man, Christian did not inquire as to whom she waited for or what held her so captivated down the road. Eleanor suspected he already knew. Instead, Christian smiled at both of the sisters and announced with great fanfare, "I've come with an invitation! An outdoor supper at my *haus* on Friday evening. Like a picnic."

He seemed quite pleased with himself, but Mary Ann hardly glanced at him.

"For all of you, of course," Christian added.

Maggie poked her head outside the window. "Even me?"

He laughed. "What type of picnic would it be without you, sweet Maggie?"

"*Mayhaps Maem* will let me leave school early!" With great enthusiasm Maggie disappeared from the window, and the sound of her voice speaking to her mother carried through the air.

Eleanor tried to hide her amusement at Maggie's eaves-dropping and inquiry as well as the sound of Christian's laughter. It was a sound she hadn't heard very often while in his presence. His intensity, so apparent in his dark eyes that seemed to watch everything without ever expressing his emotions, hindered good humor, it appeared to Eleanor. Hearing him laugh, especially at Maggie, made her realize that she may have misjudged Christian Bechtler.

"Shall we bring something, Preacher?"

He nodded, his eyes occasionally darting toward Mary Ann, who continued to display her distraction from their conversation. "Jacob Miller and his family will be there as will Widow Jennings and a few other folks from the *g'may*. I have everything covered except for dessert. *Mayhaps* you might find time to bake a pie or two?"

"Of course!" Silently, however, Eleanor couldn't fathom arriving at a picnic with so many people with just a pie or two. Dessert was as important to the meal as the main course. Certainly they would bring cookies, cake, pie, and, depending on the weather, ice cream. Fortunately, with the sewing jobs beginning to trickle in, they could afford to make extra desserts for when they visited others.

From behind the hedgerow of evergreen trees, the sound of an approaching buggy could be heard. Christian glanced over his shoulder, and when he turned back to the two women, Mary Ann had lit up, her lack of interest in anything suddenly replaced with great enthusiasm.

"John Willis has been calling," Eleanor said softly.

"Ah. I see." He looked at Mary Ann one more time. She began waving to Willis when she could see him, her attention focused strictly on him. Christian cleared his throat. "And Willis will be invited to the picnic as well."

At the mention of John Willis, Mary Ann finally turned toward Christian as if seeing him for the first time. "*Ja?*" She smiled, already taking a step in the direction of the buggy. Eleanor flushed when she saw that Willis had arrived in an open-top courting buggy, a fact that was certainly not lost on either Christian or Mary Ann. "Oh, a picnic will be *wunderbarr* fun! *Danke* for the invitation!"

And with that she hurried to the buggy. Eagerly stepping onto the footrest, she hoisted herself up so that she could sit beside Willis.

"Good day to you," Willis said in the general direction of the house. His attention, however, was on Mary Ann.

"Oh, Willis!" she gushed. "Christian just invited us to a picnic at his *haus* next Friday at supper time! Isn't that special?"

"Indeed!" He smiled at her. "Now let's go for our ride." He slapped the reins on the back of the horse, and the carriage lurched forward in such a way that Mary Ann fell against Willis, her laughter a little too loud for Eleanor's taste.

In silence Christian and Eleanor watched them leave, Mary Ann gracing them with one last wave before the buggy turned the corner and disappeared behind the trees.

"I'm afraid my *schwester* is not of the old school where emotions are kept to oneself in the interest of personal etiquette and public discretion." Eleanor sighed, turning to face Christian. Her embarrassment at Mary Ann's behavior was only countered by her wish that Christian might find happiness. "Her notions of courtship lack the common sense, I reckon, of one who has been exposed to the world. Perhaps she should gain that exposure to the world so that she can understand disappointments often follow blind happiness."

Christian remained standing there, staring at the empty lane where the buggy had just left. He seemed deep in thought for a few seconds and then, finally, said, "Such a disappointment would change her very regard for courtship, perhaps not just of one suitor but of all, *ja*?"

Frowning, Eleanor tried to make sense of his question. "I do not confess to know what the future would hold for her, Christian, should she encounter such a disappointment."

"Ah." At last he tore his gaze from the lane and looked at Eleanor, his dark eyes sorrowful and full of melancholy. "I do not wish exposure to the world for your *schwester*, Eleanor." He remained silent for a few moments as he studied the landscape. Finally he continued talking. "I don't know how much Widow Jennings has shared with you, Eleanor, but I once knew a young woman who was quite similar to your *schwester*. Her vibrancy for life equaled her energy to experience living. Unfortunately circumstances forced her to know the world all too soon, I'm afraid. I would not wish such a fate on anyone, especially someone like Mary Ann."

From inside the house Eleanor's mother called out to Christian, inviting him inside for a glass of meadow tea. He bowed his head to Eleanor, excusing himself to climb the two steps at the front door. When he disappeared inside the house, Eleanor stared after him, mulling over what he had just confided in her. While Widow Jennings had mentioned something about Christian Bechtler and a young girl, she had given no hint to the circumstances that resulted in his never marrying her. Now, based on what he told her, Eleanor's imagination ran wild, and she said a quick prayer that God would watch over her sister. After so much turmoil in their lives, an unfortunate circumstance befalling Mary Ann would be the worst of things to happen.

# ❧ Chapter Twelve ❧

Late Friday afternoon Eleanor, Mary Ann, and Maggie walked the two miles to Christian Bechtler's house for the promised picnic. Most of the road was shielded by large trees, their massive branches covered in green leaves creating a canopy of protection from the morning sun. In the distance a herd of black Angus cows grazed in a paddock, the sound of their gentle calling to each other breaking the silence of the walk.

Eleanor and Mary Ann were too tired from a week of work to indulge in much conversation. Maggie trudged behind her two older sisters, dragging her feet despite Eleanor's repeated warnings that she would scuff up her Sunday shoes. Maggie simply did not care.

"I hate walking so far," she complained, still kicking at stones in the road.

"It's good for you," was Eleanor's simple reply. "Between you at school and us sewing all week, the walk is just what we all need!"

"Indeed!" Mary Ann grumbled, reaching up to rub at her neck. "I'm tired of sewing all day. I'll become an old hunchback before you know it!"

Eleanor was glad that *Maem* had ridden over in Jacob's buggy, for the roads were hilly and *Maem* seemed especially fatigued as of late. Eleanor presumed it was from so much hard work involved in fixing up the cottage as well as the heat that seemed to linger on the second floor. Sleeping was next to impossible in the evening until the humidity dissipated around two a.m. However, as soon as the sun crested over the horizon, the air became thick once again. Today they were fortunate, as a cool front was blowing in from the north.

"I don't understand why we cannot have a horse and buggy," Maggie moaned, trudging along behind her two sisters.

Eleanor was quick to respond. "You know we cannot afford it, *schwester.*"

"Everyone else has a horse and buggy. All they do is eat hay and grass!"

Mary Ann turned around, walking backward so she could see Maggie. "*Mayhaps* your wish will come true!"

There was something about the way she said these words, a gleeful tone to her voice, that raised the red flag for Eleanor. "It's not fair to raise her expectations, only to be disappointed," she said to Mary Ann cautiously.

"Oh fiddle-faddle! I don't know why I've kept it a secret anyway. I'm not raising her expectations, and she won't be disappointed! You see, Willis has offered to give me a horse," Mary Ann blurted. "Isn't that a fine gift?"

Immediately, Eleanor stopped walking. She faced Mary Ann with a concerned expression. "You've known him less than two weeks. I'll be glad to hear that you declined his offer."

At this statement Mary Ann tilted her chin defiantly. "I most certainly did not."

"A horse!" Maggie jumped up and down. "Oh, I hope I can learn to ride it."

Eleanor tried to maintain her composure. "We cannot afford a horse, and you both know it. We also have nowhere to stable it. Even more important than the impracticality of owning a horse in our current financial state, it would be very inappropriate to accept such a gift."

"And why is that?" Mary Ann cried.

"Is there...some sort of an understanding between the two of you?"

Eleanor's question caused Mary Ann to lower her eyes.

"I thought not. And therefore the entire *g'may* would have much to say about you receiving a gift of such magnitude from Willis."

Waving her hand at Eleanor, Mary Ann continued walking. "Oh fiddle-faddle! That Amish grapevine is ridiculous and of no concern to me. Let them talk."

If Eleanor wanted to alert her sister to the fact that the Amish grapevine already was talking about her sister's untraditional relationship with Willis, she kept her mouth shut. Just the previous day Widow Jennings had visited to help *Maem* and Eleanor can peaches for their winter pantry. She had been only too happy to share the gossip regarding Mary Ann riding beside Willis in the open-top courting buggy, not just last Saturday but on Sunday too. There had even been speculation about where they had gone on Sunday because they had apparently not shown up at the youth gathering as planned. But Eleanor feared that pressing her point would only make Mary Ann more stubbornly obstinate, so she switched tactics.

"You know a horse would only be another worry for *Maem*," Eleanor cautioned. "We can barely afford enough food for ourselves, never mind food for a horse. You will refuse that gift, Mary Ann. I insist on it."

105

Like an insolent child, Mary Ann stomped her foot as she walked away from Eleanor. Yet the argument was over. The meager income they had from the interest on their small inheritance needed to be set aside for food. Without a garden at the cottage they did not have any vegetables to can, and as for fruits they had to buy them from local farmers. Over the winter they would have to rely on what little they could purchase to make up for the rest. Feeding and tending to a horse was not in their current budget.

When the three sisters turned down the lane that led to Christian's harness shop, all discussion about a horse was forgotten. Eleanor caught her breath, and stunned at what she saw, Mary Ann didn't pay attention and stumbled over a rock on the side of the road. It was Maggie who said what they were thinking.

"Is this Preacher Bechtler's *haus*?" Maggie looked up at Eleanor as if anticipating an answer. "It's—"

"Magnificent," Mary Ann completed Maggie's sentence. "I thought he merely had the harness shop. That's all that Widow Jennings said."

Eleanor tried to compose herself from the surprise that she too felt.

Before them was a large white farmhouse, complete with a wraparound porch and sizable windows on the first floor. Several of the windows looked like they were glass doors that opened onto the porch. Two large oak trees, one on the western side and the other on the eastern side, shielded the house from the midday sun. His garden, located along the back of the property, flourished with well-manicured plants. And the building where he ran his harness shop was just behind the barn, another large white building with big windows that displayed racks of various leather goods.

"When does he have time to tend to all of this?" Eleanor whispered.

"It's not as if he has any family, I reckon," Mary Ann said.

Eleanor shot Mary Ann a look, but when she detected no sarcasm in her sister's voice, she returned her attention to the house. She couldn't imagine how Christian had the time, or wherewithal, to operate such a successful harness store, tend to the *g'may* as a preacher, and manage the upkeep of the farm. From the looks of the fields in the background, he had a successful corn crop that year as well. Her respect for Christian, while already great, grew tremendously.

"Let's go," she said, nudging her sisters.

Several buggies were already parked in the area near the harness store. Mary Ann, however, quickly began searching for Willis's courting buggy. When she didn't see it, she barely greeted the others that were already gathered under the shade of the large oak tree before she began staring down the lane, searching for his arrival.

Widow Jennings raised an eyebrow at Mary Ann's obvious impatience and clicked her tongue disapprovingly. "I wouldn't have believed it, but now..."

Eleanor turned around. "Believed what, Widow Jennings?"

"Oh, never mind me," she laughed, her cheeks pinking up. "Just speaking when I shouldn't."

But Eleanor insisted.

Dramatically leaning forward, Widow Jennings lowered her voice and looked around before she spoke, as if ensuring that no one could overhear their conversation. "I heard that Willis was driving your *schwester* in his courting buggy just the other day. Sunday, I believe."

This much Eleanor knew to be true. "I scarcely find that something hard to believe," she said. "Many young people go riding in open-top buggies. And he was taking her to the youth gathering."

"*Ja, vell*, that was only the beginning," Widow Jennings said with a touch of smugness. She leaned back, as if contemplating sharing the rest of her confidence with Eleanor. Finally she continued. "It wasn't just that they were in the courting buggy. It was the fact that they did not arrive at the youth gathering, as I've already told you. Since then I've found out where they were. Apparently they were seen driving to that farm he is to inherit." Widow Jennings paused, leveling her gaze at Eleanor. "They were alone in the *haus*, Eleanor."

Stunned, Eleanor took a moment to regain her composure. Was her sister truly that *ferhoodled* in love with Willis that she would compromise her reputation by entering a house with Willis unsupervised? And not just any house but *his* future house? With such a short period of time having passed since they met and no engagement to announce, Mary Ann being alone with Willis in a house would certainly raise quite a few eyebrows and cause women to talk.

"I'm...I'm sure you must be mistaken."

"*Nee*, Eleanor," Widow Jennings said, folding her hands piously before her and standing up as straight as she could. "It comes from a very reliable source, I can assure you."

"I can assure you that if my *schwester* did go into his *haus*, nothing inappropriate happened." Eleanor wanted to believe her own words, but she knew that Mary Ann's emotions were driving her actions when her sense of propriety should be in charge. Would Willis be such a flirt as to take advantage of Mary Ann's adoration? Even though Eleanor disapproved of the couple's too obvious deep affection, she couldn't believe that Willis was such a scoundrel.

The arrival of John Willis interrupted their private conversation.

Mary Ann waved at him as he drove the horse and carriage down the lane. "He's here!" she said to no one in particular.

Widow Jennings lifted an eyebrow and gave Eleanor a knowing smile.

Christian took a few steps toward the newest arrival and greeted Willis with as much warmth as he would any visitor to his farm. But Eleanor could sense the stiffness in his spine as Mary Ann rushed past him to stand beside the carriage.

"Willis! You made me worry you wouldn't come!" she said, not caring that anyone else was nearby.

He stepped on the brake and dropped the reins onto the seat beside him before jumping down to the ground. He reached out and touched her arm, a gesture innocent yet intimate at the same time. "And miss such a lovely gathering?" He smiled at the gathered people. "Highly unlikely! I shall always be where my heart is," he declared.

Once again Widow Jennings clicked her tongue and turned away.

Standing beside Christian, Eleanor took the opportunity to redirect his attention. "I had no idea that you also farmed, Christian. When do you have time for all of the chores and responsibilities you have taken on?"

"Ah, Eleanor," he said gently. "I hire young farmers to tend the land, men who need the income to buy their own farms. It's my duty to care for God's land as well as my pleasure to help others."

"How very righteous," she complimented. It was true that farmland was increasingly shrinking in Lancaster County. Many young Amish couples were leaving the area, moving to more remote areas to start new communities in states that offered more land and fewer tourists. She often read about these new communities in the weekly newspaper, *The Budget*, and wondered what it would be like to pick up and leave. Isolating, for certain, and not something she wished to consider for her own future.

Of course, with almost three weeks gone by since their move, Eleanor often wondered about her future. Unlike Mary Ann, she was not prone to sharing her emotions so openly. The lack of communication from Edwin disappointed her, to say the least. At night she often lay awake and worried that something happened to him, although she suspected John or Fanny would have contacted them had that been the case. She missed their morning talks and evening walks. Still, she knew that God had plans for her, and she certainly would not step outside of her sense of propriety by reaching out to him.

There was no more time to discuss anything as another horse and buggy raced down the lane toward the house. With no one else expected to join the gathering, everyone turned to see who it was. The speed at which the horse ran indicated there was a problem, and Christian hurried to meet the visitor.

"Preacher!" an older man called out through the open door of his buggy. "I've a message for you." No sooner had he stopped the horse than he jumped out and thrust a white paper at Christian.

"Oh, help," *Maem* said. "I hope nothing has happened."

"Something must have happened," Eleanor said, concern etched on her face. "Otherwise there wouldn't be such urgency."

The gathering of people watched Christian, his back toward them, as they waited for a reaction. When he finished reading the letter, his arm fell to his side with the letter still clutched in his hand. After taking a moment to compose his thoughts, he turned to face them, the color drained from his cheeks.

"I must leave at once," he said, his words stressing the importance even if his tone remained even.

Widow Jennings gestured toward the picnic table, which was already covered with food. "And leave your own gathering?"

Jacob offered his own opinion. "Whatever it is can wait, *ja*?"

"I'm afraid not." He crumpled the letter into a small wad and shoved it into his pocket. "Please stay and enjoy the day."

"At your home without you?" Jacob asked. "What's happened, Bechtler? Is it one of our church members?"

"Has someone taken ill?" Widow Jennings asked.

"*Nee, nee*," Christian responded with a soft voice as if his mind had wandered elsewhere. Eleanor had never seen him so distracted. "*Vell* then," Jacob said. "If no one is ill, surely it can wait."

"Not one hour longer than it must," Christian added. He turned to the man standing beside the buggy. "You'll take me to the bus station, *ja*?"

"Bus station!" Widow Jennings could barely contain both her concern and her curiosity. With her mouth open, she turned to stare at Christian.

He, however, looked at no one. His eyes did not seem to register that everyone was watching him. "I must leave at once," he mumbled. He didn't waste any time climbing into the left side of the buggy and urged the other man to hurry.

Eleanor stepped forward. "Will you be back soon, then?"

111

Christian merely shook his head as the man turned around the horse and buggy before guiding the already sweaty horse down the lane.

"My word!" Widow Jennings said. "I've never seen such a thing!"

Eleanor walked over to her, placing an arm around the older woman's shoulder. "It must have been something dreadful to call Christian away so suddenly. I think it is best that we pray for whatever the situation is and that it is resolved quickly as well as favorably for him."

## ❧ *Chapter Thirteen* ❧

**M**AEM HURRIED ELEANOR and Maggie toward the front door. "Come, girls!" she said anxiously, gently pushing them along. She wore her black dress and apron, which made her appear austere and serious. It was Sunday, and as they did not have a horse and buggy, they needed to walk to the worship service. Given the distance and the fact that they were still new to the church district, the last thing *Maem* wanted was to arrive too late to enjoy the social time before the service.

Eleanor suspected, however, that *Maem's* jitters were also because she had something else on her mind, for, on this particular day of worship, Mary Ann was not joining them, a situation boding one thing: a private conversation with Willis that would undoubtedly result in an engagement.

The previous evening Willis had spent the better part of the evening with them. His light humor and gentle teasing had made all the Detweilers laugh. Even Eleanor had smiled when he imitated Widow Jennings with her loud laughter and penetrating questions. After their evening meal Willis had asked Mary Ann to walk with him down the lane. Later she had been only too happy to report that he asked if she would grant him some time in the late morning while the family attended worship service. Apparently Mary Ann relayed to her attentive audience of three, he had something of great importance to discuss with her.

"Now don't forget to offer him tea," *Maem* said to Mary Ann. Her giddiness at leaving Mary Ann home alone was far too apparent. She had taken time to cut some fresh wild-flowers and leave them in a plain white pitcher on the table. "I made some meadow tea and baked muffins last night."

Maggie lingered at the door, her hand on the recently painted door frame. In her light green dress she looked young and pretty, even though she had grown and it was too small for her. The dress's color offset her tan from having worked all week with Mary Ann in the garden. After clearing out the weeds and tilling the soil, Mary Ann had deemed the small plot of land halfway presentable, even though it was too late to plant anything.

"How come we can't stay to hear him propose?" Maggie asked.

"Whatever Willis needs to say to Mary Ann is a private matter," Eleanor said more harshly than she intended. A pang struck her heart at the idea of Mary Ann marrying Willis. Their acquaintance had been brief, but even Eleanor could not deny that they shared a strong emotional bond, although she felt hesitant to call it love. The one problem with Mary Ann marrying anyone, Willis or not, was that she would move away from the cottage. That thought alone made Eleanor feel especially irritated. Without Mary Ann living at home, she didn't know what she would do.

"If he's going to propose, I don't understand why he didn't just ask you last evening!" Maggie complained, pulling at the sleeve of her Sunday dress. "Then we all could miss worship service."

"Maggie!" Eleanor frowned at her. "We don't know what he wants to discuss with Mary Ann, and we could all do with a little more worship and a little less frivolity!"

Mary Ann laughed. "Frivolity? Is that what you call what we have? I think we are working just as hard here as we did at the Manheim farm. Perhaps harder." She smoothed down the front of her dress and plucked off a piece of lint. "I, for one, would much prefer working on my own farm and gardens once again."

It was the first time Mary Ann had made such a comment. Eleanor stared at her, realizing how difficult the move to Quarryville had been on her sisters. Without her job or her garden, Mary Ann's days had been spent indoors, canning food that was donated to them for winter or helping with painting the upstairs bedrooms, a job none of them liked doing. Maggie happily was excused from that chore as she had started school. And while Maggie liked her new teacher and classmates, she did lament the loss of her old friends.

"We've certainly been busy in the evenings as of late." Eleanor glanced at her sister. "Some of us more than others."

"Perhaps if you had expressed more emotion," Mary Ann said absentmindedly, "Edwin would have come calling by now."

"Mary Ann!" This reprimand came from *Maem*. "For shame!"

Mary Ann looked up at her mother, an innocent look on her face. "What? It's the truth. She's been after me so much about letting Willis know how I feel about him. What has her reserved manner awarded her? Not so much as a letter! He probably didn't even know she cared about him!"

Eleanor pressed her lips together, willing herself to remain silent.

How could Mary Ann know what she felt toward Edwin? Perhaps Edwin was more traditional in his approach to courtship, but that did not mean he didn't care for her. Of course Eleanor was also very aware that he had never made any comments or promises to her. Had she behaved toward Edwin in the manner that Mary Ann did to Willis, Eleanor would have felt not just the pain of a broken heart but also the insufferable insult of people talking about her.

Hearing Mary Ann actually suggest that his absence was her own fault, however, hurt almost as much as Edwin's silence. Eleanor turned on her heel and hurried out the door, starting the long morning walk to the worship service. Behind her she heard her mother scold Mary Ann, but it didn't soothe the sting of her sister's words.

By the time they arrived at the worship service, Eleanor had finally shaken off the hurt from Mary Ann's careless slip of the tongue. She knew how her sister felt, that Edwin's affections should have been met with more enthusiasm. But Eleanor had not wanted to presume that his friendship meant anything more than just that. In hindsight, despite her aching heart, she was grateful to have maintained her discretion, if only to shield herself from the pity of others.

Inside the Eshes' home the large gathering room was set up for the worship service. The pine benches lined the sides of the room, facing the center where the bishop, preachers, and deacon would sit. While the men waited outside, talking until the designated time, the women lingered near the kitchen. Widow Jennings stood with her two daughters, eager to greet the Detweilers.

"Such news!" she exclaimed after greeting them with a handshake and the customary kiss bestowed on each other before service. "Preacher Bechtler has yet to return!"

"Oh, help!" *Maem* pressed her hand against her chest. "I wonder what was of such great importance."

It was just the opening that Widow Jennings hoped for. Leaning forward so that eavesdroppers could not overhear, she whispered, "I reckon that it had something to do with his *dochder*."

Even Eleanor could not resist gasping at Widow Jennings's news. "His *dochder*?"

"*Ja*, his *dochder*." The widow nodded her head. "Born out of wedlock, of course."

Because she knew Christian had never married, Eleanor had already gathered that. She couldn't imagine Christian Bechtler engaged in such illicit behavior, even if it had occurred during his *rumschpringe* and before he had taken the kneeling vow to become a baptized member of the church. It didn't make sense. "I find that hard to believe."

"At least that is the way the story goes," the widow added.

*Gossip*, Eleanor thought, stiffening her back and lifting her chin. "The Amish grapevine produces more rotten fruit than any other, Widow Jennings."

"Mark my words," she replied tartly. "His love for that girl during his *rumschpringe* ruined him for any other. But she wasn't Amish and would not convert. And he would not refuse the baptism."

"That may or may not be true," Eleanor admitted. "But to jump to the conclusion that he had a child with her—"

"And speaking of out of wedlock," Widow Jennings said abruptly. There was something about how her eyes began to glimmer with a sense of self-satisfaction that disturbed

Eleanor. She quickly found out why when Widow Jennings said, "I do not see Mary Ann with you today. Is she feeling poorly?"

There was no time for Eleanor to defend her sister's honor. The door opened and the bishop walked into the room, followed by the rest of the church leadership with the exception of Christian Bechtler. Inside Eleanor fumed at the widow's insinuation, barely able to look the bishop in the eye when he paused to shake her hand.

*Oh, Willis!* she thought with anger in her heart. *What have you done to my sister's reputation?* Immediately she shifted her anger toward her sister. Whatever Willis had done, Mary Ann had certainly encouraged it. At least he was proposing to her now, and with the October baptism only a few weeks away, they could announce their plans immediately afterward.

During the entire service Eleanor could barely concentrate on what was being said. Her mind wandered to Willis and Mary Ann and then to Edwin. Without any word from him in three weeks, she held little hope of seeing him again anytime soon. She was certain that he had finally left John and Fanny's farm, for he had his own responsibilities to tend. What John was doing to manage that large farm by himself, Eleanor could only speculate. Certainly Fanny would be forced to work alongside him, and Eleanor could not help but feel a sweet justice at the thought.

The bitterness in her heart seemed to have invaded every aspect of her world.

When it came time for the kneeling prayer, she covered her face and rested her elbows on the bench, begging God to forgive her for feeling any delight in the suffering of others, even if it was only Fanny.

After the worship service *Maem* found Eleanor and whispered that they could skip the fellowship meal to return home. The anxiety she felt was certainly shared by Eleanor, so after making an excuse of feeling poorly, *Maem* led her two daughters away from the gathering to begin the walk home.

Forty-five minutes later, when they walked through the front door of the cottage, what greeted them caused Eleanor a momentary pause. Instead of Willis and Mary Ann sitting on the porch, as decorum would dictate, they were inside the house. Willis stood by the fireplace, staring at nothing, while Mary Ann remained seated in the rocking chair, her head in her hands as she wept.

"What's this?" *Maem* asked as she hurried to her daughter's side. "What's happened, Willis?"

Eleanor gathered Maggie into her arms, holding her younger sister close as if protecting her. She stared wide-eyed at Willis, imploring him to explain the situation.

"I...I must return to the family farm," he said. "Immediately."

"Immediately?" Eleanor repeated.

"When will you return?" *Maem* asked.

"I..." He looked away from them. "I don't know."

"Willis?" Eleanor gently pushed Maggie to the side and took a step toward him. "What is going on?"

"It's just that...well...they need me to help with their market stand in Maryland. I'll be there four days a week. It's just"—he hesitated, searching for the correct word—"just easier to travel from there and too far to visit here."

"Why the urgency?" *Maem* looked as confused as Eleanor felt.

"I...oh, it's something I cannot explain..." He seemed to fidget as he stood there, clearly uncomfortable with the

119

confrontation that required explanation. "Oh, why should I torment myself further!" he declared. Without another word he hurried to the door, brushing past both Eleanor and Maggie without so much as a good-bye.

Mary Ann continued to weep, and Eleanor's heart broke for her. How Willis could simply abandon her sister was beyond bewildering! His affection for her could not be denied, especially given his daily attention to her. While Eleanor might disagree with his manner of courting, she could not doubt that he cared deeply for Mary Ann.

She crossed the room and knelt before her sister, peering up at her tear-stricken face. "What happened, Mary Ann? Talk to us."

"Leave me alone!" she cried and rose to her feet. A sob escaped her throat as she ran from the room, dashed up the stairs, and slammed the bedroom door behind her.

*Maem* began to pace the floor, wringing her hands before her. "Oh, Eleanor! What awful thing has happened?"

Standing up, Eleanor shook her head. "This doesn't seem like Willis. That he adores her is more than apparent. Even I can see that."

"Will he return, *Maem*?" Maggie asked in a soft voice.

"Oh, Maggie, my dear!" They had forgotten that Maggie witnessed the unhappy exchange and abrupt departure. *Maem* hurried over to embrace the young girl.

Neither Eleanor nor *Maem* answered right away. Willis's abrupt departure and Mary Ann's unusual display of histrionics had left them both speechless. What on earth could have set him running off in such a manner? What could he possibly have said to upset Mary Ann in such a way?

"I'm not certain he will," Eleanor finally said.

"First Edwin and now Willis?" Maggie cried, the tears beginning to well up in her eyes. "I don't think I'll ever want to court someone if this is what happens!"

To Eleanor's amazement Maggie began to cry, and like Mary Ann, she ran up the stairs and slammed shut the door to her bedroom.

"Oh, help," Eleanor muttered, turning to face her mother. "Not her too!"

Her mother appeared ashen faced and in as much shock as Eleanor. "I never knew her to harbor as many sensibilities as Mary Ann."

"Such times we are experiencing," Eleanor managed to respond. "Surely something good must come out of this. I just wish I knew when."

# ❦ *Chapter Fourteen* ❧

FOR THE FIRST part of the week Mary Ann did little more than wander outside, her eyes searching the horizon as if her wishes alone would produce the image of John Willis riding toward their house. Eleanor found herself setting down her sewing at least once an hour to check on her. Each time, however, that she peered out the window, she saw the same image: the lone figure of Mary Ann standing in the middle of her garden patch, nothing but dirt beneath her feet. Occasionally Eleanor would spot her standing toward the farthest end of the garden or pacing the edge. But Mary Ann never moved from that area because it provided the best vantage point of the road.

On Thursday morning two gray-topped buggies rode up the road, each one causing Mary Ann to start and fuss until she realized that neither was driven by John Willis. They were merely neighbors dropping off some clothing. The word had spread about the Detweilers' sewing service, and women were eager to take advantage of their assistance.

"I'm off to market tomorrow at four in the morning," one woman said, her voice emotionless but the dark circles under her eyes speaking volumes. "My *maem* is watching the *kinner,* and I'll be back Saturday late. *Mayhaps* I can pick it up on Monday, then?"

Eleanor nodded her head as she wrote down the items on a pad of paper. "What type of market, if I may ask?"

"Oh, a large farmer's market in Maryland. My husband leases space there to sell meats," she answered. Casually she raised her hand to swat at a fly near her forehead. "He goes on Wednesdays until Saturday. I join him on Fridays since the weekend is the busiest time and he needs fresh inventory anyway." She sighed.

Eleanor couldn't imagine how they managed to run a small farm and a meat market stand in another state. With the husband gone for more than half of the week, the bulk of the work most certainly fell on this woman's shoulders. And with *kinner* too? "*Mayhaps* I can walk over to your *haus* and drop it off on Saturday for you," Eleanor suggested, hoping that, if nothing else, that might offer the woman some assistance.

Not ten minutes had passed after the woman left when another approaching horse was heard. Mary Ann called out to Eleanor, her voice loud and excited.

"Come, Eleanor! It's a lone rider! Come see who it is!"

When Eleanor joined her sister in the middle of the empty garden patch, Mary Ann seemed more alive and animated than she had in days. "It's him. Oh, Eleanor! I just know it's John Willis."

But the figure that approached around the evergreens was certainly not Willis.

It took Eleanor a moment to realize that she recognized the man, and only when Mary Ann gasped and cried out, "Edwin?" did she truly believe it.

He dismounted the horse a few feet from the garden, pausing to let his gaze linger on Eleanor for a moment.

"Edwin!" Mary Ann cried. Forgetting her manners, she ran up and gave him a warm hug. "We knew you would come!"

Eleanor blushed, wishing she could take back Mary Ann's words that clearly insinuated the family had talked about Edwin.

He gave a nervous laugh. "My visit is a bit overdue, *ja*?"

"Have you just come from Manheim, then?" Mary Ann asked, excitement in her voice. "How do my gardens look? And the flower beds? Has Fanny been maintaining them? Oh, how I miss seeing gardens!"

"*Ach*, Mary Ann," Eleanor finally spoke, chastising her sister. "Such questions! I'm sure they look no different from the gardens around here."

Mary Ann responded by giving Eleanor a sharp look and gesturing to the empty garden plot. "We don't have any gardens here!"

Choosing not to respond, Eleanor lifted her eyes to look at Edwin. Something about the way he stood before her caused a conflict of emotions within her. While her heart continued to beat rapidly, she noted that he seemed more reserved than he had been when they left Manheim. In fact, with the dullness in his eyes, he looked downright unhappy.

"Uh...*ja*, your gardens remain quite pretty," Edwin responded at last. "But they are not as beautiful as when you tended to them. Although I haven't been there for a week or so."

Eleanor heard her mother approach the front door, and when she saw Edwin, she hurried over to greet him, a bright smile on her face. "What a welcome surprise!" she said as she shook his hand. "Have you just come from Manheim, then? How does your sister fare?"

He seemed to fidget, his feet shuffling in the grass. "Fanny does quite well, I'm sure, although I haven't been there for a short while."

"Oh?"

"I've returned to Narvon to visit with my family and some...friends," he said, avoiding eye contact with them. "I thought to visit with you on my way back." He paused. "To Manheim."

This news pleased their mother, and her smile broadened. Eleanor knew why. Quarryville was quite remotely located from both Narvon and Manheim. Such a visit—and on horseback!—spoke of an endearment for the family, more than words could express.

"*Vell*, do come inside and join us for dinner," *Maem* said, gesturing toward the house. "It's almost ready, and I'm sure there is much news to catch up on!"

Inside they seated themselves, Edwin in the rocking chair, and Eleanor continued to watch him, curious about Edwin's distant manner. At first she thought he might be nervous and embarrassed at the delay in his promised visit. Now, however, she wondered if something was wrong. He wrung his hands and continued to avoid her eyes.

"Is everyone well at Manheim and Narvon?" she asked, paying attention to how he shifted his gaze to look at her and then looked down at the floor.

"Oh *ja*, everyone is fine," he responded. "My *bruder* is managing the farm for me while I help John and Fanny." He hesitated for a moment. "I do believe your departure has helped Fanny gain a finer appreciation of the hard work involved in maintaining a farm."

Mary Ann snickered, and Eleanor gave her a stern look.

"Farmwork is hard, indeed," Eleanor said. "But I miss it. We've nothing to do with farming here, but we have kept busy sewing clothing for people in the community."

*Maem* hurried over and handed Edwin a glass of meadow tea. "That was Eleanor's doing. Quite a fine idea. Helps some of the people and earns us some extra money."

Edwin looked at her at last. His eyes brightened for a moment. "Was it, now?" He smiled for the first time in a way that appeared genuine. "Why am I not surprised?" He turned his attention toward her mother. "Are you getting on well here, then?" he asked.

"Oh, indeed," *Maem* said.

"Except for having to visit and dine at the Millers!" Mary Ann added in a callous manner.

Both Eleanor and *Maem* stared at her, too surprised by her complaint.

"It's more than anyone should have to bear," she said defiantly. "Widow Jennings, especially!"

"Mary Ann!" Eleanor couldn't keep herself from responding. "How can you say such a thing? They have been nothing but kind and gracious in welcoming us here!"

Rolling her eyes, Mary Ann said, "But the payment for that is listening to their constant prattle and bearing their continuous prodding into our private lives! Why, they practically chased John Willis away!"

Edwin sat up in his seat. "John Willis? I don't think I know anyone named Willis."

"Oh, but you shall," Mary Ann said with complete confidence.

"I see."

For the rest of his visit Edwin's reserve slowly melted away and he seemed much more like himself. At one point *Maem* and Mary Ann left the house to go outside, walking down the lane to meet Maggie on her return from school. Eleanor felt awkward, sitting alone with Edwin. The length of their separation from each other certainly created some discomfort, but Eleanor noticed how Edwin tried to minimize his distance and make up for lost time.

"I suspect I will be taking over my *daed*'s farm in the spring," he said slowly.

"You don't sound happy about it," she heard herself say, immediately wishing she hadn't made such an intimate observation.

"I...I reckon I'm not as happy as I'd like to be," he admitted.

She wanted to ask why, but decorum held back the question. Instead, she merely said, "I'm sorry to hear that, Edwin."

He was about to respond when Maggie burst through the door. Like Mary Ann, she jumped into Edwin's arms and gave him a sisterly embrace.

"I knew you'd come!" she gushed. "No matter what the others thought and said, I just knew it!"

Eleanor did not need a mirror to know that her cheeks flushed pink once again.

Edwin laughed at the greeting bestowed on him by Maggie. "I did promise I would, didn't I, now?"

"What took you so long?" Maggie demanded, a playful pout on her lips.

"I...uh...I had some things to take care of in Narvon." And, once again, that sorrowful look returned to his eyes and an invisible wall seemed to separate the former Edwin from the Edwin that now sat before them.

Mary Ann and *Maem* had just walked into the house when he said this, and before either one of them could inquire further—for Eleanor could clearly see they both wanted to ask—she quickly changed the discussion.

"How long will you be visiting?"

Edwin shifted his weight in the chair and clasped his hands before him as his eyes looked at the small clock hanging over the window in the kitchen. "Regrettably I must return today. I borrowed the horse from a friend of mine in Georgetown." He paused. "I'm considering purchasing the horse, so he let me ride here to visit with you. My driver is picking me up in just an hour, so I shall have to leave shortly."

"But I haven't had time to visit with you!" Maggie cried in alarm.

Eleanor reached out her hand and gently took Maggie's. "Now Maggie, you should be grateful that Edwin stayed so long just to see you! Surely he could have left long before now. You should thank him and not complain." She smiled at Edwin while still holding Maggie's hand. "Your visit here has been the highlight of our week, for sure and certain. And you must send our regards to John, Fanny, and little Henry."

Within the quarter hour, Edwin said his good-byes, and Eleanor walked with him outside to where his horse grazed. Their parting was friendly but with no promises on his part to return and that distant look remaining in his eyes. As he rode the horse down the lane, he never looked back. Eleanor sighed, knowing what had not been spoken. Whatever she felt for Edwin and whatever she hoped he felt for her, Edwin Fisher's visit had been strictly to fulfill a promise and not for any other reason.

"Seriously, Eleanor!" Mary Ann scolded when she returned to the house. "Could you have been any colder toward him?"

Stunned, Eleanor stared at her. "Cold? What do you mean?"

"Clearly he would have stayed. You only had to ask! Maggie could have slept in *Maem*'s room. Why, he looked so sad and unhappy! I'm sure I know the reason why!"

Gritting her teeth so that she did not say what she wanted to, Eleanor waited, knowing that Mary Ann, never one to be shy with words, would volunteer her opinion without being asked.

"If he questioned your affections for him before, he certainly suspects now that you have no more interest in him than you would in an older *bruder!*" Mary Ann said with a sharp tone in her voice.

No longer could Eleanor stay silent on the matter. She narrowed her eyes, her attention only on Mary Ann. "Better that than to throw myself at him and have the whole *g'may* talk about how forward I am!"

Mary Ann caught her breath and Eleanor turned, walking back to the door. She needed time alone to clear her head. Despite her pointed response to Mary Ann, Eleanor wasn't so certain that there wasn't an element of truth to her *schwester*'s accusation. Perhaps Edwin did not understand how she felt for him. Had her own sense of propriety driven away the one man she had hoped to love for the rest of her life?

# ❦ Chapter Fifteen ❦

MARY ANN TRUDGED behind *Maem* and Eleanor as they crossed the side field toward the Millers' house. Up ahead Maggie chased a butterfly, tripping once and disappearing before she stood up, brushed off her dress, and started running again.

"Why, exactly, must I come along? I'm not feeling well, you know," Mary Ann complained, dragging her feet through the tall grass. "I could just as well stay home, rest, and even sew!"

"You hate to sew," Eleanor said over her shoulder.

"Not as much as having to take a meal with that obnoxious Widow Jennings and her mousy daughter!"

"Mary Ann!" *Maem* scolded her for her impertinence. "Such cheekiness! I know I raised you better than that!" But when *Maem* turned back around, Eleanor thought she saw the hint of a smile on her mother's face.

Over a week had passed since Edwin's unexpected visit. Eleanor certainly had felt the pangs of grief mixed with guilt during the initial days. She kept thinking about the idea that he might have missed seeing her fondness for him. Had she truly been so proper that he might have mistaken propriety for apathy? At night she couldn't sleep. She lay on her side, her back to Mary Ann in the bed they shared.

With eyes wide open she stared into the darkness and kept thinking over every conversation she had with Edwin. She hunted her memory for clues that might indicate the flaw in her behavior that caused him to be so reserved.

No one seemed to notice her fatigue, and for that she was grateful. She kept her worries to herself, not even sharing them with Mary Ann, who had already made her opinion well known. There would be no compassion from her sister, that was for sure and certain. In the meantime her silence allowed Mary Ann the privilege of stealing the spotlight as she vocalized her pining for Willis while simultaneously planning for her as-yet-to-be-mentioned wedding.

The previous day, when Jacob had stopped down to invite them to Saturday supper, *Maem* had quickly accepted on behalf of the four of them. Eleanor presumed her mother's quick acceptance had a lot to do with the morose behavior of one daughter and the precipitous prattle of the other. Now, as the Detweiler family walked toward the big white farm-house, Eleanor felt a sense of relief. It was good to leave the cottage and socialize with others, even if the socializing was often one-sided.

"Come in, come in!" Widow Jennings cried out, flinging open the front door before they had even reached the entry walkway. A small child was draped over her shoulder, its head hidden beneath a crocheted blanket. Clearly the child was sleeping, which didn't seem to hinder Widow Jennings from talking. With a broad smile, her happiness at seeing the Detweilers more than apparent, she motioned them inside. "We've such a surprise for you today!"

Once inside the house, Eleanor found herself leading the way into the great gathering room that connected with the Millers' kitchen. Leah Miller was busy at the stove, so involved in preparing the meal that she barely did more than wave to acknowledge their arrival. Widow Jennings, however, hurried over to the sitting area and sat in the rocking chair, continuing to hold her grandchild in her arms. Her loud, boisterous voice did not wake the sleeping child, a fact that surprised Eleanor but did not seem to interest anyone else in the room.

"*Danke* for the invitation," *Maem* said to Jacob, who sat in his own recliner by the propane lantern. Despite the sun not having set, the hissing noise and bright light of the flame flooded the room.

"What's a gathering without our family?" he said cheerfully. Then he motioned to where three women sat on the sofa on the far side of the sitting area. "Family makes every occasion special, for sure and certain."

Eleanor smiled politely at them and waited for an introduction. Two of the women were younger, both refreshingly pretty in a plain sort of way. As for the older woman, there was nothing remarkable, or even memorable, about her appearance. She had deep creases on her forehead and her nose looked bulbous. However, there was a sparkle in her eyes as she looked at the newcomers, her eyes pausing to rest on Eleanor.

"Let me guess! The Detweiler sisters!" she said and laughed good-naturedly.

"Come, come, girls!" Jacob said, waving his hand for them to step closer. "What's this shyness routine? I want you to meet these fine young ladies!"

Eleanor did as instructed while Mary Ann had to nudge Maggie, who was prone to shyness around strangers. Meanwhile *Maem* excused herself to help Leah in the kitchen.

"This is my sister-in-law, Charlotte, and her nieces, Lydia and Annie," Jacob declared. "They arrived just this morning to visit for a few days."

"We've heard so much about you from *Mammi!*" Charlotte said, shaking Eleanor's hand with more enthusiasm than was necessary.

It took Eleanor a moment to realize that she referenced Widow Jennings as her mother, a fact that startled her since Widow Jennings rarely talked about her first daughter, let alone mentioning a second. And her appearance was nothing at all like her mother's. While Widow Jennings's hair was white from age, Charlotte had brown hair pulled back so tight that her part was almost an inch wide. And from the looks of it she enjoyed her desserts a little too much, for her waist was so rotund that, for a moment, Eleanor thought she might be pregnant.

Even more distressing, however, was the comment that Charlotte and Widow Jennings had had discussions about the Detweilers. For just a moment Eleanor wondered what Widow Jennings saw when she looked at her mother and sisters. She knew from comments Widow Jennings made about others that she was not prone to holding back her opinions. Certainly Mary Ann's behavior had been a topic of conversation, as Eleanor had warned her it would be.

Charlotte, however, didn't seem to know that she was unknown to Eleanor and the rest of the Detweiler family. "We've heard so much about the Detweilers, haven't we, Lydia? Hmm? Annie?"

Lydia gave a soft smile. "Oh *ja*, we have."

"It's nice that you could visit," Eleanor said politely. "And on such a beautiful day."

"And I simply can't wait to go for a walk after dinner!" Charlotte clapped her hands together, more like a child than an adult. In fact, if it weren't for the weathered look on her forehead and the corners of her eyes, Eleanor would have thought she was younger than Lydia or Annie, and they both appeared to be no more than twenty. "I just love the outdoors. And walking. When you don't live in the country, you forget how delightful the walks are! Such beautiful scenery and all of those birds!" She gasped and clasped her hands together. "I love watching all of the birds, especially the ones in the haylofts. You'd think they'd be starting their migration, though, wouldn't you?"

"Do you live nearby, then?" Eleanor asked, more out of politeness than interest.

"Oh, heavens, no! We're up on the other side of Honey Brook," Charlotte gushed.

"And, regrettably, I shall be returning with them when they leave," Widow Jennings said. Eleanor wondered whether her regrets were for leaving Quarryville or for having to battle Charlotte to commandeer the conversation.

Charlotte seemed immune to the double meaning of her mother's words. "You do so love Honey Brook, don't you, *Mammi*? It's so different from down here. We live just close enough to town—if you can really call it that!—to walk there. Of course what is there to see in Honey Brook? Although they do have that one Chinese food restaurant on 322! But who wants to walk through town anyway? Especially in the winter. Dreadful winters!" She made a face. "I could do quite well enough without all that snow, couldn't you, *Mammi*?"

Widow Jennings groaned and rolled her eyes. "Heavens, yes! I think next year I shall go down to Pinecraft in Florida! I have two *schwesters* with homes there."

At this Charlotte laughed, although it sounded more like a giddy giggle. "You say that every year, *Mammi*, and then you never do it! I suspect you like Honey Brook just as much as you like Quarryville!"

"Mark my words, Charlotte! One of these days I shall make good on my threats!"

Mother and daughter laughed as if sharing the greatest joke between the two of them. Eleanor immediately saw the resemblance, if not in looks then at least in personality. Like her mother, Charlotte talked a lot, more often about nothing than something, however. The constant chatter seemed to fill the air and lighten the mood.

"Honey Brook?" Mary Ann said, her face lighting up at the name. Eleanor could see that the wheels of her mind were turning, and she suspected she knew why. "Isn't that near Narvon?"

Widow Jennings laughed and leaned forward to touch Charlotte's knee. "Suddenly Honey Brook doesn't seem so desolate and far away to one of our guests!"

"Oh, now, *Mammi*!" Charlotte replied. "I won't even try to guess who the lucky young man is to have captured Mary Ann's attention!"

Mary Ann flushed and looked away. Eleanor felt a small sense of satisfaction in her sister's embarrassment, although she would have preferred for Mary Ann just to remain silent about Narvon in the first place. Almost two weeks had passed without so much as a word from John Willis. Mary Ann sent letters every two days, sneaking out of the house when she thought *Maem* was napping and Eleanor not paying attention. In the afternoons when Maggie brought in the mail, Mary Ann would hold out a moment of hope that

Willis responded, only to be gravely disappointed to learn he hadn't.

"Perhaps the Detweilers might come visit us in Honey Brook, hmm?" Widow Jennings offered on behalf of her daughter.

"What a *wunderbarr gut* idea!" Charlotte turned to her two nieces. "Isn't there a big fund-raiser coming up soon?"

Lydia, the younger of the two women, nodded her head. Her pale skin reminded Eleanor of a porcelain doll. It was more than apparent that Lydia did not live, or work, on a farm. "Oh *ja*. The firehouse fund-raiser! We promised to donate baked goods to help them raise money." She looked at her sister. "Right, Annie?"

"That's the perfect occasion!" Charlotte said, ignoring Annie's attempt at a response.

"I want to go too!" Maggie said, too loud for a soon-to-be young woman.

Eleanor gave her a look to be silent. No one needed to remind Maggie that she had school, and even more important, if all the girls were to go, *Maem* would be left home alone. That was something Eleanor simply could not allow to happen.

"They always have such a gathering for the bake sale!" Charlotte seemed pleased with herself for having thought of the idea to include Mary Ann and Eleanor. "I dare say that neither one of you girls will walk home that evening!"

At this Widow Jennings held up her hand. "Now, now, *dochder*! Don't set your sights on introducing either one of the Detweilers to your Honey Brook men. It appears that both are spoken for!"

"You don't say!" With a wide smile Charlotte stared at both Mary Ann and Eleanor. "Dare we ask the names of these soon-to-be unavailable men?"

Widow Jennings could barely contain herself. "We have quite the mystery around the one of them," she said. "All we know of Eleanor's intended is that his name begins with *F*!"

"*F*?" Charlotte seemed to think about this for a long minute. "Frederick? Francis?"

This time it was Jacob who spoke up. "Wasn't there a young man riding through here just the other day? Fisher was his last name."

Simultaneously Widow Jennings and Charlotte gasped.

"The *F* name at last!" Widow Jennings cried and leaned over to playfully tap Jacob on his arm. "I told you it wasn't necessarily his first name, didn't I?"

Eleanor felt the heat rising to her face. Fortunately her *maem* called her over to help in the kitchen. As soon as she started to walk away, she could hear the conversation shift to something else and said a silent prayer of gratitude. If they had begun inquiring further and mentioned Edwin's first name, she knew that she'd have no hope of responding in a way that maintained her privacy.

Mary Ann and Maggie went outside to watch the Millers' children while Eleanor helped her mother and Leah with the food preparation. The distraction kept Eleanor's mind from wandering to her worries about Edwin and her mortification of Jacob revealing Edwin's last name. If earlier she had thought the social outing a pleasant diversion, she now felt differently.

"Dear Miss Eleanor," a soft voice said from behind her.

Eleanor turned, surprised to see Lydia standing there, that same soft smile on her face.

"I have been so looking forward to meeting you. And I'm delighted to hear that you'll be coming to Honey Brook. I've heard quite a bit about you."

Politely Eleanor smiled. "Widow Jennings can be rather kind with her compliments."

"Oh no," Lydia said. "Not from my *grossmammi*. We share a mutual acquaintance, it seems."

"We do?"

Lydia nodded, the simple untied strings from her white prayer *kapp* brushing against her shoulder. "*Ja*, we do. The Fishers."

Eleanor caught herself from reacting. "My sister-in-law, Fanny?" She couldn't imagine Fanny saying anything nice about her or any of her family, unless it was to praise them for moving out so expeditiously.

"Her family, *ja*," Lydia said. "And I do so want to discuss something with you. I've heard how practical you are in both thought and action."

*Practical.* The word hung between them, and Eleanor could not help but translate that to mean that she had a reputation for being proper and refined in matters of outward appearances. Too proper and refined, Eleanor scolded herself, according to Mary Ann. The accusation continued to haunt Eleanor as, even now, she felt the harsh sting of self-reproach.

"I was wondering," Lydia began, walking a step behind Eleanor as she set the table, "how much you know about Fanny's mother."

"Fanny's *maem*?" Caught off guard, Eleanor paused. Why would Lydia be interested in her? "I've met her once or twice, if I recall rightly, but I know very little about her."

"*Ach.*" Lydia stopped following Eleanor for a second and stared into the distance. She appeared distracted and disappointed at the same time.

Continuing with setting the table, Eleanor glanced over toward Lydia's aunt Charlotte and sister Annie. Charlotte was as animated, if not more so, than her mother while Annie merely sat there on the sofa, quiet and demure with nothing to contribute to the conversation. While curious as to why the two sisters had accompanied their aunt, Eleanor knew better than to ask. One thing she did know was that there was something odd about Lydia, especially how she lingered around her without offering to help. While Lydia appeared to present a righteous front, her lack of action spoke louder than her facade.

"You must think I'm terribly forward for having inquired about your relationship with the Fisher family," Lydia said at last.

Eleanor forced a small smile. "Truly I hadn't thought about it either way."

Lydia, however, seemed intent on talking about it. "I don't want you to think me too presumptuous in presuming such intimacy since we have just met."

Eleanor merely made a soft noise in the back of her throat in response. While she hadn't thought that before, she now wondered why Lydia was bringing more attention to the very behavior she worried that Eleanor thought poorly of.

"I...it's just that..." Lydia smiled demurely, and at once Eleanor sensed something was amiss.

"Truly, Lydia," Eleanor said. "I thought nothing of the inquiry. Fanny is, after all, my sister-in-law. If you are familiar or wish to be familiar with the Fishers, it is only natural that you would inquire. Think nothing of it."

Glancing around to make sure no one was watching, Lydia took Eleanor's arm and led her toward the hallway. Once they were alone, Lydia focused her attention on Eleanor and lowered her voice so that no one could overhear. "I am familiar with the Fishers, but I have yet to meet the mother. I was hoping that you might know something about her character." She wetted her lips as if they were unusually dry and with apparent great effort continued talking. "You see, I have no one to confide in and I have heard so much about you. I feel that I can trust you."

Eleanor felt discomfort with the implied soon-to-be confidence. She knew nothing of this woman and did not want to be intimate with her. However, she wasn't certain how to respond. "Lydia, surely you could confide in your *schwester*."

"*Nee*, I cannot."

With a sigh Eleanor said, "While I don't know your secret that needs confiding and I'm not one to want to be privy to such things, I can assure you that my lips will never speak of whatever you wish to tell me."

Apparently that was just the answer Lydia wanted to hear. She lit up and leaned forward. "I'm to marry into the Fisher family this autumn."

It took Eleanor a moment to comprehend what Lydia had just said. There were only two young men of eligible age. "You're to marry Roy Fisher?"

Lydia laughed a little too loudly and pressed her hand against Eleanor's arm. "No, silly. I'm to marry Edwin Fisher. Didn't he tell you? I thought he had said you'd become such good friends." She turned her gaze on Eleanor and seemed to examine her closely—too closely.

Eleanor tried to remain calm, but she knew that her eyes widened and the color drained from her face. Was it possible that Edwin fancied Lydia? Or had he been engaged to her all along? "No, Edwin never told me. When...when did you become acquainted with him, if I may ask?"

Suddenly Lydia seemed animated as her nervousness disappeared. "Why, a few years back! He courted me during our *rumschpringe*. Since they live two church districts away, I have yet to meet his *maem*, you see. I have heard she is rather opinionated, and, *vell*, I was hoping you might have some pointers for me. I do want her to like me! So very much!"

As Eleanor realized the implication of Lydia's words, she began to feel light-headed and dizzy. All of this time she had been so confident that Edwin cared for her, and then, after his visit last week, when he appeared so unhappy and distant, she feared that it was his perception that she lacked interest in him. Now, however, she learned that, all along, it was Edwin who was not interested in her!

"Oh my," she whispered to herself.

"*Kum esse!*" Leah called from the kitchen.

Lydia tightened her grip on Eleanor's arm. "Promise to never speak a word?"

Barely able to move, never mind think, it was all Eleanor could do to respond with a simple, "*Ja*, of course."

For the remainder of the visit Eleanor sat quietly next to Mary Ann, neither young woman more than picking at her food. Their silence went unnoticed by their host and his mother-in-law as they gossiped and joked with Charlotte and the others. With nothing else required of Eleanor except the occasional smile or halfhearted attempt at laughing, she could think of only one thing: the pain that she felt in her heart as she realized Edwin Fisher was not just lost to her but had never been hers to begin with.

# ❧ *Chapter Sixteen* ❧

OR THE NEXT few days Eleanor remained extra pensive, trying to focus on the chores around the house and the sewing for their growing client base so that she could forget the feeling of distress that filled her chest. She often found herself washing already clean dishes or resewing a tear she had already repaired, forcing her to take out precious stitches and redo her work.

At night she read the Bible, her eyes often scanning the same line over and over again without comprehending the verse she read. And after she blew out the small kerosene lantern on her nightstand, she lay on the bed, staring into the darkness, her mind racing and her heart beating. With sleep eluding her, she arose feeling wearier than when she retired the evening before. And each day repeated the cycle.

After the shock of hearing Lydia's confession, Eleanor found that she could think of nothing else. Her mind replayed the joyful manner with which Lydia had shared her secret. How unjust when one person's joy creates painful angst in another!

Try as she might, Eleanor could not make sense of Edwin and his behavior. She also found it difficult to think of him as a man without scruples, for only a dishonorable man would lead a woman to think he favored her company over others.

That was when she began to wonder if she had been wrong. Could it be that she had misread Edwin's conversations and glances, his smiles and attention, and that he had only been pleasant and polite? Or had Mary Ann been right in claiming that she should have expressed herself more openly in case Edwin was interested in her but doubted her feelings for him? What if he didn't know how she felt? And if he had known, would he have called off his engagement to Lydia? Still, knowing now that he had been engaged to Lydia that entire time brought Eleanor full circle, as she returned to the question of whether she had misread Edwin's feelings.

At those moments, when the disappointment in Edwin rose deep within her broken heart, Eleanor doubted her own ability to judge the character of others. Perhaps people she thought were good, truly righteous, and honorable were not. She knew everyone had sin, for only Jesus was perfect, but for her entire life, Eleanor had believed that, for the most part, people were good at their core.

Now, after all that had happened in such a short period of time, she wasn't so sure.

She wondered about Christian Bechtler, who had yet to return after his abrupt departure from his own picnic. No one seemed to know where he was, or perhaps it was that no one seemed to care. He was a man everyone was so glad to see yet no one seemed to talk about. Of course Eleanor remembered that Widow Jennings had confided in her that Christian had a sullied past involving a young woman. Yet, in the short time she'd known him, Eleanor sensed that he was righteous and good-hearted, a man of God and not the world. Could her opinion of Christian be in error too?

And, of course, she couldn't help but consider Willis. His lack of correspondence with her sister worried Eleanor, especially when she watched Mary Ann. Her sister still waited by the mailbox each day, although her numerous letters to him remained unanswered. The look of despair on her sister's face as she walked back toward the house, her feet dragging along the dirt lane and her hands empty save for the occasional bill, made Eleanor wonder at Willis's callousness. Had he intentionally deceived her sister?

That he fancied Mary Ann, Eleanor had no doubt. She knew that a young man could not fake the emotions he displayed toward a woman. Not in such an open manner anyway. His words, his actions, and even his looks in Mary Ann's direction all indicated that his feelings were true and honorable. However, Eleanor was baffled by one question. If Willis truly loved her sister, why hadn't he responded to Mary Ann's letters?

By Thursday *Maem* was beside herself with the quiet that had fallen over the house. She alone had noticed Eleanor's subdued behavior, but as always, she refused to interfere when it came to personal matters. Eleanor appreciated that. The last thing she wanted was to disclose the secret she had so innocently promised to keep.

However, it didn't help that Mary Ann began to sulk around the house, unable to focus on sewing or tending to even the most basic of chores. A dark cloud seemed to linger over her head, her mood black and her spirits down. She took to mumbling under her breath as she paced the floor waiting for the postal truck. Her appetite suffered as well, and she hadn't eaten one morsel of food since the day before last. No matter how much Eleanor tried to coax her to help with the increasing pile of clothes clients dropped off, Mary Ann barely even acknowledged her. Instead, she continued pacing the floor until exhaustion forced her to sit down for a few minutes. With each passing day, her hope seemed to fade just a little bit more.

The noise of an approaching car engine broke the silence and caused Eleanor to look up. She glanced at the clock on the wall. Two o'clock.

"The mailman's here, Mary Ann," she said softly, returning her attention to the garment in her hand.

Slowly, and without any indication of excitement, Mary Ann stood up from where she had been sitting and walked to the door. Her feet shuffled against the floor and her shoulders hunched over as she disappeared outside.

Eleanor wished she could ease her sister's burden, but she had her own issues to contend with. Besides, their approach to courtship had been so different that Eleanor wasn't certain how to comfort her. While there was not much Mary Ann could do now, Eleanor often wondered just how much her sister should *not* have done. Perhaps Mary Ann's willingness to be so open about their courtship had simply scared Willis away.

"Poor thing," *Maem* said, watching Mary Ann from the open door. "She's suffering so. I just don't understand this Willis! Such a good reputation and from a fine family. And his interactions with Mary Ann...why, I thought for certain they would be wed this year!"

Eleanor was about to respond when she heard another voice, one she easily recognized. Widow Jennings must be walking down the lane with Mary Ann. Her loud voice and easy laughter filled the air, increasing with each step. Finally she seemed to burst into the room, her energy filling every corner of the house.

"So busy working!" She shook her head and clicked her tongue as she assessed the different piles of clothing Eleanor was working on. "And inside too? Tsk, tsk. On such a beautiful day!"

Eleanor glanced at her mother and then at Widow Jennings. "The sun is hard on the eyes when sewing," she said.

"True, true." Without being invited, Widow Jennings sat down in a chair by the kitchen table. "I bring an invitation!" She smiled broadly and looked at each of the three women. "One that, I dare say, shall bring a smile to some very sober faces in here!" Reaching into a pocket of her dress, she withdrew a white envelope. "My *dochder*, Charlotte, invites all of you to accompany me to Honey Brook. For the firemen's fund-raiser!" She handed the letter to Eleanor. "Just think. The festival is next Saturday. We will leave on Thursday and have a baking party in the afternoon on Friday. Their church service is Sunday, and I can personally attest that their preachers are as good as, if not better than, our own!"

Mary Ann rolled her eyes, and Eleanor shot her a fierce look of reproach.

"We'll have to return on Monday. But what a fun time we shall have, hmm?" She smiled mischievously as if she had one last secret to share with them. "*Ach*, I almost forgot. Charlotte is fairly certain that a John Willis is in the area, visiting with a neighboring family. Without doubt, if that's truth, he will be in attendance."

At this last bit of news Mary Ann gasped. Her eyes sparkled and she hurried over to Eleanor, grabbing for the letter. Her eyes scanned the piece of paper, and, when finished, she looked at Widow Jennings with a new admiration. "Of course we will go!" Then, realizing that she hadn't asked for permission, she turned toward her mother. "Right, *Maem*?"

For a moment, their mother hesitated, her mouth opening slightly as she looked from Widow Jennings to Mary Ann to Eleanor and back to Mary Ann. "I...I don't think we can. Maggie..." She didn't finish the sentence. She didn't have to. Maggie was back at school, and it would not be wise to pull her out for so many days when the school year had just started.

"But..." Mary Ann's eyes widened and a panicked look passed over her face.

"There are not buts about that, Mary Ann."

Eleanor took a deep breath, waiting for what she knew was the inevitable.

Widow Jennings scratched at the whiskers under her chin. She seemed to be thinking, and Eleanor knew exactly about what. "*Mayhaps* there's another way," Widow Jennings said. "Let me take Mary Ann and Eleanor. They'll be quite helpful preparing for the fund-raiser, anyway. We'll need to bake a lot, and Lydia would be rather disappointed if they didn't attend." She looked at Eleanor in particular. "She's rather fond of you girls, it seems."

Immediately Mary Ann's expression changed from panic back to elation. "*Ja, Maem*! That's a *wunderbarr gut* idea!" She glanced at Eleanor, a pleading look in her eyes as if begging her sister to speak up on behalf of this idea. "Right, Eleanor? You always say we don't do enough charity work in the community!"

"I had meant our own community, Mary Ann," Eleanor said in a soft voice.

Mary Ann's eyes appeared to bulge out of her head, and she mouthed something. It took Eleanor a second or two to realize that she was begging with a silent word: *please.*

"But," Eleanor added slowly, "helping other communities is *gut* too." If she had not been so desperate to cheer her sister, she would have vigorously resisted the idea. To be thrown into Lydia's company for days at a time would be torture indeed.

Mary Ann gave a little jump before containing her excitement. Widow Jennings, however, had noticed. Smiling, she nodded her head. "Now, if your *maem* will agree, I can ride over to use the phone at the Yoders' farm down the lane," she said expectantly. "Jacob's barn phone is broken and he's not desiring to fix it, you know."

What was there to say? Eleanor knew that *Maem* had been backed into a corner. However, she also knew that her mother wanted Mary Ann to be happy. If happiness was to be found in Willis, the young man she loved, why would anyone stand in the way of her being able to reconnect with him? Besides, Eleanor knew the feeling was mutual. Even though she continued to wonder at his silence in the weeks since he departed, she knew Willis shared Mary Ann's feelings. Anyone could have seen it, especially Widow Jennings.

"I reckon it's all right," *Maem* acquiesced, shifting her gaze from Mary Ann to Eleanor. "On one condition, however."

Mary Ann bounced on the balls of her feet, her hands pressed together in front of her chest as she eagerly awaited her mother's final approval. "Anything, *Maem*. Just say it and it will be done!" Widow Jennings laughed, and even Eleanor found a way to smile at the instant change in her sister's conduct. Seeing her excitement was a welcome change from watching her descent toward depression.

*Maem* pressed her lips together and lifted her eyebrows, staring straight at Mary Ann. "You may go with Widow

Jennings, my *dochder*, but I sure don't want to be the one to share the news of your trip with Maggie."

Eleanor shook her head, smiling at Mary Ann's enthusiasm while dreading Maggie's reaction to the news that once again she would have to stay behind instead of joining the older sisters in doing something "fun." However, in the back of Eleanor's mind, she had a foreboding feeling that the dark cloud that lingered over both her and Mary Ann's heads would not disappear just because of a trip to Honey Brook.

# ❧ *Chapter Seventeen* ❧

ELEANOR STARED OUT the window of the large car as they pulled into the driveway of the Peacheys' house. Just as Charlotte had described, the little cream-colored house was located within walking distance of the small town of Honey Brook, but the town was really nothing more than a few commercial buildings along the busier section of the main road.

Their street seemed quiet, and off in the distance, Eleanor could see the remains of what must have been a very large field of corn belonging to an Amish neighbor. Soon the left-over cornstalks would fade to brown and be cut down, with tiny stubs left in the ground until the earth was plowed for next year's crops.

Seeing the farm in the distance helped Eleanor release some of the tension she felt as the driver stopped the car in front of the Peacheys' residence.

It was a pretty house with flower boxes outside each of the windows that faced the road and a covered porch with two white rocking chairs. Large hanging ferns provided some privacy from the ever-present prying eyes of summer tourists, although Eleanor sensed that, like most areas of Lancaster County, there were fewer tourists now that the summer season was over. Children were back at school, and most of the *Englischers* had used up their vacation days. That meant that life could proceed at a normal pace.

"Here we are, girls!" Widow Jennings announced as she opened the passenger-side door and started to extract herself.

"Indeed," Eleanor said softly.

She hadn't wanted to travel to Honey Brook and certainly did not want to stay there for an extended visit. She knew how close it was to Narvon, and while she hoped Mary Ann could reconnect with her beau, Eleanor certainly did not fancy running into any members of the Fisher family. Subdued and quiet, Eleanor took a deep breath before getting out of the car. It would be a long few days in the company of Widow Jennings and her equally talkative daughter, Charlotte, of that she was sure and certain.

For all of Eleanor's apprehensions, Mary Ann seemed more vibrant than she had since Willis's unexpected departure from the cottage in Quarryville. During the car ride she had tapped her fingers on the seat between them as she looked out the window, watching everything and seeing nothing, Eleanor suspected.

No sooner had they been greeted by the Peachey family and shown to their rooms than Mary Ann excused herself and hurried to the mailbox, to Eleanor's embarrassment. Watching from the window, Eleanor could only shake her head at her sister. After placing a small envelope in it, Mary Ann raised the red flag to indicate that the postal person should pick up a letter for delivery.

Eleanor didn't have to ask whose address was on the envelope. She knew it was addressed to Willis.

"Really, Mary Ann," Eleanor whispered when her sister returned to the house from the mailbox. "We haven't even been here ten minutes! Where is your restraint? And when will he receive it anyway?"

Ignoring her sister's harsh reprimand, Mary Ann breezed past her and hurried up the stairs to unpack her bag in the room assigned to them.

"Tsk, tsk," Widow Jennings said from the doorway of the sitting room. "A husband won't be caught without some display of prudence."

Eleanor fought the urge to roll her eyes.

"I dare say," Charlotte called from the sitting room. She stood at the window, gazing outside. "I can't believe our good fortune! There is Lydia on her way to visit!" She laughed and clapped her hands together. "How wonderful to have a house of merriment once more!"

"Once more?" Surprised at her hostess's choice of words, Eleanor looked over at Charlotte. "Why once more?"

"*Ach*, we haven't had so many visitors since our first *boppli*! We used to have so many! But once the first *boppli* comes along, everything changes! And then a second and a third and a fourth!" Charlotte laughed gaily. "With so many *kinner*, the energy in our house has just chased the visitors away, it seems!" She turned toward her husband, leaning over to tap his arm. "Right, my dear?"

Her husband sat in his ratty brown recliner, the local newspaper in his hands. At Charlotte's question, his expression remained dour. "*Mayhaps* you chase them all away with your prattle," he mumbled, more to himself than to anyone else.

His comment shocked Eleanor. Raising her head, she looked at him, only partially surprised to see that he continued reading the paper. For a moment she wondered if she had heard him correctly, for he remained perfectly calm as if he had not spoken at all.

However, she knew his words were not imagined when Charlotte responded, "Oh, help! Listen to you!" She laughed and waved her hand at him. "Chasing away visitors! *Maem*, did you hear him?"

Widow Jennings did not respond; she merely raised an eyebrow and pursed her lips.

"A deaf man could hear you," her husband said under his breath and turned the page of the newspaper.

Despite Eleanor clearly hearing his words, Charlotte seemed oblivious to the lack of affection and, in Eleanor's opinion, outright ill-mannered behavior displayed by her husband. She continued chattering, declaring more than once her happiness in seeing both of the Detweiler sisters and asking Eleanor about her mother and younger sister at least two times. Before they could answer, she laughed and changed the subject, talking to her mother again.

Three young boys ran into the room and raced toward their father, who merely scowled at them, shooing them away in an abrupt manner that indicated his lack of affection toward his wife extended to his offspring. When they began to run around his chair, laughing loudly as they tried to grab at each other, Eleanor quickly understood why.

"Oh, honestly!" Charlotte shook her head and gave a quick *tsk-tsk* with her tongue at her husband.

Eleanor thought she heard him grunt.

"Come, boys," Charlotte said, her arms opened wide and a smile on her lips. Immediately the boys stopped their rough-housing and hurried to their mother's side. The way they stared at her made Eleanor suspect they had not spotted the stranger when they ran into the room. "Meet Eleanor

Detweiler. Now you boys will mind your manners while the Detweilers are here, *ja*?"

The eldest of the three boys nodded his head, his eyes wide as he stared at the stranger seated before his mother. The other two boys remained silent, the smallest of them lifting his bare foot to scratch the back of his leg with his toe. Eleanor suspected that not one of the three knew much about minding their manners at all, especially when their father looked up from the paper and, on seeing his wife doting over his sons, rolled his eyes and shook his head.

"Now run along and play outside." Charlotte watched as they scampered toward the door, each one trying to out-race the other as they hurried to escape the confines of the house. Once the back door slammed shut, Charlotte sighed and turned to Eleanor. "Such good boys. I absolutely dote on them!"

Eleanor wasn't certain about that, and when Charlotte's husband grumbled under his breath, she thought she heard the word *spoiled*, an assessment that she thought might be a touch more accurate than Charlotte's description of her sons as "good."

Forgetting about her three sons, Charlotte switched her attention back to Eleanor. In the hallway Mary Ann's footsteps on the stairs announced that she was returning downstairs. "But they are too young and not as interesting as you young women!" Charlotte said, her expression lighting up as Mary Ann entered the room. "Isn't it so, *Mammi*?"

Widow Jennings nodded her head. "Oh, *ja*!" She leaned forward and directed her next comments toward Eleanor and Mary Ann, who took the empty seat beside her sister. "It was a sad day when Charlotte was married. I had no more young women to marry off!"

Charlotte laughed, covering her mouth with her hand in delight.

"But now I have both you and Mary Ann to see properly settled!"

Eleanor bit her tongue from responding that she didn't want or need Widow Jennings's help in securing a husband. God would do that for her according to His plan, not hers. But not wanting to sound ungrateful, she remained silent, although she was certain her cheeks turned pink.

Fortunately she didn't have to respond, and the conversation was interrupted by a knock at the door.

"Who's that, Charlotte?" Widow Jennings asked.

Without wasting one second, Charlotte quickly rose to her feet and crossed the room. "Oh, *Mammi*! We have so much baking to do for the fund-raiser tomorrow. What's a baking party without more people?" With that she disappeared into the hallway toward the front door.

Widow Jennings leaned back in her chair and took a deep breath. "She always was my social butterfly!" The satisfied look on her face expressed her pleasure with Charlotte. "Not like Leah," she added. "At least Jacob makes up for that!"

To Eleanor's dismay Lydia swept into the room, her angelic face and sparkling eyes immediately seeking Eleanor's. "Oh, we've been so looking forward to this!" She greeted Charlotte and Widow Jennings before directing her attention solely to Eleanor. "I think this will be a great weekend! It's so nice to visit with good friends. And for such a *wunderbarr* cause, don't you think?"

While Eleanor wouldn't consider any of the women in the room good friends, she did smile at the enthusiasm with which their visit was greeted. And even though she felt the pain of knowing Lydia was courting Edwin, Eleanor tried to look past her own suffering to see the good in the woman. Baking for charity was not something malicious and ungodly people did. Besides, she could only blame herself for having misread Edwin's friendship for something more. That was not Lydia's fault, Eleanor reminded herself.

But try as she might, Eleanor still had a hard time warming up to Lydia. Whenever Lydia tried to work alongside her, Eleanor remembered that Lydia was Edwin's fiancée. Unbeknownst to the other women in the kitchen, Eleanor's heart broke over and over again during the course of the afternoon.

She tried to focus on baking chocolate chip cookies and double fudge brownies to donate to the local firehouse for their fund-raiser. Thankfully the atmosphere in the kitchen was one of camaraderie and friendship. Forcing Edwin from her mind, Eleanor listened to Charlotte and Widow Jennings banter back and forth, telling stories about different people in their family. And while Eleanor considered it gossip, she couldn't help but smile at their expressiveness in describing the events.

"A skunk in the house?" Lydia covered her mouth when she laughed just a little too gaily for Eleanor's taste. "And it sprayed them?"

Charlotte nodded her head. "*Ja*, they had to replace the sofa and everyone took baths in tomato juice!"

Even Mary Ann laughed. "Oh, help! I couldn't imagine such a scene!"

Widow Jennings used a spatula to remove the latest batch of cookies from the metal sheet, transferring them onto a wire rack to cool. "When you live in the country, you need to keep the screen door shut! Otherwise you never know what will wander in!" She looked up and made a face. "Including people!"

Charlotte opened a cabinet, and not finding what she was looking for, she sighed. "Eleanor, would you mind running down the basement steps, please? I must have left my containers down there at the bottom of the stairs. I need at least six of them for transporting these to the firehouse tomorrow."

"I'll help her," Lydia volunteered.

The last thing Eleanor wanted was time alone with Lydia. Unfortunately it was the one thing Lydia seemed to seek out all day. Now, as they walked down the basement stairs to an area of the house where Lydia could bare her deepest and darkest secrets to her, Eleanor felt even worse. Her heart ached at the thought of Lydia standing before her *g'may*, Edwin on her right side, as the bishop read the vows of matrimony. Being near Lydia made it even harder on Eleanor. But true to her nature she maintained her composure and smiled at the woman who guided her toward the basement.

"Oh, Eleanor," Lydia gushed when they got to the bottom of the staircase. "Such news! I have been practically exploding so that I could share it with you."

Eleanor braced herself.

"You'll never guess who has returned to his family home!" Like a young teenage girl on *rumschpringe*, Lydia clapped her hands together and bounced on the balls of her feet. "Edwin! And I am certain he will attend the event tomorrow! Won't that be just *wunderbarr*?"

"Certainly," Eleanor managed to say, her eyes scanning the shelves for the containers. While she tried to remain calm and unemotional, her insides churned. How could she possibly face Edwin knowing he was to marry Lydia? The pain and humiliation of having thought he was truly interested in her, then finding he was already committed to another, was greater than any person should bear.

Lydia's giddy mood suddenly changed. A cloud seemed to pass over her face, and despite having found the containers, Eleanor felt compelled to linger a moment to inquire further.

"Are you all right, then?"

"*Ja*, I reckon," Lydia said with an overly dramatic sigh. "It's just that…*vell*…something has happened and I feel so terrible." She walked toward the shelves where the canned goods and unused Tupperware containers were stacked. She reached up and ran her finger along the tops of the neat rows of canned chow-chow, applesauce, and meats. "When Edwin was away helping his sister, Fanny, and brother-in-law, John, with the farm, I met his brother, Roy."

"Oh?"

Lydia nodded and turned around to face her. "He attended a youth gathering and asked to take me home. I didn't want to hurt his feelings, Eleanor, so I went. How uncomfortable that will be after Edwin and I marry! Roy will be ever so embarrassed since he sought me out," she tittered. "Obviously Edwin never told him that he was courting me. So what am I to do, Eleanor?" She looked up at Eleanor with her large brown eyes. "I hate to offend him or to hurt either brother. I do love Edwin so!"

Eleanor forced a small smile. "I am sure you do, Lydia." She reached up for the Tupperware and handed one container to Lydia. The irony of Edwin's intended seeking relationship advice from her was not lost on Eleanor. Given the state of her own heart, she was, after all, the last person to advise another on matters related to love. "I'm sure Roy will understand when"—she paused as she tried to gain the strength to say his name—"Edwin announces your betrothal to the family."

Delighted with Eleanor's response Lydia laughed and clutched the container to her chest. "Oh, you've made me feel ever so much better! I simply couldn't have my future brother-in-law think I snubbed him as inferior!"

When Lydia turned and walked toward the stairs, a new lightness in her step, Eleanor took a deep breath. Was that the reason Edwin had never told her about his betrothal to Lydia? Had he felt that she, Eleanor Detweiler, was inferior and therefore easy to snub? For a moment her heartache turned to anger and disappointment. How could Edwin have treated her in such a callous manner?

But just as quickly, the negative thoughts disappeared.

Carrying the plastic containers in her arms, Eleanor started up the stairs to return to the kitchen. She couldn't blame Edwin for the way she felt. He had neither asked for her affection nor misled her in any way. He had offered friendship, not marriage. He had shown kindness, not disdain. Yet as she ascended the staircase, she couldn't help but wonder why, despite his proper conduct that defied the need for any reproach, she still felt such an aching pain deep within her heart.

# ❧ *Chapter Eighteen* ❧

ARLY IN THE morning on Friday Eleanor sat outside on the porch, working on embroidering a small white handkerchief. A cool breeze blew from the west, and with the sun rising behind a large tree, it was the perfect morning for some reflection. Charlotte had already insisted that everyone take a nice long walk over to her sister-in-law's farm down the lane for morning muffins. Mary Ann had eagerly agreed, hoping she might see Willis drive by in his buggy. Eleanor, however, begged off, and to her surprise, no one made a fuss over her staying behind.

She had watched as Charlotte, Widow Jennings, and Mary Ann herded the small children down the sidewalk and away from town. With each step they took, Eleanor had felt a little more relaxed. When they vanished from sight, she had rested her head on the back of the rocking chair, engaging in a private conversation with God as she prayed for the strength to survive until Monday.

"*Gut morgan*," a male voice said from the sidewalk just beyond the porch.

Surprised, Eleanor looked up and, to her further astonishment, saw Christian Bechtler approaching the steps to the front porch. "Preacher!" She set down her embroidery and quickly stood up to greet him halfway, her hand outstretched to shake his. "How *wunderbarr* to see you!"

He gestured toward the rocking chair, indicating that she should sit. Politely he waited for her to be situated before he joined her, occupying the remaining chair. "I ran into Charlotte the other day. She told me you were visiting for the fund-raiser."

"I didn't know you were staying in Honey Brook," Eleanor said. "You've been greatly missed at Quarryville. I trust all is well?"

Christian averted his eyes and seemed to ponder his response. After a hesitation he nodded. "*Ja*, I am well. I do apologize for my abrupt departure the other week." He looked up, forcing himself to meet her eyes. "I had some unfortunate news, Eleanor. Nothing less would have torn me away from my *g'may* and my business."

She had never doubted that and felt certain that all of the church district felt the same way. Still, that had not stopped others from speculating and whispering about what could possibly have kept Christian Bechtler away for so long. Eleanor, however, had not inquired, and if she heard the whispers, she merely walked away or changed the subject.

Christian cleared his throat and looked around as if searching for other people. "You are alone, then?" he asked.

"*Ja*," Eleanor said. "The others have gone visiting. We'll be baking more this afternoon for the fund-raiser, so the time alone in the house is precious, indeed."

He smiled a soft and gentle smile that spoke of his understanding her need for some peace and quiet, an escape from the constant chatter of Charlotte and the ruckus of the boys.

"I'm sorry Mary Ann isn't here to see you," Eleanor added. "She will be sorry to have missed you, for sure and certain."

At this comment, a dark cloud passed over his eyes and he lifted his chin. "Ah, Mary Ann," he said in a low voice. "I am, in fact, glad she is not here, Eleanor. It is you to whom I wish to speak."

"Me?" Eleanor frowned, his admission startling her. What could Christian Bechtler possibly want to see her for?

Christian stood up, his hands clutched behind his back as he began to pace the length of the porch. He seemed lost in thought again, and Eleanor gave him that time to gather his words. Whatever he wanted to say, it was apparently difficult. She could hardly imagine why Christian Bechtler would have sought out her company for something of such obvious importance.

"Mary Ann," he began. "Is she"—he stopped pacing for a moment—"is she still intent on Willis?"

Biting the corner of her lip, Eleanor slowly nodded her head. She suspected how she felt about Mary Ann, and despite their age differences she had hoped there might be a connection between the two. His maturity and level-headedness would counter Mary Ann's propensity for drama and emotional outbursts. While she wanted to spare his feelings, she almost knew that honesty was the best policy for her response.

"I'm fairly certain the answer is yes, Christian."

"And, would you say, if things were not to work out as she intends, that she would be heartbroken?"

Eleanor nodded slowly. With Mary Ann's heart so intent on Willis as her future husband, there was little room to doubt that, should things not work out as she intended, she would suffer gravely, both internally and externally.

The thought made Eleanor cringe.

He nodded and began pacing again. "I will pray that her heart heals quickly."

His words struck Eleanor as being very cryptic. Eleanor had not thought highly of Willis for leaving her sister in such an emotionally distraught state. But Christian had not been in Quarryville when Willis left. Had word traveled about his desertion? Of course, Eleanor realized suddenly, Christian must have heard about it from Charlotte.

"I trust from your words that you have heard of his leaving almost as abruptly as you did," Eleanor responded at last.

This caught Christian off guard, and he stood still. "I have not."

"Then you must be referring to something else." Eleanor got to her feet and walked toward Christian. "Please, tell me what you know. I fear my *schwester*'s heart is quite vulnerable right now."

For a long moment he contemplated her request, his eyes searching hers. There was a look of pain on his face, and Eleanor knew that whatever he needed to tell her, he did not *want* to share. However, he nodded once again. "I'm afraid I must start at the beginning, Eleanor, so that you understand everything."

"Oh my," she whispered. "The beginning of what?"

The pacing began again. He ran his hand along the porch railing, tapping his fingers nervously against the corner pillar before he turned back. "When I was a young man, I fell in love with a woman." He looked up, his cheeks turning pink. "You may have heard of this, *ja*?"

Eleanor nodded once.

"*Ja, vell*," he continued. "She was so much like Mary Ann. She loved gardening and spoke her mind. Her emotions could never be contained. But she refused to take her kneeling vow. My parents feared I would leave the church, so they sent me to Ohio to work for my *daed*'s second cousin in his harness store. He claimed he wanted me to have more experience with making harnesses, but I knew the truth. When I returned…" He took a deep breath before he said, "I learned that she had given birth to a child. A baby girl."

Eleanor gasped. This was a part of the story she had not heard, and she was shocked at the instant thought that perhaps the illegitimate child might be Christian's.

He quickly put her fears to rest when he recognized the very thought that plagued her. "Everyone thought the child was mine." He paused, giving Eleanor enough time to realize the amount of pain Christian must have experienced if people speculated in such a manner. "Despite my protests, the bishop brought me before the elders with my parents present. The bishop asked me to confess what I knew. I explained that I had never known that woman. Not like that. My punishment for a crime I did not commit was shunning."

"Oh, Christian!"

He nodded his head. "It was difficult because I knew the truth. The *boppli* was my *bruder*'s. I did not tell his secret."

"How awful!" She could not imagine the man that stood before her experiencing such a horrific event. It would be traumatizing to say the least.

"But"—he held up his finger to indicate there was more to the story—"one night, my *bruder* did not come home. He left with the woman and the baby…A month later, a letter came explaining that my *bruder* married her and it was his *boppli*. They had moved to Philadelphia. They had a hard life, Eleanor. God knows I prayed for them, despite my broken heart." He placed his hand over his chest. "When I heard that my *bruder* died, I went searching for his widow and the child. It took me over a year, and when I did, I brought them back to Honey Brook. At that time the mother was sick and her prognosis was as dire as my *bruder*'s. She made me promise to watch over the child, a promise I made and kept all of these years."

Despite the tragic nature of his tale Eleanor remained silent, unable to speak or offer her empathy. She could tell from his hesitant manner that there was more to this story, and she could only presume that it would eventually get back to Mary Ann. She could not, however, imagine how.

"The child, a *dochder*, grew up with her maternal grandparents, but I helped financially support her and I checked on her as often as I could. She, like her own mother, grew into a beautiful and passionate young woman, wanting nothing more than to live life and be loved." He inhaled and shut his eyes. "*Mayhaps* it was the loss of her *maem* or possibly the change in her lifestyle when she moved to the farm that made her rebel."

"She was raised by her Amish grandparents, then?"

He pressed his lips together, the muscles in his cheek twitching ever so slightly. "*Ja*, she was. And they are most conservative, Eleanor. A shocking change for any child, I reckon. Despite everything I could do to help her, in the end she made her own decisions." A car drove past the house, and Christian waited until the rumble of its engine dissipated down the road. Then, when they were once again standing in silence, he said, "At fifteen she was rebellious against the Amish faith and apparently vulnerable to sweet words spoken by someone who gave no thought to her future."

Eleanor frowned. She suspected that his words were intentionally vague. A fifteen-year-old girl? "I don't think I understand," she said.

165

Christian opened his eyes and stared directly at her. "When I was called away, I learned that she, like her mother, became pregnant out of wedlock, Eleanor. And the father..." He let his words linger and waited.

Slowly, like the morning sky changing colors as the sun rolls out of a night of slumber, the meaning of his words dawned on Eleanor. A fifteen-year-old girl? Having a child out of wedlock? Sweet words? As the pieces to his story began to fall into place, she slowly recognized how this terrible story connected to her sister. And when the full meaning became clear, she gasped, reaching out to hold on to the railing to steady herself. "Willis!"

Christian nodded his head. His expression told her that he had taken no joy in sharing the sordid details of his niece's misdeeds.

"Oh, Mary Ann!" Eleanor whispered. Her mind raced, hearing the words of Widow Jennings and seeing Mary Ann's defiance. Was it possible that Willis was such an ungodly man that he would have tempted Mary Ann to follow in the same path as Christian's niece? Hadn't Mary Ann gone to Willis's aunt's house unchaperoned? Her defiance when reprimanded had shocked Eleanor at the time. Now the memory of it gave Eleanor something to worry about. "You don't think..."

"What I think and what may or may not have happened are irrelevant, Eleanor." He straightened his shoulders. "Willis's *aendi* learned of his indiscretion as well as his denying any accountability or responsibility to my niece or the *boppli*. I have learned that his *aendi* promptly disinherited him. The families kept everything very quiet, but if he ran off abruptly, I imagine it was related to all of this. You must understand that I tell you this with the greatest of reluctance. It is with

Mary Ann's emotional well-being in mind that I confide this story."

"Is...is he marrying your niece?"

Christian shook his head. "*Nee*, she is both a young woman and a child at the same time. Besides, she is not Amish, and marrying her would result in him having to leave the Amish church. That would mean shunning with no chance of exoneration. He has, after all, taken the kneeling vow." Christian took a deep breath and exhaled before he turned to look at Eleanor. "As if this situation were not bad enough, Willis has refused responsibility for the *boppli*."

Eleanor could not imagine what she would say to Mary Ann. How could she break the news to her sister that Willis had defiled a young girl and abandoned his own child? "I had been so certain he loved her," she whispered.

"Of that I cannot speak my thoughts. His affections seemed genuine, Eleanor. But his intentions may not have been." He reached out and touched her arm. "I tell you this to protect your *schwester*, not in the hopes that the information might aid my own pursuit of her interest. I am not such a fool as to think that Mary Ann's affections for Willis would shift in my direction should she learn this tale."

Long after Christian departed, Eleanor sat on the porch alone, pondering his words. She could hardly believe the story Christian had shared with her. Was it possible that John Willis was righteous on the outside but such a scoundrel on the inside? To take advantage of a young girl in such an unbiblical manner was beyond reprehensible! And to think that Christian's niece now would have a child to care for without the benefit of a husband.

Eleanor stared into the distance, her mind trying to wrap around this information that Christian had shared with her.

The thought that John Willis, the man her own dear sister favored over all others, had such a dark side made Eleanor feel a pit in her stomach. She would have to tell Mary Ann, but she didn't know how to begin such a sordid tale. Would Mary Ann even believe her? Or would she simply think Eleanor was, once again, seeking to block her undisguised pursuit of Willis?

# ❧ Chapter Nineteen ❧

T HE PARKING LOT behind the firehouse and the block in front of it were both closed off to motor vehicles and buggies. A crowd of people, both *Englischers* and Amish, gathered there, slowly meandering around the tables set out by the different vendors. Eleanor stood behind the table where Charlotte had set out their baked goods for display and sale. Mary Ann lingered by the front of the table, her eyes constantly scanning the crowd as she sought out the only person Eleanor hoped she did not find.

"Where is he?" Mary Ann muttered, brushing off something from the front of her black waist-high apron. She had taken extra time to get ready today, preening in front of the small mirror to make certain every hair was smoothed back and her prayer *kapp* pinned perfectly so that the heart shape lay just right against the back of her head. "I'm sure he will be here!"

Eleanor tried to maintain a level head. She had struggled with Christian Bechtler's tale, wondering whether she should share it with Mary Ann. After a long, sleepless night Eleanor decided against telling her. Whatever had happened between the two of them, Mary Ann did not need more pain than she would feel when she realized that Willis had not returned correspondence with her for a reason.

Trying to distract her sister, Eleanor bent down and pulled out a large box filled with baked goods. "Mary Ann, I could use your help," she said, standing upright and looking at her. "We should unpack more bread. It seems to be quite popular."

Ignoring Eleanor, Mary Ann continued gazing into the crowd. She even stood on her tippy toes to peer over the heads of the crowd, not even moving out of the way of two women who needed to pass through.

"Honestly, Mary Ann!" Eleanor snapped. She hadn't expected to react like that to her sister, but the knowledge that Willis was such an unscrupulous man coupled with Mary Ann's ignorance of his character irritated her. "You look more forlorn than a whimpering child. Please pay attention and help me!"

Eleanor's harsh tone snapped Mary Ann out of her single-minded mission to find Willis. She glared at Eleanor and stomped around the table. "Is restocking bread really so difficult, Eleanor?" She bent over the box and began rifling through it to find what she needed. When it wasn't in that particular box, she shoved it back under the table and reached for another box of baked goods. With a lot of huffing and puffing, she began unpacking more of the wrapped bread. "There!" She stood up and faced her sister. "Are you happy now, then? There is your bread!"

"Mary Ann!"

Without hesitation she returned to her post and continued searching the crowd for Willis.

Eleanor rolled her eyes and rearranged the loaves of bread so that the table looked more orderly. She was about to say something else to Mary Ann, to scold her about her obvious lack of interest in the fund-raiser when that was why they were there, when she felt a presence behind her.

Spinning around, she almost knocked into Christian Bechtler. "*Ach*! Christian! You startled me!" she cried out, half laughing.

He steadied her by placing his hands on her shoulders. "I'm sorry, Eleanor. I didn't mean to," he said, his eyes darting in Mary Ann's direction. She hadn't even turned to acknowledge him, although Eleanor doubted she was aware of anything other than the longing of her own heart. "I see that everyone is doing well here," he said, a solemn tone to his voice.

Deflecting the unspoken question about Mary Ann, Eleanor gestured toward the table. "Might we interest you in some baked goods, Christian?" she teased. "The bread is doing quite nicely."

"Ah, the bread." He exhaled and turned his attention to their table. He assessed the baked goods with a serious expression on his face, as if studying a horse before an auction. "Such uniform baking, I must say. I would be remiss in denying others the sweet taste of fresh white bread. So I shall pass on your offer today, Eleanor."

She laughed, aware from Charlotte that he had already made a hefty financial donation to the firehouse and certainly did not need any food since he was staying with a local Amish woman who would have been offended if he purchased bread elsewhere. "I imagine the other people who purchase the bread today would thank you if they could," she said lightly, "so I shall express their gratitude for them."

He smiled, obviously enjoying the teasing banter. For a moment Eleanor caught a glimpse of a different side to Christian, and she realized that there was more to this man than anyone suspected. His devotion to his niece touched her, as did the story of how people thought he had fathered her out of wedlock. Instead of calling out his brother, Christian

171

had remained a man of righteous substance, displaying an amazing strength in letting the gossip spread, rather than feeding into it. She suspected that he had not wanted to add more to the Amish grapevine. His silence on the matter must have convicted him in the eyes of others until the truth came out about who the real father was.

Eleanor was convinced that his handling of the situation was the real reason Christian Bechtler, a lifelong bachelor, had been nominated for the role of a preacher within the church district. He was, after all, a true role model to others on how to behave under such trying circumstances.

Her thoughts were interrupted when she heard her sister cry out, "There he is!" Mary Ann turned to look at Eleanor, the ecstatic joy on her face undeniable. "Oh, Eleanor! He's here! I knew it!" Without waiting for a response from her sister, Mary Ann dashed into the crowd, heading in the direction of John Willis.

"Mary Ann! No!"

Eleanor dashed around the side of the table and chased after her, trying to dodge the different people without shoving them. She kept her eyes on the back of her sister's prayer *kapp*, knowing that if she lost sight of Mary Ann, she'd never find her again.

A break in the crowd displayed exactly what Eleanor feared. Mary Ann stopped short, and just as Eleanor ran up behind her, she shouted, "Willis!"

At the sound of his name he turned in her direction. For a moment Eleanor saw a glimmer in his eyes as he recognized Mary Ann. In that split second Eleanor wondered if Christian Bechtler had been mistaken. What if his entire tale was merely gossip gone awry? The way that Willis looked at Mary Ann...Eleanor saw love in his expression.

But as soon as it came, it disappeared, the suddenness of his initial reaction to seeing her replaced with a new expression, one Eleanor never would have imagined Willis to feel toward Mary Ann: resolute coldness.

Mary Ann didn't notice that people were staring at her. Instead, she ran up to Willis and grabbed at his arm, her face beaming as she sought to meet his gaze. She stood far too close to him, and he took a slight step backward, withdrawing his arm from her grasp. Instead of greeting her with joy, he extended his hand for her to shake, a proper yet surprisingly impersonal response.

The gesture startled Mary Ann. She looked at his hand and then back up into his face quizzically. "Willis?"

"It is good to see you again, Mary Ann." His voice was cold and unfamiliar. Even Eleanor could hardly believe her ears. "I trust you and your family are faring well?"

"What is this about, Willis? Haven't you received any of my letters?"

The color drained from his cheeks and his eyes shifted in another direction. That was the moment Eleanor realized he was not alone. A young Amish woman stood next to him. With her pale pink dress and rosy cheeks, the blond woman looked more like a little doll than a real person. Her heart-shaped prayer *kapp*, much larger than Eleanor was used to, looked like a halo framing her face.

"I have not received anything," Willis said. "You will give your best to your *maem*, *ja*?" And with that he turned his back on her, returning his attention to the group of people standing around him, the young woman reclaiming her space next to him.

Eleanor stood behind Mary Ann, gently placing her hand on her sister's shoulder. "Let's go," she whispered.

"I...I don't understand."

Guiding her sister back toward their table, Eleanor kept ahold of her arm. Mary Ann did not speak, and when Eleanor looked at her, her eyes stared at nothing, her face completely devoid of any expression. The noise of the crowd seemed to disappear around them. Instead, all Eleanor heard was the echo of her sister crying out Willis's name and seeing the look in his eyes. It broke her heart to remember how quickly his expression had changed from love to coldness.

Back at the table Charlotte stood beside Widow Jennings. Neither one seemed to notice that Eleanor had her arm placed around Mary Ann's shoulders. With her color drained from her face, Mary Ann did not look up to greet either woman. Instead, she stared into the distance, and Eleanor knew her sister was trying to understand what had just happened.

"Where have you girls been?" Widow Jennings asked, a slight edge of irritation to her voice.

"I apologize. We've only been gone a few minutes," Eleanor said, still tending to Mary Ann. "Have there been many people?"

Widow Jennings dismissed her with a wave of her hand. "Oh, that's of no consequence. I do, however, want to tell you what I have learned!"

Eleanor started to shake her head, trying to indicate to Widow Jennings that whatever she had to say, now was not the time. Certainly she had some news about John Willis. Whatever gossip she had, Mary Ann certainly did not need to hear it now.

Oblivious to Eleanor's head motion the widow took a step forward so that she could stand closer as she prepared to share her news. Over the widow's shoulder Eleanor noticed Christian Bechtler approaching the small group. He looked concerned and stared directly at Mary Ann. Certainly he had witnessed some of what just happened.

At the very moment he stood behind Widow Jennings, the widow leaned forward, and with her eyebrows knit together in a frown and her lips pursed together, she said in an angry tone, "All the hopes that we put into that John Willis for our Mary Ann are shattered! He's to wed some young girl whose *daed* is giving him the farm! I dare say that his *aendi* will be rather put out by that news!" She shook her head, unmindful of Mary Ann's reaction.

Beside her, Mary Ann fell limp against Eleanor, the soft sound of an intake of breath barely audible. Eleanor tightened her hold on her sister's shoulders, trying to hold her up.

"A scoundrel, I tell you," the widow added. "The worst sort of Amish man!"

And with that Mary Ann began to swoon, her legs slowly collapsing beneath her. Eleanor called out her name, doing her best to keep her upright. Quickly Christian Bechtler stepped forward and swept his arm beneath the falling young woman. Eleanor felt the weight of her sister's body against her disappear as Christian lifted her into his arms.

Mary Ann fell against him, her eyes shut and her head limp, hanging to the side. Eleanor gasped, reaching out for her sister's hand, holding it as Christian carried the unconscious Mary Ann through the throngs of curious onlookers.

It was only when Eleanor looked back that she saw Willis still standing with his soon-to-be wife on the other side of the parking lot, completely unaware that the announcement of his upcoming wedding had just destroyed Mary Ann's heart and quite possibly the chance for her ever to love again.

# ❦ *Chapter Twenty* ❦

"HAS SHE EATEN yet today?"

Eleanor looked up from where she sat at the kitchen table, the Bible open before her. For the past three hours the quiet of the house gave her time to read and reflect, the perfect distraction from the events of the previous day. She had been reading through her favorite verses of Psalm 34:

> The eyes of the LORD are on the righteous,
>   and His ears are open to their cry.
> The face of the LORD is against the ones doing evil,
>   to cut off the memory of them from the earth.
>
> The righteous cry out, and the LORD hears,
>   and delivers them out of all their trouble.
> The LORD is near to the broken-hearted,
>   and saves the contrite of spirit.
>
> Many are the afflictions of the righteous,
>   but the LORD delivers him out of them all.

Earlier everyone else had departed to attend worship service at the neighboring farmhouse. Knowing that she wouldn't leave Mary Ann, no one bothered to ask if Eleanor intended to join them. That hadn't sat well with Charlotte, and for a few minutes she tried to convince herself that she needed to stay with the two Detweiler sisters. Luckily for Eleanor, her husband insisted that Mary Ann was in capable hands and that Charlotte simply could not leave him alone with three young boys.

After they had finally left, Charlotte still fussing and clucking her tongue over leaving the two young women alone, Eleanor stood for a few minutes in the center of the kitchen and prayed. She needed God's support. Her heart felt heavy, both for her own loss as well as her sister's. She knew God's plan would reveal itself when and if He intended. However, the heavy feeling in her heart made her pray for deliverance. She wasn't certain how much more she could bear.

The last several months had been long and painful for the Detweiler family. So much change, all unexpected and emotionally draining. But after she finished praying, she reminded herself that at least they had each other. And as past trials had proven, together they could survive anything.

But now Widow Jennings and Charlotte had returned from worship at the neighboring farmhouse. From the looks of it they had returned ahead of Charlotte's husband and children. They hovered around the kitchen table, looking at Eleanor with concern etched in their faces.

"She has not eaten," Eleanor admitted. In fact, Mary Ann had barely moved. She had lain in the bed, her back to the door, and merely stared at the wall. No matter how much Eleanor tried to coax her to eat or drink something, Mary Ann had not responded.

Charlotte wrung her hands before her. "Oh dear, what a dreadful visit this has been for poor Mary Ann."

For a moment Eleanor thought Charlotte would begin her fussing all over again. She prepared herself for another round of fretting. Fortunately her mother thwarted it by scowling and pointing out the positive side to the distressing situation.

"It's best she learned of his true character now," Widow Jennings said. "Mary Ann, like many others, will survive a broken heart. She may feel as if her world has collapsed, but she will doubtless pull through."

"Such trouble, such trouble," Charlotte mumbled. "And to think we were to visit with the Glicks down the road a spell." She pondered this for a moment and then looked up at Eleanor. "You don't think Mary Ann will be interested in visiting, then? I haven't been there in almost two months. I was so looking forward to going."

Since the previous evening, when Christian Bechtler had brought them back to Charlotte's house, Eleanor seated in the back of his buggy and Mary Ann seated beside him with her head pressed against his shoulder, there had been no response from Mary Ann. The only thing she finally did was weep, a terrible sound, one Eleanor had never heard before. Soft, silent, and serious, Mary Ann's weeping lingered far into the night. Eleanor had slept with her arms around her sister, holding her as tight as she could and praying for God to lift this burden from her sister's heart.

"*Nee*, I do not think visiting is on Mary Ann's schedule today," Eleanor responded.

The last time Eleanor checked on Mary Ann, she had been sleeping. When Eleanor placed her hand on her sister's brow, she heard her whisper Willis's name. Her skin took on a translucent appearance, the lack of any color in her cheeks making her appear sick, almost deathly looking.

"I do believe I should go check on her." Eleanor rose from the table and started to walk toward the staircase.

Holding up her hand, Charlotte stopped her. "*Nee*, Eleanor, wait for a moment. My niece Lydia was right behind us. She was quite intent on seeing you." She turned toward her mother, the plight of Mary Ann quickly forgotten and her focus on what she deemed more important: social niceties. "Such a great thing, *ja*? The budding relationship of young friends."

The smile on her face and the happiness in her voice contrasted far too greatly with the heartache being felt by Mary Ann at that very moment. Knowing that she could not, and would not, say anything to Charlotte, Eleanor excused herself and hurried up the stairs, eager to see how her sister fared after the past hour of solitude. Behind her she heard Charlotte continue talking to her mother about how much she missed her own friends from her days as a young woman.

At the door Eleanor rapped lightly and turned the doorknob. She let it swing open and peered inside. Mary Ann sat on the edge of the bed, still facing the wall with her hands folded on her lap and her shoulders hunched over.

Slipping through the opening, Eleanor quietly shut the door behind her and hurried over to her sister's side. She sat on the bed and reached out her hand to take her sister's. "Mary Ann," she said in a soft voice, "you need to eat something, *schwester*. You'll take ill if you don't."

"I am already ill," Mary Ann replied.

The comment caught Eleanor off guard. She studied her sister for a long moment and noticed Mary Ann's pale skin and the dark circles under her eyes. For the first time Eleanor felt a moment of panic. "What do you mean you are already ill?" Silence met her question, leaving Eleanor's imagination free to run wild. "Oh, Mary Ann!" she gasped. "Please tell me that Willis did not..."

"*Nee!*" Mary Ann said, the hint of force spoken in that one word immediately reassuring Eleanor that her worst suspicions were unfounded. "But my behavior. Everyone knew. He knew." She spoke these words in a whisper. "I'm so ashamed of myself."

Rubbing the back of her hand, Eleanor tried to reassure her. "You had no reason to doubt his intentions, *ja*? He openly courted you too."

"*Ja*," Mary Ann affirmed. Then she paused. "*Nee*." She reached up with her free hand and rubbed her forehead. "Oh, I don't know what I believe anymore. Did he? Or did I misinterpret his intentions? *Mayhaps* he never had any true feelings for me, only lust. The uncertainty will haunt me, Eleanor. I...I let myself..."

When Mary Ann hesitated, her eyes shut and her face turned toward the light of the window, sunlight brushing across her cheeks. For all of her bravado and assertions in regard to the way relationships should be, she was still an innocent young woman, just shy of eighteen years of age. But the shadows of wisdom aged her in ways no woman should know.

"You let yourself what?" Eleanor prodded.

With a long sigh Mary Ann turned to look at her. The emptiness of her eyes startled Eleanor. Gone was the spark, just as Christian Bechtler had asked about the other day. "I let myself believe. That is my sin, Eleanor. Nothing further." And with that she sank back down into the bed, her head turned to the side and away from Eleanor. When it became clear that Mary Ann was finished speaking on the matter and wanted to be alone, Eleanor did the only sensible thing: she left the room.

*Which was worse,* she wondered as she walked down the stairs. *To love someone without it being known or to love someone without it being returned? Perhaps there was nothing to compare, for they both caused the same amount of heartache.*

By the time Charlotte and her mother left to continue their Sunday visits with neighbors, Lydia arrived. She waited patiently in the hallway to see her aunt and grandmother leave before she shut the door and turned around, smiling at Eleanor but avoiding her eyes. Something about the way Lydia walked into the room and, without being asked, sat down in the recliner near the wall caused Eleanor to wonder about the exact purpose of this visit.

With her back to the doorway Lydia waited patiently for Eleanor to join her. The strained look on her face led Eleanor to believe that Lydia had heard the story of Willis and Mary Ann, a fact Lydia wasted no time to confirm.

"Oh, Eleanor, I'm so terribly sorry for your *schwester!*" Lydia said. She clutched a handkerchief in her hands and twisted it around her fingers. "What a horrible thing to happen to her! She's such a lovely young woman. I do, however, wonder if she had been a bit more discreet, if she might have saved herself some of the speculation."

"Speculation is just another form of gossip," was the only response Eleanor could give without sounding bitter or irritated. It didn't surprise Eleanor that Lydia was so forthright in expressing her opinions. What did surprise Eleanor was Lydia's comment about discretion. Hadn't Lydia shown a complete lack of discretion when she confided so quickly in Eleanor? The insinuation that Mary Ann may have contributed to the situation was clear. And Eleanor felt defensive for her sister's honor. "Neither one is fine in the eyes of God."

When Lydia shrugged off her rebuke with silence and tightened lips, Eleanor knew her initial instincts about Lydia had not been misguided, and she had been right to resent the intimacy Lydia had forced on her. Eleanor had tried to move beyond her own broken heart and crushed dreams, recognizing that, technically, Lydia could not be blamed for them. But to listen to her judge Mary Ann's situation? If Eleanor were not someone who honored God's wish for peace among His people, she would have given Lydia a piece of her mind.

Oblivious to Eleanor's inner turmoil, Lydia returned to her favorite subject: herself. "I'm so thankful that, unlike Willis, Edwin is ever so trustworthy. Still, I'll be glad when Edwin finally speaks to the bishop. This secrecy is so difficult to maintain. We have had to behave with such discretion to conceal our relationship that it has become a terrible burden!"

"I...I can imagine." Eleanor knew only too well how painful her own secrets felt. Between facing this woman who was engaged to the man she loved, holding the story that Christian had confided to her, and comforting her sister until the wee hours of the night, Eleanor's shoulders felt heavy under the enormous weight of secrets.

"That's why I'm just so glad, Eleanor, that you and I have become friends." Lydia smiled when she said this, and for the first time Eleanor realized Lydia was not quite as pretty as she had originally thought. She no longer saw the pale skin, devoid of freckles or sun damage, or the pretty smile with perfectly white teeth. Instead, she saw a young woman who, despite having been raised on a farm, probably had not known a day of hard work in her life. Lydia's thirst for someone—anyone!—to confide in meant that she did not have a lot of close friends, and that, in and of itself, told Eleanor a lot about this woman. The fact that Lydia had immediately sought out Eleanor's friendship from the very beginning told Eleanor something else about her: their differences were far too great for a true friendship to form between them. And Eleanor suspected Lydia knew that, which made her wonder all the more why any confidence had been shared with her in the first place.

She began to wonder if Lydia worried that Edwin's affections had strayed. Perhaps she sought to keep him for herself by asserting her own claim on him. And while she began to realize Lydia might also be experiencing a touch of the emotional turmoil Eleanor felt, she took no comfort in that. After all, regardless of how Lydia fretted over Edwin's loyalty to her, Eleanor knew that if he had proposed to Lydia, regardless of the circumstances or timing, he would never go back on his word.

The gentle ticking of a clock hanging on the wall was the only noise in the room as Eleanor tried to think of something to say.

"Shall I fetch you some coffee?" Eleanor asked, getting up before Lydia could answer. She hurried over to the kitchen and turned on the stove before she filled the silver kettle with water. While she waited for it to boil, she opened a cabinet to retrieve two mismatched coffee cups. Setting them on the counter, she sighed. *If only Lydia would have left with Charlotte and Widow Jennings!* she thought. The last thing Eleanor needed right now was to sit and entertain the young woman. She would have much preferred to be alone so she could tend to Mary Ann.

The hinges of the front door squeaked. Curious to see who had arrived, Eleanor turned toward the doorway just as a figure appeared. To her amazement she recognized the man right away. But just as quickly her amazement turned to dismay: Edwin Fisher's timing could not have been worse.

"Eleanor!" Edwin said as he crossed the room in three strides and stood before her. He reached out, placing his hand on her arm. "I've only just now heard that you were in Honey Brook! I would have come to visit before now had I known."

Too aware of Lydia's curious gaze as she peeked around the side of the recliner, Eleanor took a step back, letting his hand fall from her arm as she gestured toward the sitting area. "Edwin, I do believe you are familiar with my visitor, Lydia?"

Edwin's initial reaction looked to be of disbelief, especially after he pivoted on his heel and saw her now standing by the chair. He stumbled over his words, his eyes shifting from one woman to another. "I...oh..."

Lydia helped him overcome his awkwardness. She stepped forward and held out her hand for him to shake. "*Ja*, we do know one another," she said, her eyes focused on his. "It's so *gut* to see you again, Edwin Fisher." For a moment, her hand stayed there, suspended between them.

Reluctantly, and with one last look at Eleanor, he finally shook the outstretched hand. "Indeed. Likewise, Lydia." He released her hand and shuffled his feet. "*Ja*, *vell*, I was only stopping in to say hello, being on my way home from worship service. I was...*ja*, *vell*, I was only on the way home, and I best keep going so that I'm not...uh...late."

Immediately Lydia stepped forward, standing closer to Edwin than propriety normally allowed. It spoke of an intimacy that was reserved for courting couples. "Perhaps you might escort me home too, as I was just getting ready to leave. It's been such a while. I'm sure we have much to catch up on."

The whistling of the kettle on the stove interrupted her words. The three of them looked in its direction, the two empty mugs on the counter clearly revealing Lydia's fib about leaving. But true to character, Edwin merely nodded his head and took a step toward the door. "Of course," he said. "My buggy is right outside the door."

With great bravado Lydia smiled at Eleanor and practically pranced across the floor toward the door. She exited first, leaving Edwin to follow. His hesitation to do so led Eleanor to believe he did not wish to take her home. And when he glanced over his shoulder at her, she knew he felt as uncomfortable as she did. Eleanor understood why. What type of righteous man would mislead a woman when promised to wed another? She knew the answer: none.

Yet, as much as her heart ached, Eleanor simply could not find herself in a position to hate him. She suspected that if she knew Edwin the way she thought she did, there was more to the story than a philandering young man looking to make conquests of innocent Amish women. *No,* she thought as she turned off the stove and listened to the sound of Edwin's horse and buggy pull out of the driveway. *Edwin was not a philandering young man. That role was left for Willis, who had apparently left a string of broken hearts in the wake of his very dangerous selection of amusement.*

# ❧ *Chapter Twenty-One* ❧

Back at the cottage the gray clouds lingered overhead, hiding more than just the sunshine. Since their return from Honey Brook five days ago it seemed as if no light shined within the four walls; the outside gloominess penetrated the house. During the first few days Mary Ann did little more than sit in the rocker and stare out the window. She refused to eat, and no amount of coaxing from Eleanor or *Maem* would convince her otherwise. While Mary Ann's silence drew the attention and empathy of the rest of the family, Eleanor suffered quietly.

On Monday morning Christian Bechtler had arranged for a driver to bring them home earlier than had originally been planned. He also managed to return with them. His concern over Mary Ann touched Eleanor. Quiet and unassuming, he tended to her sister's needs, knowing that he could expect nothing in return for his efforts. The purity of his affection was the most honest form of love Eleanor had ever witnessed. Yet Mary Ann did not respond to him, or anyone else for that matter.

Every day he stopped by the house after he finished his work. He brought flowers, a different bouquet every afternoon, and handed them to Eleanor before he went over to greet Mary Ann. After a few minutes of trying to elicit a reaction, Christian would reach out and gently touch her shoulder before leaving again, a sorrowful look on his face.

"Has she improved at all?" he had asked on Friday before he left.

"She's walking a bit more," Eleanor admitted. "Mostly pacing. She's not talking so much, but she is eating."

"*Vell*, that's a good start." He cast one more forlorn glance in her direction. "To see her suffer so, at the hands of such a callous, deceitful man." The anger in his voice startled Eleanor. In the short time she had known Christian, she had viewed him as a calm, righteous, and forgiving man. Yet now his words reflected something that bordered on resentment and blame. While she did not disagree with him, she saw him in a different light. Instead of being a man who was only rigidly committed to following God's Word, he could also feel deep emotion for people. It was a side of him she found quite moving.

By the time Saturday rolled around, the clouds had moved in and a chill clung to the air. To Eleanor's relief Mary Ann stopped staring out the window and stood up, unexpectedly announcing her intention to walk before the sunset.

Maggie jumped up and started for the door. "I want to go with you."

"I want to go alone," Mary Ann replied. She moved across the floor, her shoulders down and her face pinched. She had lost so much weight that her dress, a pale pink one, hung from her shoulders, the straight pins that held it shut unable to hide that fact. Without her sparkling eyes and quick-witted retorts, Mary Ann was just a shell of her former self.

"It's going to rain, Mary Ann," Eleanor said. "I don't think you should walk alone."

Sarah Price

"It's not going to rain," she replied in a soft but even voice, heading for the door, her bare feet brushing against the floorboards.

"You always say that," Maggie whispered, her eyes wide as she watched the ghostlike form of her sister cross the floor toward the door.

"And it never does." Without another moment to let anyone further argue with her, Mary Ann walked out the door.

Eleanor, *Maem*, and Maggie stared after her, watching as Mary Ann walked past the front window, pausing to look at her garden, and then continued toward the lane. She turned right, disappearing behind the hedge and from sight.

No one spoke, too astonished that Mary Ann had not only arisen from her seat but left the house to take a walk. *Perhaps,* Eleanor thought, *this is the beginning of her healing.* She knew, all too well, that it took time for open wounds of the heart to recover. Her own injury was still in need of time to get better.

"I dare say that I'm just unable to think straight," *Maem* said at last. "Such a horrible thing, this Willis leading on our Mary Ann. To think we held him in such high regard and favor!"

Fortunately no one seemed to know the entire story, and Eleanor was not about to volunteer it. She wasn't certain if Mary Ann would feel better or worse if she knew Willis had fathered a child out of wedlock, denied responsibility, and been disinherited because of it. The woman he intended to marry was certainly not holding his affections the way Mary Ann had. But had he married Mary Ann, he would not have gained a farm and would have had no way of supporting her. He had chosen to marry another woman for practical reasons, of that Eleanor was sure and certain. It was not an uncommon decision for an Amish man, and Eleanor suspected it was better for Mary Ann to recover from that injury instead of having to discover that he was not a righteous man at all.

Still the debate continued to rage through her as she worked on her sewing in the quiet of the kitchen with her mother and sister.

"Knock, knock," a male voice called through the open door.

Maggie ran over to the door, eagerly greeting their now-daily visitor, Christian. "Preacher!" she shouted, happily taking the bouquet of flowers from him. "You'll never guess what has happened!"

He smiled at her. "You passed your test yesterday at school?"

She laughed. "*Ja*, of course. But this is something even better!"

"Maggie, don't crowd him so," *Maem* scolded gently. "And bring me those flowers. They will need some water."

"How do the Detweiler women fare today?" Christian asked, quickly scanning the room with his eyes.

"Quite well, Christian," Eleanor responded. "Seems like Mary Ann is doing a bit better today."

He raised an eyebrow. "That is *wunderbarr gut* news, indeed! Where is she, if I might ask?"

Maggie plopped down at the table and pressed her face against a hand, leaning toward Eleanor. "She went for a walk. And without me!"

Eleanor nudged her gently. "You always complain about going for walks with her. She has to practically drag you each time!" She returned her attention to Christian. "I'm surprised you didn't see her. She left on the lane just fifteen or so minutes before you arrived."

The color drained from his face and his back stiffened. "I did not see her. And the rain has begun. Did you not notice?"

All three heads turned to look at the window. As Maggie had predicted earlier, the rain was falling. However, it fell in such a way that it did not hit their windows. At least not yet.

"Oh!" Eleanor stood up and hurried over to look outside.

"And lightning storms are headed this way. I could see them over the valley, which is why I walked here instead of bringing the buggy." He joined Eleanor at the window and peered over her shoulder, squinting as he stared. "She would turn back, *ja*?"

*Maem* began worrying, her hands clasped together and one thumb rubbing the palm of the other hand. "We should never have let her go alone!"

Christian walked over to her and placed his hand on her shoulder. "I shall go fetch her. Don't worry."

His words seemed to reassure *Maem*, but only a little, for she still looked frightened as he headed toward the door.

"Which direction, Eleanor?"

"I...I don't rightly know, Christian. She turned right at the hedge, so certainly in that direction."

He nodded his head and disappeared through the door, being careful to shut it behind him as the rain began to downpour, the sound of the rapid cloudburst on the roof now echoing throughout the room. No one spoke as Eleanor and Maggie crowded around the window, staring outside and searching for any sign of Mary Ann. Besides the rain the only noise was the rhythmic ticking of the clock on the wall and, to all of their alarm, the loud clap of thunder.

"How far away is it, then?" Maggie asked, peering anxiously into Eleanor's face. "I counted two seconds. Is that two miles?"

Eleanor swallowed. "*Ja*, so they say."

"Will she get struck by lightning?"

"Maggie!" *Maem* stood up so quickly from the table that her chair fell over backward. "Don't say such things!"

The rebuke frightened Maggie even more than the lightning storm. Eleanor reached over and put her arm around the young girl. "She'll be fine, Maggie. God will see her home safely. And *mayhaps* that would make us all feel better. To pray, *ja?*"

They stood together and bent their heads, silently praying to God for the safe return of their sister. Eleanor added the extra prayer for her sister to never find out about John Willis so that the hole in her heart could begin to close. While she knew that she would accept whatever God planned for her sister, as well as herself, she suspected asking for it might not hurt, either. If nothing else, it made her feel better, knowing that she had unburdened her fears onto the shoulders of the Almighty.

The rain began to fall so hard that it streamed down the windows, making seeing anything beyond the glass almost impossible. It looked as if someone had created a waterfall along the roofline and poured an endless stream of raging water along the front of the house. The sky lit up, and almost immediately a booming clap of thunder followed.

Maggie screamed and ran to her mother, burying her head in her shoulder. "I heard it sizzle!" she cried. "Oh, Mary Ann! Come home!"

"Christian will find her," Eleanor said, hoping to reassure Maggie as well as her mother. "He cares for her so."

Regardless of her reassurance the three of them paced the floor and, in silence, worried to themselves. Eleanor continued to look out the window, hoping to see her sister walk up the lane, but to no avail. After ten minutes had passed, she moved to the door, peering outside and searching, in vain, for Mary Ann. The rain continued to fall, and the lightning storm lingered overhead, each electrifying crack followed by a horrifying boom from the thunder. *Maem* began to weep, her head in her hands, and Maggie sat down in the rocking chair, not speaking as she pushed with her feet, back and forth, waiting.

Another five minutes passed, and Eleanor saw something in the mist of the storm. A figure moving toward the house. Dressed in all black, the man seemed to move slower than normal. His arms were burdened by something heavy, and as he approached the house, Eleanor could see that he carried the limp form of her sister.

"Christian!" she cried, and with total disregard for the storm she ran out the door and raced toward him.

"Stoke the fire and get the *haus* warm!" He hurried as fast as he could with Mary Ann in his arms.

Eleanor did an about-face and ran back to the house, her feet slipping twice on the grass. She called out to her mother that Christian had found Mary Ann, but from the look on her mother's face when she reached the house, she could tell that her mother did not hear her. "Hurry, *Maem*," she instructed. "We need warmth in the house. She's soaked through and through."

"Mary Ann?"

"*Ja, ja*, he found her."

"Thank the Lord!" *Maem* cried, her hands pressed together.

Ignoring her mother's praise, Eleanor pointed toward the wood pile and snapped at Maggie, "Get some wood on that stove so that she can dry off," she said, hurrying to the back bedroom she shared with Mary Ann. It was damp and cold in that room, but Eleanor knew it was the best place for her sister. At least she could be covered with quilts and prayed over, her family tending to her needs. And, in the future, Eleanor knew she would take better care of her sister, not permitting her to leave the house unless she was chaperoned. But as she turned down the bed, Eleanor suspected that her sister would not want for a chaperone again in the future.

She hurried back into the living area just as Christian entered the house carrying Mary Ann, his hair plastered to his head and his shirt clinging to his chest. The look on his face merely confirmed what Eleanor already knew: he was a man in love. Whether Mary Ann returned the affection did not matter to him. His actions had already proven that, for him, love was not merely a delight or a diversion. For Christian love was a sacred gift from God, and regardless of whether he loved in vain, he would act with honor and integrity.

"She's freezing!" he cried out as he entered the house. "Warm clothes and blankets. Quick!"

His command of the situation caused a flurry of activity. *Maem* followed him into the bedroom, and Maggie ran to the trunk in her mother's room for blankets. As soon as Christian set Mary Ann on the bed, Eleanor quickly removed her boots while *Maem* began unpinning her dress. Discretion mandated that Christian step out of the room, although Eleanor noticed his reluctance to do so, his worry for Mary Ann far greater than his prudence.

"She'll be fine," Eleanor reassured him.

He nodded and stepped out of the room, concern still etched on his face.

They moved quickly, undressing Mary Ann and covering her with blankets. *Maem* rubbed at her arms while Eleanor took a towel to Mary Ann's head, trying to dry her long hair so that her head did not stay chilled.

Christian must have been working on starting the fire in the main room, for the smell of raw smoke began to infiltrate the bedroom. Maggie lingered by the door, her eyes wide and frightened. Eleanor heard her ask, "Was she hit by lightning?"

"*Nee*, Maggie," Christian responded. "I found her lying down near the woods in the back fields. She was fine but drenched."

Eleanor caught her breath at his words. *Of course,* she thought. The back fields were where she had met John Willis. She should have known that was where her sister would go. But to be lying down during a rainstorm? The chill in the air coupled with the rain would surely make her sick, especially since she had lost so much weight recently and wasn't eating properly.

"Oh, Mary Ann," she sighed to her sister, uncertain whether she could actually hear her. "What have you done now?"

# ❦ Chapter Twenty-Two ❦

FOR THE NEXT week Mary Ann remained in bed. *Maem* gave up her first-floor bedroom so Mary Ann could remain near the main room, making it easier for the rest of the family to tend to her needs.

The family maintained a vigil over Mary Ann. Someone sat with her around the clock, dabbing at her feverish forehead and forcing her to accept some broth. The bishop visited along with other members of the *g'may*, and Eleanor had no doubt that the news of Mary Ann's illness had spread far and wide.

Through their visitors other news quickly began to infiltrate their house. Widow Jennings was only too eager to whisper of Willis having married that woman just the Tuesday after the fund-raiser. It had been a quiet affair, which had struck Widow Jennings as odd. Amish weddings usually were all-day events, with hundreds of people visiting to celebrate.

"And when his *aendi* heard the news," Widow Jennings had said in a raspy but quiet voice as she leaned forward so that Maggie could not hear, "she was rather put out! Apparently she went to the bishop with some news that"—she glanced over her shoulder at Maggie—"is unfit for young ears to hear. But I've heard tell that John Willis has been shunned!"

"Shunned?" *Maem* gasped and put her hand to her chest. "Surely that can't be so?"

But there was no time for further explanation. A man's footsteps on the stairs interrupted their conversation. Christian had arrived and, with his usual somber expression, his concerned eyes drifted down the hallway toward the room he knew Mary Ann occupied. "How is she today, then?"

Eleanor was thankful for his appearance. The last thing she wanted was her mother to learn about Willis and his out-of-wedlock baby. It was news that would eventually be whispered in the shadows of every Amish home, not just in their *g'may* but also in surrounding ones too. But Eleanor just didn't want to deal with her mother's reaction and risk her sister overhearing.

"She's doing the same, I fear."

Eleanor stood up from where she had sat, and to her relief Widow Jennings made a quick apology that she needed to return to her own house and could stay no longer.

As expected, Christian sat by Mary Ann's bedside, the door open for propriety's sake, and read to her from the Bible. He spent over an hour at her side, his deep voice just a mere murmur as he read to her, occasionally pausing to wipe her brow with a cool cloth. But as the sun began to shift in the sky, he knew he couldn't stay longer. With great reluctance he vacated his place by her side.

"Eleanor," he said when he came back into the kitchen. "She seems to have lost her will."

Eleanor glanced at her mother, who was busy preparing some soup to take into Mary Ann. "She will find it again, Christian." Looking back at him, she met his eyes. "She must. I don't know what I would do without her."

He hesitated before he added, "Nor I."

An hour after Christian had left, Eleanor sat in the rocking chair and worked on some sewing. *Maem* and Maggie had retired to bed for a late afternoon nap, both of them exhausted from staying up with Mary Ann throughout the night.

Eleanor was not expecting anyone to visit. So when she heard the sound of horse hooves pounding on the lane, she set aside her work and hurried to the door. Peering outside, she squinted to try to make out who approached their house. She hoped the sound of the traveler did not disturb her mother from sleep, especially since the rider seemed in a hurry, quite unlike the usual lazy clip-clop of a horse and buggy. The urgency of the rider also gave her a moment's pause, and she hoped nothing untoward had happened to someone else in the *g'may*. She had quite enough on her hands with Mary Ann still unwell.

Eleanor grabbed her black woolen shawl and wrapped it around her shoulders before opening the door. The days were much cooler now that autumn was well under way. A gust of wind pushed the door out of her hand and almost slammed it against the wall, but she caught it with her foot.

Just as she stepped onto the front porch, she saw a chestnut horse round the bend, the rider, a man, bent over and heading directly for their house. Now Eleanor worried that something was indeed wrong. Perhaps a messenger had come to fetch them or to tell them bad news. Her mind began to sort through the different situations that might warrant such a hurried approach to their house.

Quickly she shut the door behind herself and walked down the steps to the grass in front of the house. She started walking toward the moving figure of the horse and man until she was a good distance from the house. And that's when she recognized the man atop the horse, a man she thought she would never see again and, in many ways, had hoped for the same.

"Good day, Eleanor," Willis said as he stopped his horse. Still holding the reins in his right hand, he jumped down to stand before her.

Eleanor stood there, unable to speak as she stared at the sight of the shunned man.

"I...I trust that you are well?" he asked in a voice humbler and far more timid than the Willis she knew from the past.

Eleanor crossed her arms over her chest and glanced in the direction from whence he had just arrived. Perhaps Willis had come to visit Jacob and missed the turn. Surely he had not come to visit any of them! "I have no time to spare with the likes of you," she said in a firm voice. She turned to leave, but he called out her name.

"Please Eleanor, I beg of you!"

She stopped walking and turned back, her arms still hugging her chest as if to still the rapid beating of her heart.

"I must have a moment of your time," Willis said as he took a step toward her, the horse following behind him.

"A moment?" With great apprehension she considered his request. Besides the fact that she had yet to consider forgiving Willis, her biggest fear was Mary Ann's reaction should she happen on Willis standing outside their cottage. However, Mary Ann still slept and was unlikely to awake anytime soon. And Eleanor could not deny that she had some degree of curiosity as to why, exactly, John Willis would have shown up on their doorstep. Even more important was Ephesians 4:31–32: "Let all bitterness, wrath, anger, outbursts, and blasphemies, with all malice, be taken away from you. And be kind one to another, tenderhearted, forgiving one another, just as God in Christ also forgave you." With a sigh she leveled her eyes at Willis and said, "Fine, Willis. But please be quick about it."

A look of relief washed over his pale face. It struck Eleanor that the handsome young man who had so fervently courted her sister had disappeared, leaving behind a shell of a man whose hair needed a good trimming and whose eyes were shadowed by dark circles that had previously not been there.

"I've come to inquire about Mary Ann," he gushed as he took another step toward Eleanor, almost as if he were trying to inch his way closer to the cottage. Recognizing this, Eleanor stood her ground and did not move. "I...I heard at our *g'may*'s worship service this morning that she has been ill this past week. Is this true?"

*What right,* Eleanor wanted to say, *do you have to inquire about the well-being of my* schwester? Her refusal to respond only caused Willis to continue his inquiry.

"Eleanor, my very soul is tortured at the thought that she is in grave danger," he pleaded. "I must know the truth. I pray morning, noon, and night for her recovery. Take me out of my misery and update me on how her health stands."

Reluctantly Eleanor conceded. "She is sleeping comfortably right now, and despite having a fever, we have every reason to believe she will make a full recovery."

He sank to his knees, the reins of the horse now looped around his right arm. "Praise God," he murmured. "An answer to my prayers."

Disgusted with his display of emotion, especially in light of the impact his roguish behavior had on the very situation that he inquired about, Eleanor frowned. "If that is all you have come to inquire about, I will be thanking you to leave now, Willis. I fear the friendship and camaraderie that was once felt between us exist no longer."

"But wait! Please! I...I have to unburden myself of the weight on my shoulders," Willis cried out, dropping the horse's reins and stepping forward to take Eleanor's arm in his hand.

"For your benefit or hers?" Eleanor asked, pulling her arm free from his grasp.

"Hers." He paused. "Mine. Oh, I just don't know, Eleanor. I just want to explain what happened, to beg of some mercy from your family. If you could only understand what, exactly, happened, *mayhaps* you would not hold such a grudge against this poor man. *Mayhaps* you would even find some compassion for me."

*Compassion!* she thought. *Most unlikely, indeed.*

When he realized that she was standing there, waiting for him to proceed with his explanation, he suddenly became flustered as if he hadn't actually expected to convince Eleanor to listen to him. Now that he had her attention, he tugged at his collar and began to pace just a little, the constant motion helping to ease his mind as he began to share his story with Eleanor.

"When I first met her, the day she was kicked by the horse," he started, "I had no further intention than to be friendly and welcoming to the family. I knew that I would, one day, inherit my *aendi*'s farm and, as such, we would be neighbors of sorts. I had no desire to take the friendship further with your *schwester*. She was, at the time, an object of intellectual amusement and nothing more. Besides, I knew that I would need to marry a woman with some sort of family backing to even begin to properly manage my *aendi*'s farm."

Eleanor gasped. Not only had Willis just admitted to having no intention of courting Mary Ann, but he also admitted that he sought a woman of means! "This is outrageous! I fail to see how this will lead me to find any sort of compassion!" she said reproachfully.

Stunned by her words, Willis looked up, red-faced, and held his hand in the air. "*Nee*, Eleanor, the truth is that, despite my intentions, I cannot deny that my feelings for Mary Ann quickly grew, like the mustard seed in the ground. It grew fast and spread wide until Mary Ann was all that I could think about." He removed his straw hat and ran his fingers through his hair before he turned away from Eleanor. "You have no idea the torturous nights, the agonizing conversations I had with myself—discussing and debating the emotional tug at my heart that contrasted so sharply with my logical needs for a future."

Eleanor stared at him, unblinking and mouth open at his confession.

"And, after I could not take it anymore, after I lost debate after debate, I knew I had only one choice, and that was to marry her." He turned around and stared at her. "I had every intention of proposing, Eleanor, that very day that I went away. But, you see, my *aendi* learned about a most unfortunate"—he paused and lowered his eyes—"situation, one that I dare say you must have learned about from the ever-growing Amish grapevine."

"I dare say that it is beyond *unfortunate*," Eleanor said, emphasizing the word *unfortunate*.

Willis raised his eyebrows. "*Ach, ja*, I see." He shook his head as if dismissing something troublesome. "You have learned of the situation then?"

Eleanor lifted her head and said nothing.

201

"I beg of you to consider the source who, I am certain, presented it as though I am the scoundrel and she the victim. There is little to no consideration for the role played by the young woman in question. Was it a lack of understanding or a lack of concern for her own well-being that she finds herself in such a condition?"

Eleanor could barely look at him. Listening to his self-serving account of the facts made her feel physically ill. A grown man defending his own actions against a young woman who was not even yet in her *rumschpringe*? "A condition? Her life is ruined, Willis!"

"As is mine!" he snapped back. Then he took a deep breath and looked up toward the sky, frustration etched into his face. "Do you not understand? I could not marry the girl—she is not Amish. I would have been shunned! And, once my *aendi* disinherited me, I could not marry Mary Ann! So now I find myself in the worst of all situations! I am left in a loveless marriage, shunned by my community, and living miles away from the very woman I wish, oh so fervently, that I could wake up beside every day. Not a second passes that I do not long for Mary Ann—"

Abruptly, Eleanor held up her hand to stop him from continuing. "*Nee*, Willis. Say no more on this subject, or else you will have more sins to confess to the bishop. Shunned or not, miserable or not, you are, after all, a married man now." She quoted, "But I say to you that whoever looks on a woman to lust after her has committed adultery with her already in his heart."

"Married?" he scoffed. "In name only."

"That is not my concern," she said.

"Eleanor, I beg of you! Have compassion! I have been shunned. I cannot sleep in the same room with her, eat at the same table, or even ride in a buggy with her. It is like two strangers living under the same roof."

While, admittedly, Eleanor felt moved to feel some level of pity for Willis, she also knew that a man so emotionally distraught could easily overlook his own contributions to the events leading up to his current circumstances. And pushing aside her empathy, she knew Willis was one of those men. Still, she was not cruel of heart and could not continue to point out his flaws. Clearly he was feeling the pain of shame for his actions.

"What would you have me do, Willis?" Eleanor finally said, hoping to bring closure to this unexpected meeting. With each passing second she feared Mary Ann would awake and see Willis standing in their front yard. And if Maggie spotted him, that too would present an awkward situation that Eleanor would prefer avoiding.

"I am a man with a ruined reputation, Eleanor. There is little I can do to change that," he said in a forlorn voice. "But if you should have mercy on me to let Mary Ann know the truth, what my intentions truly were, perhaps then I could at least rest in the future, knowing that the hatred she must feel for me is decreased, no matter how slightly."

Eleanor glanced over her shoulder toward the house. There was no sign of movement or activity, but she was starting to become anxious for Willis to depart the property. If Christian unexpectedly returned round the bend and saw her speaking to the very person who had defiled his niece and destroyed his friend, there was no telling what the ramifications might be.

"Willis," Eleanor said, "I will share this information with Mary Ann when and if the time is right. Knowing my *schwester*, she has already forgiven you. Her heart has always been large and filled with compassion. Perhaps knowing that will help you rest easier."

Willis stood there, his hat clutched in his hands. He fiddled with it as he reflected on what Eleanor had just said. Finally he tilted his head and stared at her. "But you will tell her? You must promise me."

With a firm shake of her head, Eleanor responded, "*Nee*, Willis. I will do nothing of the sort. I would no sooner make a promise that I am not certain I can keep than I would tell a lie."

Any indication of hope on his face seemed to evaporate as she spoke. "I...I see," he said, but she could tell from the tone of his voice that her response had not been what he anticipated. She could not fathom what he had actually expected when he took it upon himself to visit. As a married man his communication with any single woman, especially Mary Ann, was inappropriate. As a shunned man he shouldn't be communicating with anyone in the community at all.

"If there is nothing further to discuss, Willis—and I cannot imagine there is—I will bid you good-bye," she said, thankful that the conversation was over at last.

He hesitated before turning back to his horse and retrieving the reins. He cast one last look over his shoulder, first at Eleanor and then at the house, before he mounted the horse and reluctantly rode away.

Eleanor watched as his horse carried him back down the lane from which he had arrived just minutes earlier. Unmoved by the visible slump in his shoulders, she remained staunch in her resolve to stay true to her word. She knew only too well the strength of first love. With Mary Ann's precarious emotional and physical condition being so precarious,

Eleanor did not want to present her sister with any reason to feel sympathy or connection to Willis. Despite her current troubles Mary Ann had a promising future, unblemished by any permanent stain, especially now that the truth was known about Willis, even if only by a few people. Eleanor had no intention of relaying any information to her sister unless it was to Mary Ann's benefit, not Willis's.

# ✤ Chapter Twenty-Three ✤

O VER THE NEXT few days Christian remained increasingly vigilant, a constant presence at Mary Ann's side. Eleanor suspected he had learned of Willis's unexpected visit to the area—perhaps someone had seen Willis riding to or from the Detweilers' home. Regardless, Christian was not taking any chances and he stayed at Mary Ann's bedside, sitting on a ladder-back chair and reading to her from the book of Psalms and the Song of Solomon. His voice carried throughout the house while *Maem* made batch after batch of chicken soup, which Eleanor repeatedly tried to force Mary Ann to accept.

When she continued to refuse the food, it was Christian who offered to try to convince her to eat. He took the bowl from Eleanor, and with gentle words and coaxing, he pleaded with Mary Ann to accept the liquid so that she could regain her strength. In the early evening of the second night, she opened her eyes and looked up, a strange expression on her face as if trying to recognize him. When she did, she frowned and moved her head, just slightly, to look at the ladder-back chair with the open Bible on the seat.

"You—" she said in a soft voice, barely audible. Her eyes were wide and bright, studying his face as she spoke. "You came for me."

Christian nodded his head once. "I did."

"You found me."

Another single nod, his eyes never leaving her face.

Something changed in her expression. It softened with what Eleanor suspected was an understanding. Mary Ann seemed to be thinking, perhaps remembering the series of events that led up to this moment. When she refocused on Christian, she looked wide-eyed and enlightened. "You've been here the whole time." It wasn't a question, merely a statement. And with that she accepted the soup from Christian's hand and her recovery truly began.

Eleanor blinked back the welling of tears in her eyes and turned her head to look out the door. She recognized that enlightened look on her sister's face. Certainly Mary Ann finally understood something that had been so obvious but completely overlooked by her during the past weeks of her pining for Willis. While she had been so focused on following her heart in such a public manner, she had missed seeing another who followed his, just in a quiet, more subdued way. Eleanor suspected that her sister's fancy for the dramatic romance now recognized the unspoken suffering of Christian Bechtler, who had watched from the sidelines as the relationship between Mary Ann and Willis developed. Certainly that knowledge would change the way she thought of him.

Leaving the room, Eleanor walked to the kitchen, pausing once to glance over her shoulder. From the kitchen she could still see them, Christian seated beside Mary Ann, gently feeding her spoonful after spoonful of soup. Now it was Mary Ann's eyes that never left his face.

"Oh my," her mother whispered, watching the scene from the kitchen. She reached out and touched Eleanor's arm. "Perhaps tragedy will lead to something good after all, *ja?*"

Eleanor nodded her head and gave a soft smile. "I do believe so," she whispered back. "And she'll be all the better for it."

The two of them clasped hands, content in the knowledge that Mary Ann's care was in the hands of someone who loved her as much as they did. Maggie, listening to the conversation from the kitchen table, looked confused, but for once she remained quiet, most likely for fear of being told to leave the house and play outside.

For the next two hours Eleanor worked at catching up on their sewing orders, enlisting Maggie to assist since, clearly, Mary Ann could not. They sat at the table, working under the light of the propane lantern that hung overhead, hissing and sending enough heat from the flame that *Maem* had not needed to start a fire.

Christian left the bedroom door cracked open when he withdrew from Mary Ann's side and retreated toward the front door. "She's doing much better, I think," he said as he reached for his hat, which he had hung from a peg in the wall near the door. He spun it several time in his hands as he looked down the small hallway toward the bedroom where Mary Ann rested. "Regrettably I must depart for the time being. But I shall return. Is there anything I can bring for you? Medicine from town? Supplies?"

Eleanor smiled at him and shook her head. "*Danke,* Christian. You've done more than you will ever know. How can we ever repay your kindness to our dear Mary Ann?"

Christian glanced at her mother and then back to Eleanor before he slid the hat on his head. "It's no more than any other man would do," he said modestly, and then, with a dip of his head, he opened the door and disappeared into the afternoon sun.

"Such a fine man, that Christian Bechtler," *Maem* said as she stood near the window and watched him unhitch his horse from the hitching post. "How fortunate we are that he found her that day." She shuddered. "I cannot bear to consider what might have happened."

"Then don't, *Maem*," Eleanor scolded. "God took care of Mary Ann, and that is all we must consider, not the what-ifs."

For a long moment *Maem* and Eleanor stood there, each one reflecting on the unusual change of circumstances. In such a short period of time, their hopes that Mary Ann would marry had shifted from Willis to Christian Bechtler, and while originally thought to be an unlikely pairing, it now seemed to be the most sensible matching for Mary Ann.

"Hello, there!"

The sound of a male voice startled them. Eleanor turned toward the door to find Jacob standing there with a bright smile as he shook off his coat and hung it on the very peg from which Christian had just retrieved his hat. "How fare the Detweiler women today, then?" His eyes fell on Maggie. "No school for you today, eh?"

She shook her head.

*Maem* spoke up. "We're all so concerned for Mary Ann. It wouldn't do her any good to sit in the schoolhouse worried about her sister all day."

Jacob nodded, crossing the room to the kitchen table. He paused momentarily and glanced out the window where Christian's buggy was just now rounding the bend. "Ah, but I suspect from what I hear that things are taking a turn, *ja*?" He chuckled. "And definitely for the better, no doubt."

Neither *Maem* nor Eleanor said anything in response.

"*Vell*, that's right *gut* to see some spark of hope in Preacher!" He leaned back in the chair, his broad frame causing it to creak beneath his weight. "About time some lovely young woman recognized the size of that man's heart. Will do him good too. He's been too long alone and is far too *gut* a man to be *left* alone!"

"Coffee?" Eleanor asked, hoping to change the direction of the conversation.

He waved his hand. "*Nee*, but *danke*, Eleanor." He looked around the room, his eyes taking in every detail, from the green window shades to the pretty dishes displayed on the fireplace mantel. He seemed satisfied and sighed. "How comfortable and fine this cottage has become. I knew that it only needed a little bit of love to be transformed. Like everything in life, I reckon."

*Maem* smiled at the compliment, the first genuine smile Eleanor had seen on her face in days. "*Danke*, Jacob. It has become a *wunderbarr* home for my family, indeed."

"Speaking of family," he said, positioning himself to start a new conversation. "I come bearing interesting news. Leah spoke with her *maem* on the phone this morning."

"Oh? How is Widow Jennings?" *Maem* asked, joining Jacob at the table.

"Quite fine, although I imagine her well-being was not mentioned during the conversation, for there was much news to discuss of greater interest." He looked at Eleanor and raised an eyebrow, his eyes never leaving hers. "Seems our Lydia is to be married two weeks from this coming Thursday. The wedding was announced after worship service this past Sunday."

Standing at the kitchen counter, Eleanor felt as if her stomach twisted and her heart fell. She tried to remain stoic, bracing herself to deal with her mother's reaction after Jacob left. Ever since Lydia had confided in her, Eleanor had been praying for the strength to face the moment when the engagement of Lydia and Edwin would become public knowledge. Unfortunately she now realized that no amount of prayer and preparation could have prepared her. Perhaps deep down inside she had hoped that it would never come to fruition. Now, however, she knew that the news was no longer secret.

"Oh my!" *Maem* clapped her hands together. "A wedding? I'm sure we'll be thrilled to attend!"

Even Maggie seemed overjoyed. She grinned at the news and bounced on the balls of her feet, doing her best not to shout out or cheer. "I love the desserts at weddings!" was all she said.

Jacob laughed at her comment and rubbed his protruding stomach. "I tend to agree with you there, Maggie! Perhaps too much!"

*Maem* smiled at the joke. "Weddings are such great fellowship, *ja*! It will be nice to have something positive to look forward to attending. I hadn't known that she was seeing someone, however. Do we know who the young man is?"

"Indeed we do. Seems she has been secretly courting a young man for quite some time. I believe you know him." He paused and, once again, looked over at Eleanor. When she lowered her eyes, he took a breath and returned his attention to *Maem*. "Edwin Fisher is the man. I believe he is the *bruder* of your Fanny. Apparently they had an understanding that dates back to their *rumschpringe*."

The news caught *Maem* off guard. She gasped and raised her hand to cover her heart. "Edwin Fisher?" Her eyes immediately shifted to Eleanor. "Our Edwin Fisher is to marry Lydia? Oh..."

Maggie could not contain herself. "That can't be! He and Eleanor..."

"Shush, Maggie," Eleanor snapped, interrupting her sister with a fierce tone that said much more than she wanted to share. When both *Maem* and Maggie quieted, Eleanor did her best to compose herself, and with as much poise as she could muster, she said to both of them, "We should all be quite happy for their good fortune to find each other."

Maggie's mouth opened, and for a second she stood there staring at Eleanor as if disbelieving what she heard. But Eleanor remained resolute in her stance that if she accepted what she could not change, it would be easier for the rest of the family to follow her example.

Jacob nodded his head at her words. "They will need support too." He lowered his voice, most likely to indicate that he was about to share information of a sensitive nature since there was no one around to overhear. "Apparently Edwin's mother was not as understanding as you, Eleanor. She does not care for Lydia, says she's not a *gut* farmer's wife. And she was put off by the story of such a long, secret engagement. Seems his *maem* now refuses to let him take over the family farm and claims that it shall be given to his younger brother, not Edwin."

For a brief moment Eleanor shut her eyes. She increasingly believed that Lydia was a foolish and manipulative young woman who had likely prodded Edwin into a commitment before he was mature enough to know better. Yet Edwin would never go back on his word to Lydia. He was not that type of man. While Eleanor knew very little about Fanny and Edwin's mother, she could only presume that the woman had a very strong hand in the family decision-making process. With Lydia more engaged in womanly pursuits such as baking and needlepoint, her lack of interest in farmwork would mean that, until their children were of an age to help, Edwin would labor on the farm alone. And the farm, one of the larger ones in the area of Narvon, was much too special to the Fisher family to have it fall apart because of a bad marital decision on the part of the Fishers' son.

Jacob let his hand fall down, hitting the top of the table, a sound resonating in the silence of the room. "So there you have it, the fall of two young men who did not choose wisely." He stood up. "I'm sorry to be the one to break the news." He said this while looking at Eleanor for the third and final time. "However, it's best to learn now about the true nature of these men."

"*Danke*, Jacob," *Maem* said in a strained voice.

"Now, I best be going to tackle my evening chores." He walked to the door, where he paused to lift his hat from the peg and place it on his head. "Have a good evening, then."

The room remained silent long after he left. Eleanor waited for the questions, wishing she had a place to go for private reflection. With no barn to retreat to and Mary Ann in their bedroom, Eleanor's only option was going for a walk. Still, she'd have to come back eventually. It was better to just get it over with, she told herself.

"How long have you known?" *Maem* asked at last.

"A few weeks, I reckon."

"And you said nothing?" *Maem* didn't wait for Eleanor to respond. "You knew yet you went to Honey Brook? You baked goods alongside Lydia? You listened to your *schwester*

213

with her false hopes that Willis would come back to her? Oh, Eleanor!"

"It's all right, *Maem*," Eleanor heard herself say. She knew she spoke the words only to reassure her mother. It would take a long time for those words to be spoken in truth.

"But Edwin loves Eleanor!" Maggie cried out, the disbelief in her voice giving way to tears in her eyes. "I know he does!"

At a time when Eleanor should have been comforted, she went to her sister's side and hugged her instead. "Edwin and I are right *gut* friends, Maggie. There is no need for tears."

Maggie clung to her, the tears falling freely now. "If this is what happens during courtship, I don't ever want to do it!"

Despite the pain in her heart Eleanor gave a mournful laugh as she rubbed at the young girl's back. "Now, Maggie, don't be so silly." She pulled back and squatted so that she could stare into Maggie's eyes. "If *Maem* had felt that way, she never would have married *Daed*. Then where would we be?" She smiled and wiped away Maggie's tears with her finger. "Everything happens for a reason. God's reason. In due time, *mayhaps* we will learn why, if He chooses. If this is what God intended for them, then I'm happy for Edwin and Lydia."

"Happy or not, I will not go to that wedding!" *Maem* declared.

*Maem*'s defiance surprised her, although Eleanor had already made up her mind that she would not attend if asked. So she raised no argument with her mother's words. Instead, she took a deep breath, knowing that the next few weeks would be long and painful as she wondered about the flurry of activity happening in the lives of Edwin and his soon-to-be bride, Lydia.

Although this was the beginning of the wedding season, Eleanor suspected that the announcement came as much of a surprise to Lydia's family as to Edwin's. Most parents suspected or were even told in advance of the bishop announcing the wedding at church service. With all weddings falling on Tuesdays or Thursdays, the family had little time to prepare the house, the guest list, and the food. If the Fisher family was in an uproar about the wedding, Edwin would be stuck inviting all of his family's guests by himself.

Despite how she felt emotionally, Eleanor couldn't help but feel a little compassion for him. All because of a promise made long ago, certainly when he was too young to know better, he now faced a lifetime of honoring it.

# ❧ *Chapter Twenty-Four* ❧

ELEANOR EXCUSED HERSELF and started to head toward the stairs, hoping to retreat to the bedroom she normally shared with Mary Ann. With Mary Ann staying downstairs, Eleanor knew she could find comfort and solace in her bedroom, if nothing more than a few private moments to come to grips with her feelings. However, just as she put her foot on the first step, she saw that the door to *Maem*'s room was open and Mary Ann stood in the doorway, a blanket wrapped around her shoulders as she leaned against the frame.

"A wedding?" Her large eyes and pale face seemed to drain of even more color. "Please tell me it's not more news about..."

"*Nee!*" Eleanor shook her head. "It is not about John Willis. For once, Mary Ann, it has nothing to do with you." She started to climb the steps but stopped when Mary Ann put her hand on the stair railing.

"But *Maem* sounded so angry! Whoever could it have been about?"

Eleanor drew in her breath. "She spoke of Edwin Fisher's marriage, Mary Ann." Then she climbed the rest of the stairs, not once looking back to see if Mary Ann followed.

She did.

"Edwin?" Surprised at this name being in the center of their discussion, Mary Ann slowly followed Eleanor into the second-floor bedroom. "Edwin Fisher? He's to be married?"

Eleanor stood by the window, staring outside so that she did not have to look at her sister. For once she just wished her sister would go away. The last thing Eleanor wanted was to rehash the details from this horrible news.

"Eleanor? What's going on?" she insisted.

"He's marrying Lydia, Mary Ann." Her voice sounded flat and emotionless. Inside, however, she cried at the very thought that their engagement was now public knowledge and sure to proceed to marriage.

"Lydia?" Mary Ann exclaimed. "But he loves you! Of that I am sure!" When Eleanor did not respond, Mary Ann walked to her and touched her arm. "Is this true, Eleanor?"

Still refusing to look at her, Eleanor nodded.

"And how long have you known?"

Finally Eleanor turned to face her sister. "Lydia was quite kind in confiding in me from the very beginning of our relationship, Mary Ann."

Mary Ann's mouth opened and she gasped. "Yet you never said one word to me!"

"*Nee*, Mary Ann," Eleanor said. "She asked me to keep her confidence. I could not go back on my word, even though I often thought of doing so."

"Oh!" Mary Ann sank onto the side of the bed and shut her eyes. "How could I have been so blind?" she asked rhetorically. "All this time I was thinking only of my own pain." She raised her eyes to stare at Eleanor. "And you have been so calm and cheerful at all times. You have supported me, even when you did so by putting yourself in her presence! How selfless you are, Eleanor!"

"Do not suffer on my account, Mary Ann," Eleanor pressed her. "I wish Edwin nothing but the greatest of happiness. More importantly I recognize that his conduct was flawless. Despite my own imagined hopes, I provoked my own disappointment through my presumptions of more than just friendship between us. And I take comfort that I did not cause others to suffer when I learned the truth. Why should others be afflicted from the pain of my misunderstanding?"

"But I shall suffer, Eleanor! Why, I begin to understand now, at least more so than I did before," Mary Ann exclaimed. "During all this time, you knew and remained silent. You bore the pain of heartbreak as no other! With composure and discretion. And during my time of need, you supported me. I shall hate myself forever for not having been there for you. For not having seen beyond my own problems and worries to recognize yours!"

She leaped to her feet and wrapped her arms around Eleanor, holding her as tight as she could. "Oh, *schwester*," Mary Ann cried. "Forgive me my impertinence and selfishness. I shall never complain again about John Willis! You have acted in a way that no one can find fault with, even if Edwin has!"

Eleanor extracted herself from her sister's embrace. "You need to understand something," she said in a tone that hinted at reproach. "Edwin is doing the right thing, Mary Ann. If he had backed away from his promise to Lydia, regardless of how long ago and under what circumstances he made it, I would think all the worse of him! A man without principle is no man at all."

Mary Ann sighed. "Oh, Eleanor, don't we know that to be true?"

Eleanor turned once more to the window, staring aimlessly out of the glass panes while Mary Ann put her arm around her older sister's shoulders. For a long while they stood like that, the two sisters looking at nothing. Then Eleanor shut her eyes and rested her head against Mary Ann's. Despite her facade of cheer and strength it would take her a long time to overcome the disappointment of Edwin's marriage to Lydia. For unlike Mary Ann, Eleanor had no Christian Bechtler to comfort her or show her the compassion of a man of true principle.

Still, in true form, Eleanor felt only happiness for her sister. If one thing came from the realization that there had been no sense and even less sensibility to their initial selection of men, at least Mary Ann had found a stalwart supporter in Christian Bechtler. Their unlikely pairing may not have occurred if Mary Ann's heart had not been broken, her eyes opened, and her character matured.

*God's plan*, Eleanor thought as she felt Mary Ann's arm tighten around her shoulder. God's plan, indeed.

# ❧ *Chapter Twenty-Five* ❧

CHRISTIAN SAT ON the edge of the chair, his knee almost touching Mary Ann's as she rocked back and forth in the rocking chair. With a blanket tucked under her chin, a flush of red covered her cheeks, and she reached up to push down the cover, never once removing her eyes from attentively staring into his face.

Eleanor kneaded some dough, her hands covered with flour as she listened to Christian's solid voice as he read out loud from Mary Ann's Bible:

"How fair you are, my love!
　How very fair!
　Your eyes are doves behind your veil.
Your hair is like a flock of goats,
　streaming down the hills of Gilead.
Your teeth are like a flock of shorn ewes
　that have come up from the washing,
all of which bear twins,
　and not one among them has lost its young.
Your lips are like a scarlet thread,
　and your mouth is lovely.
Your cheeks are halves of a pomegranate
　behind your veil.
Your neck is like the tower of David,

built in rows of stone;
on it hang a thousand shields,
   all of them shields of mighty men.
Your two breasts are like two fawns,
   twins of a gazelle,
   that feed among the lilies.
Until the day breathes
   and the shadows flee,
I will go away to the mountain of myrrh
   and the hill of frankincense."

He continued reading, his voice low and soft but with an inflection that maintained Mary Ann's attention. She seemed to linger on the edge of her chair, waiting breathlessly for him to continue reading. And when he did, she seemed to relax, listening to each and every word he spoke, a soft smile on her lips.

Her deliberate concentration on both the Scripture being read as well as the man reading it was not lost on Eleanor. Working at the counter, her body positioned so that she could watch Mary Ann's reaction as well as hear Christian's reading, Eleanor smiled, pleased with how rapidly her sister seemed to be recovering. Five days had passed since Jacob's visit to the house with his announcement that had stunned the rest of the family. Having been unwillingly prepared for it in advance, thanks to Lydia sharing her secret, Eleanor had been able to maintain her composure even as the fateful Thursday approached.

By now Edwin would be in the throes of preparing for his wedding, and Eleanor did her best not to think of him. She knew there was no sense in pondering the what-ifs and what-could-have-beens. Edwin Fisher was, after all, off-limits to her now, for soon he would be someone else's husband. To wallow in self-pity would do no one any good, neither Eleanor nor anyone else in her family. So she pushed him out of her mind and focused on other things, such as the transformation in her sister.

To bide her time and force her heart to recover, Eleanor found that watching the budding relationship between Christian and Mary Ann filled her with a healing happiness that felt as if it spread throughout her entire body. While the feisty and opinionated Mary Ann of the past seemed to have disappeared, a new Mary Ann emerged from the ashes, one who showed compassion and reverence for the man she credited with saving her both physically and emotionally. Eleanor often wondered if she might add spiritually to that list as well.

Despite Mary Ann's steady improvement Christian continued his daily visits. The only change was that, rather than stay all day by her bedside, praying over her and waiting for her to respond, he curtailed his visits so that he stopped by only during the late afternoon. With her health slowly being restored and no need to worry that she might take a turn for the worse, Christian knew it would not be proper to visit with her in a bedroom. By the afternoon Mary Ann would be sitting in the kitchen area among the other family members, thus enabling his visit to adhere to the strictest of propriety and at no time compromise her reputation.

His thoughtfulness did not go unnoticed by Eleanor, although she spoke of it to no one. Instead, she continued to observe Christian and Mary Ann with great optimism, which only grew when Eleanor noticed the change in the timing of his daily visits clearly worked in Christian's favor. As she grew stronger and more alert, her depression slowly lifting along with her spirits, Mary Ann began to miss his presence and looked forward to the steadfast manner of his company. She seemed to wake in the morning with only one thing on her mind: Christian's visit. By the time she dressed and sat in the rocking chair, her eyes would alternate from watching the clock to staring out the open door. Her impatience for his arrival would be matched only by her lengthy sighs and frequent tapping of her fingers against the arms of the chair.

Today, however, she made her frustration known to him. When he shut the Bible, Mary Ann reached out her hand and pleaded with him, "Please keep reading, Christian. I so enjoy listening to your soothing voice"

He glanced down when she placed her hand on his arm. For a moment he seemed to contemplate her touch, and while he did so, she made no attempt to remove it. When he finally raised his eyes to look at her, the glow on his face said more than words could. Eleanor saw something in addition to love in his expression; she saw hope.

"Ah," he said slowly as he placed the Bible on his lap and reached out to gently cover her hand with his own, "but that is the beauty of tomorrow, Mary Ann. The anticipation of what is yet to come!"

She thought for a moment and then searched his face, that pleading tone still in her voice when she asked, "You *will* come tomorrow, won't you, Christian?"

"Tomorrow is Sunday, my dear Mary Ann."

"But we don't have worship tomorrow."

He gave her a soft smile. "You are correct. It is our off-Sunday."

"Then you will still come?"

He tilted his head slightly and watched her, his adoration and devotion to her more than apparent in his expression. Slowly, he nodded his head. "We have much more to read in the Song of Solomon, do we not?" He held the Bible for a moment, his hands wrapped around it as if holding a cherished gift. Eleanor suspected he was holding it like that not just because it was the Bible but because it was Mary Ann's Bible. Reluctantly he held it out for her to take from him. When Mary Ann took it, her fingers brushed against his.

Eleanor looked away, wishing the room was larger so that they could have some privacy. She remembered how Mary Ann used to complain about Christian's long-winded, monotonous sermons. She knew her sister would most likely never complain again. Her image of him had changed, and she had seen through the exterior of an older, single man who remained calm in the worst of situations and displayed little emotion. She had found the inner man, one who remained devoted to those he cared about, dealing with the most unlikely of adversaries and situations while he waited patiently for the tide to shift in his favor.

"Until tomorrow then, Mary Ann," he said as he stood.

She smiled at him, her eyes taking him in before she looked down at the Bible in her hands.

Christian started to walk out of the room, heading toward the front door. He hesitated, however, before he opened it. He looked over his shoulder at Mary Ann, who sat with the Bible on her lap, her fingers tracing the very place he had just touched. Satisfied that she was fine, he cleared his throat and met Eleanor's gaze. "If I may, Eleanor, I'd like to have a word with you. There is something I need to discuss."

Surprised, Eleanor nodded and gave the dough one more good knead and then placed it in a wooden bowl to rise. She covered it with a kitchen towel before quickly washing her hands under the faucet. Pieces of dough fell from her fingers, the water washing away the dry feeling of flour that clung to the sides of her fingernails.

As she followed him outside, she dried her hands on her black apron, wondering at the formality of Christian's request to speak to her. She didn't doubt for a moment that the discussion was not about something but, rather, someone, and she braced herself for what she suspected he wanted to talk about with her. Certainly his request to marry Mary Ann would not come as a surprise to any of the women in the Detweiler family. It did, however, seem surprising that he would request an audience with her and not *Maem*.

After being in the house all morning, Eleanor felt refreshed by the cool autumn air. The bright yellow and red leaves had fallen a week ago, and now only the brown oak leaves remained, along with the pale green of the silver maples. When the breeze blew, the drying leaves rattled and some of them broke free from the tree branches and floated through the air.

Eleanor stood before Christian and waited for him to speak. She thought of how Christian and Mary Ann started their relationship, Christian comparing her to a love long lost and Mary Ann not even thinking of him at all. The bittersweetness of the moment caught Eleanor off guard as she realized that, despite all of the pain Mary Ann had felt over the past few weeks, God had provided her with a man who far exceeded John Willis in every way possible.

"I must ask something of you," Christian started, enunciating each word slowly and deliberately. He seemed nervous, shuffling his feet and clutching his hands behind his back. "It is quite important, and I can only ask this of you. No one else."

Eleanor tried to hide her amusement at this anxious side of the usually confident and calm Christian Bechtler. "What is it, Preacher?"

"I have heard about the plight of your friend, Edwin Fisher," he said.

Immediately the smile disappeared from her face. She had expected a discussion about him and Mary Ann, not a mention of the one person she truly hoped to forget. "Edwin Fisher?"

If he was aware of the pain that Eleanor felt at the mention of Edwin's name, he did not show it. Instead, Christian merely nodded his head. "The one and the same, *ja*."

"What...why is his story of importance to either one of us?" she managed to ask, despite being flustered. She could not imagine any circumstance in which Edwin Fisher would be of concern to Christian Bechtler and even less to her!

"Ah." Christian held up a finger as if to make a point. "A man who stands by his principle, regardless of his true affections, is a righteous man, indeed."

She blushed, remembering the sacrifice Christian had made so many years ago. Although in a different situation, Christian had demonstrated the same characteristics and been rewarded with doing so when he was nominated to be one of the preachers for their church district. At the same time, she remembered the plight of his niece, the very woman who now had a child both fathered and denied by John Willis.

"I understand Edwin Fisher has been removed from the family farm and has no means of supporting himself in the way he had intended," Christian said. "I find that most troublesome, Eleanor, for a man who stood by a promise made so long ago. The respect I have for his commitment is quite great. There should be more men like him in the world, wouldn't you agree?"

She forced herself to nod once in recognition of Christian's questions, but she could not speak. How could she argue with Christian's perspective while denying her own angst at Edwin's upcoming nuptials? In her mind she recalled Lydia on the very first day she brought Eleanor into her confidence. Surely Lydia must have had an ulterior motive for doing so, especially since they had only just met. Yet now that Lydia was marrying Edwin, Eleanor could only wonder why Lydia felt threatened at all. She made up her mind that Lydia was just a silly woman with confidence issues. Clearly Lydia had nothing to be concerned about for Edwin stood by her, even in the face of losing his parents' farm.

"I've thought about this man since I heard of his disinheritance. It has kept me awake at night, and only recently was I able to come up with an idea."

"An idea?" she echoed incredulously.

"*Ja*, a proposition for this young man."

She could hardly imagine what Christian had in mind.

"It turns out that my own tenants at the farmhouse are moving west to join with that Colorado Amish community."

"Colorado? You mean the settlement headed by Ephraim Troyer?"

He nodded his head solemnly. Many people were moving west, joining smaller communities of Amish with greater access to land. Colorado was one of the latest places that seemed to attract aspiring farmers from Pennsylvania. "I've corresponded with Troyer over the years since he moved there. It's a *gut* place with a lot of inexpensive land out there. With what my tenants have saved, they intend to buy a 120-acre plot to farm. A *wunderbarr* opportunity for them to create something to pass along to their children and grandchildren."

"Of course," she said. "But what does Edwin Fisher have to do with that? Or me either, for that matter?"

"I should like you to write him a letter, extending my personal invitation for him to move to my farmhouse and take over the farm."

Eleanor could hardly believe what she was hearing. The generosity Christian was bestowing on Edwin—and Lydia too, for that matter—conflicted with Eleanor's realization that she would have to live in the same community as Edwin and his new bride. To see them at worship service every two weeks? To watch them as their family grew? Surely that was more than she could bear.

"Why me, Preacher?"

"I seem to recall that you were quite friendly with him." There was no malice or suspicion in his words. With his rapid departure from Quarryville and his concern over helping his niece, Eleanor doubted that Christian knew anything from the lips of Widow Jennings or Jacob Miller about her association with Edwin Fisher. And if he did, he was gentleman enough to keep it discreet.

"His sister married my half *bruder*," she said at last, feeling it was the safest comment to make, admitting the reason for being friendly with him without admitting the extent of that friendliness. "I know he is a good worker, for he helped at my *daed*'s farm when John took it over from us."

"So I suspected. Of course, if you feel good about Edwin, then I take that as the highest of recommendations. And since I am not very familiar with Edwin Fisher, he is more apt to accept the offer if it comes from a friend." He leveled his gaze at her. "That is why I'd like you to pen the letter. The *grossdaadihaus* is certainly large enough to accommodate a young family for several years. I'm sure Edwin and his *fraa* would be quite content there."

How could she possibly say no? After everything Christian had done for the family, especially for Mary Ann, Eleanor knew she had only one choice, and that was to say yes. However, reaching out to Edwin to invite him to bring Lydia to Quarryville would be one of the hardest things she had ever done. To put pen to paper and draft a letter that remained friendly yet distant, personal yet professional, interested yet aloof? What Christian asked of her was more than she thought she could do, but she knew she could not deny him.

"Of course, Christian," she said, hoping her voice held no emotion to give away how much she dreaded this favor he asked. "I'd be happy to write this letter for you."

# ❧ *Chapter Twenty-Six* ❧

*October 26*

*Dear Edwin,*

*I trust that all is well with the upcoming wedding. Maem and I will be sorry to not be able to attend. Unfortunately, as Fanny and John may have relayed to you, Mary Ann has been ill, and we feel it best not to leave her unattended. Please know that we send our best wishes.*

*I am writing to you at the request of Christian Bechtler, one of our preachers and also the owner of a harness-making shop in Quarryville. While personally unknown to you, Christian Bechtler is the finest of men with a sincere offer to you that you might take over the management of his farm.*

*After becoming aware of our family connection, he asked that I write to you. He learned of the circumstances with which you now find yourself out of work. Conveniently, he has a farm that has been in his family for generations. His tenants are moving away, and the house will be empty.*

*Christian has asked that I convey to you his desire that, if you are still in need of employment, perhaps you might consider taking over the management of his farm. With almost 100 acres of beautiful fields to plant hay and corn, it would be a wonderful place to start your new life.*

*Should this be something of interest, I have included a slip of paper with his information so that you might contact him directly.*

*Again, best wishes from all of us.*

*Prayers and blessings,*
*Eleanor Detweiler*

She stared at her handwriting on the plain sheet of white paper. The blue cursive words seemed forced and unfeeling. It was her tenth try at penning the letter. Nine other pieces of paper were scattered in crumpled wads near the garbage basket. No amount of writing those words made anything seem sensible. How could she possibly write to Edwin to alert him of this offer when the last thing she ever wanted was to speak to or hear from him again? Each drafting of the letter made her fight the emotions that welled up in her throat and threatened to engulf her. The only concession she could make to her own feelings was to avoid any direct mention of Lydia in the letter.

Two days had passed since Christian asked her to write the letter to Edwin. Two long days of Eleanor trying to draft the letter in her head. Each time that she thought she had formed the correct words to use, she began to write them down on paper only to realize that she didn't like them after all. Now Eleanor feared that more days would pass before she actually drafted something even remotely acceptable by her standards, much less have the emotional strength to mail it.

The previous day when he visited, Christian had not asked whether the letter was finished, for which Eleanor was thankful. She would have been embarrassed to admit that she struggled to find ways to put the offer into words. Each time she tried, she merely saw Edwin's face and heard Lydia's laugh, neither of which brought her any closer to writing the letter. Now she figured she was on borrowed time, and she knew she had to tackle this letter without further delay.

Just a short time ago, at exactly two thirty, Christian had arrived at the cottage with his buggy. He seemed to be a creature of habit, arriving at the same time every day. His consistency was admirable and apparently appreciated by Mary Ann, who began to preen a bit each afternoon at two o'clock in preparation for his arrival.

Today, after spending fifteen minutes inside the house visiting with Mary Ann, *Maem*, and Eleanor, Christian had suggested that Mary Ann take in the fresh air. With glowing eyes she had started to get up from her chair when *Maem* began fretting out loud.

"Oh, it's so chilly today. There's a bitterness in the air," she said. "I'd hate to see her catch cold so soon after recovering."

"The change of scenery will benefit her more than the cold will harm her," Christian countered politely. "Besides, I made certain to bring along a quilt in case the air is too cold for her."

Reluctantly *Maem* had agreed and Eleanor had stood at the window, her arms wrapped around her waist as she watched Christian hold Mary Ann's elbow, gently guiding her to the buggy. The compassion he continued to show to her sister made Eleanor feel confident that an announcement of their upcoming wedding would be shared with the family soon.

Mary Ann could hardly keep her eyes off him when he was there, his attention devoted to ensuring her comfort. Yet Eleanor noticed that other than Mary Ann's unfettered awareness of Christian's presence, she displayed none of the girlish infatuation she had exhibited with Willis. In fact, just the night before, Mary Ann sat in bed, her pillow propped against her back as she read through the very verses Christian had read earlier that day. When Eleanor made a comment about how well Christian read Scripture, Mary Ann merely smiled but said nothing. *What a difference*, Eleanor had thought. Gone was the love-filled boasting and starry-eyed daydreaming, replaced with a sensible young woman with a private demeanor. She reminded Eleanor more and more of herself each day.

Now, in the quiet of the kitchen, Eleanor sat at the table with her head bent over the paper as she reread it one last time.

"What are you writing, Eleanor?" *Maem* asked as she entered the kitchen carrying a basket of folded laundry. She set the basket on the table and began folding the items she had just pulled from the wash line. "You've been at it for two days now."

Eleanor sighed and slid the letter into an envelope. "Nothing of much importance. Just a letter to an old friend," she said.

What did it matter, she wondered, how the letter was worded? Her words would not change the situation. After all, Edwin would soon have a wife, and Eleanor knew that moving on was her only option. If a word was out of place or a statement just a little unclear, it was not such a big deal anymore. She didn't need to care what he thought of her penmanship or wording. All that mattered was that she fulfill her promise to Christian Bechtler.

"I suspect your sister will have an announcement for us," *Maem* said, as if reading Eleanor's mind. She plucked the small pile of freshly washed and folded kitchen towels from the table and carried them over to the cabinet drawer where she stored them. After she shut the drawer, she stood there staring at the wall for a long, thoughtful moment. "And I'm happy for Mary Ann. Christian has proven himself to be rather devoted to her care, don't you think?"

Eleanor nodded as she opened her address book and looked through it for the Fisher family's address in Narvon, which she quickly wrote on the envelope. While she wasn't certain he was living there, she suspected that someone would get the letter to him. "How fortunate that Mary Ann finally understood how strong Christian's admiration is for her."

"Admiration?" *Maem* laughed, shutting the drawer with a quick shove of her hip. "Oh, Eleanor, sometimes you are too practical for your own good. That man is besotted with her! If he wasn't so mature and godly, he'd be a *ferhoodled* young man, for sure and certain!"

"Who's *ferhoodled*?" Maggie pranced through the front door, shedding her sweater and dropping her lunch bag onto the floor. She ran over to the counter and started to reach for an apple from the fruit bowl. *Maem*, however, reached out and grabbed her hand.

"Please pick up those things you dropped on the floor, Maggie," she said, pointing to the sweater and lunch bag. "That's not where they belong now, is it?"

"No, *Maem*."

Eleanor stood up, and with the envelope in hand, she hurried to the door. The postal truck came by the mailbox just a little after Maggie's return from school. She wanted to be certain to mail the letter today so that she didn't have to struggle with rewriting it for an eleventh or twelfth time that evening. Just knowing that the letter was out of her hands would make her feel less apprehensive about having written it at all.

Eleanor discovered that the mailbox was already filled with several letters from the past few days. Unless they were expecting letters, they usually walked out to fetch the mail just once or twice a week. To her surprise, there was a letter in the mailbox addressed to *Maem* from Widow Jennings, who remained with her daughter Charlotte in Honey Brook. Placing her own letter in the now empty box, Eleanor raised the red flag before hurrying back to the house, suspecting she knew what Widow Jennings had to say that could not (or, rather, would not) have been shared through Jacob.

Bracing herself, Eleanor handed the letter to *Maem*. "*Vell* now," *Maem* said as she set the empty laundry basket in the hallway. "I'll be curious to see what she has to say then." She sat at the table and slipped her finger along the flap. The letter fell onto the table, and Eleanor could see that it was just two sheets of paper.

*Maem* picked them up, and after retrieving her reading glasses from her apron pocket, she began to read the letter to herself. Her lips moved as her eyes traveled along the small, cursive handwriting. Just a few lines into the letter, she gasped and covered her mouth with her hands. "Oh my!"

"What is it, *Maem*?"

"I...I can hardly say."

Maggie ran over, clamoring to try to see the letter. She stood on her toes, peering over *Maem*'s shoulder. When *Maem* tried to shoo her away, Maggie peeked over her other shoulder.

"Go on outside with such energy," Eleanor scolded her.

"*Ja*, out you go! Go run to Jacob's for some fresh milk. We're almost out." *Maem* seemed just as eager to have Maggie leave the room as Eleanor, the former unaware of the news the letter would bring and the latter far too aware that it was nothing a young girl should hear.

"Aw, why? I want to hear too!"

*Maem* lowered the letter and leveled her stare at Maggie. "And that's exactly why you are being sent to Jacob's! It's not for your ears."

Kicking at the floor, Maggie turned around, grumbling about how she never got to hear any of the good gossip as she sulked out the door.

"That child!" *Maem* said disapprovingly, clicking her tongue and shaking her head.

"What's the news, *Maem*?"

Raising the letter again so that she could read it, *Maem* began to summarize what was written. "I don't want to give credence to what Widow Jennings was saying about John Willis, but it seems it is true. John Willis has been shunned."

"Really?" Now it was Eleanor's turn to hurry to the table. She leaned over her mother's shoulder and began to read the letter for herself.

"*Ja*, that's what she says." She pointed to a section of the letter. She handed the letter to Eleanor and sank down into one of the kitchen chairs. "Finish reading it, Eleanor. I don't think I dare do it myself!"

It had taken well over a week, but John Willis's shunning was public knowledge at last. Only now the details of his behavior were being whispered about among households throughout the country, for sure and certain.

"Apparently he has been more worldly than is permitted for a man who has taken the kneeling vow," Eleanor said, trying to disguise her previous knowledge of this news.

*Maem*'s mouth opened, and she reached out to retrieve the letter from Eleanor. Her eyes quickly read the rest of the letter. "Oh my! A young *Englische* girl? A *boppli*? Why, she's not more than a child herself!"

She set down the letter and stared at Eleanor. "The girl's uncle and Willis's *aendi* contacted the bishop?"

While *Maem* tried to grasp that information, Eleanor struggled with the only piece of news she had not previously known: Christian had gone to Willis's bishop. Eleanor caught her breath, and like her mother, she covered her mouth with her hand. Standing up, she tried to make sense of what she had just learned. If Christian had not informed the church of Willis's behavior as soon as he learned of it, why would he have told on him now? There was only one answer for that: Mary Ann. Certainly seeing Mary Ann heartsick and broken had upset him so much that he finally decided the suffering of two young women warranted more than divine interference; it also called for community intervention.

"And Willis denied it at first until confronted by the uncle and the girl." *Maem* set down the letter and looked up at Eleanor. "Have you ever...?"

"*Nee*," Eleanor replied. She had never known anyone who was shunned by the church. Yet it was always an unspoken possibility that hung over the heads of every member. As a child, she had always worried that someone she knew would be shunned. When she had taken her kneeling vow, she learned about the strict discipline of the church for members who strayed from living plain. Venturing into the worldly ways of the *Englische* held consequences. Shunning was the most extreme sanction for materialistic behavior that did not conform with the Amish lifestyle.

"His poor *fraa!*" *Maem* lamented. "Such an unsuspecting lamb to be taken in by such a wolf in sheep's clothing!"

Eleanor wanted to respond that clearly Willis's wife was not the first young woman to be taken in by Willis's smooth words and handsome looks. In fact they had their own poor unsuspecting lamb who had fallen prey to his charms. Remaining silent, however, seemed the best option.

"In all my years, I've never heard such a story. And to think that Mary Ann was intent on marrying him! Oh, help!" *Maem* folded the letter and shoved it back into the envelope as if the mere touch of her fingers to the paper burned her skin. She slipped it into her apron pocket as she looked up at Eleanor. "Best not let Mary Ann see this. No sense in even bringing up his name, never mind spreading the gossip about him."

Silently Eleanor agreed.

She couldn't imagine how Willis would manage to live with his new wife and her family. They could not eat at the same table or even share the marital bed. The scandal of Willis's promiscuity—and with a young girl at that!—most certainly would sour his relations with his new family. And Eleanor could hardly imagine what the young wife must feel about discovering her husband was a philanderer who refused to accept responsibility for a baby he had fathered. Even if Willis confessed his sins to the congregation and the ban was lifted, it could take years, if not a lifetime, for his relationships with family and friends to return to some degree of normal.

Perhaps this was one of the reasons God had intervened and saved Mary Ann from such a tainted relationship. The thought struck Eleanor, and immediately she wondered if that had not been part of God's plan. Yes, Mary Ann had felt terrible emotional pain over humiliating abandonment by a man she thought loved her and would marry her. Yet certainly it was better for her to have loved a man that rejected her for another woman than to have married him only to learn that he was guilty of so many grievous sins. The shame of the former was nothing compared to the dishonor and pain associated with the latter.

And indeed, Eleanor further realized, God had used the pain to teach her *schwester* a valuable lesson: life is best lived with a strong dose of humility and an even stronger amount of maturity. Only by feeling the pain of such heartbreak was Mary Ann able to recognize—and value—the godly character and steadfast love of Christian, a man she had heretofore overlooked. Indeed, the ways of God were often mysterious, but in this case, at least, Eleanor caught some glimpse of His plan and could only bow her head in humble gratitude at His work in her *schwester*'s life.

# ❧ *Chapter Twenty-Seven* ❧

ELEANOR AND *MAEM* knelt by the kitchen chair while Mary Ann stood on it, her arms outstretched to the sides as they pinned the hem of her new light blue dress. *Maem* held six straight pins between her lips while Eleanor measured to ensure that the hem remained straight. With a small fire in the fireplace, the kitchen smelling of burnt wood and freshly baked bread, the room felt warm and cozy on this cold November day, as much like home as their former residence at the Manheim farm.

"My arms are getting tired," Mary Ann complained.

"Oh, hush now," Eleanor retorted. "You only get married once, Mary Ann, and you must have the perfect dress!" She took a pin from her mother and gently slid it through the fabric. "And this color of blue is perfect, indeed. Now turn around, *schwester*, so I can see the other side."

As expected, Christian had proposed to Mary Ann on their buggy ride over a week ago, and the wedding was scheduled to take place on Tuesday. With only slightly more than two weeks between Christian asking Mary Ann and the actual wedding, everything had been a flurry of activity since then. Fortunately Jacob insisted that the wedding be held at his farm, since the cottage would not accommodate the three to four hundred guests that would, undoubtedly, stop by for the day-long activities. His ever-quiet wife volunteered to help organize the food preparation, which left *Maem* and Eleanor the task of making her wedding dress.

"Christian has been even more attentive since you agreed to marry him," *Maem* said happily through her pressed-together lips. "I wouldn't have thought that to be humanly possible." She pinched a section of the hem together, assessing how even it was when compared to the rest. Satisfied, she removed a pin from her mouth and stuck it through the fabric. "I don't think I've ever seen a groom who took such satisfaction from pleasing his intended. Oh, Mary Ann! Such a *wunderbarr gut* marriage you will have."

Mary Ann blushed and merely said, "He is the best of men."

Eleanor sat back on her heels and looked up. "I do believe the hem is finished. Lower your arms. Let's see how it sits now."

Once her arms were lowered, Eleanor assessed the hem with a critical eye. "Hmm, I think we may have gotten it on the first try."

"Thank the good Lord!"

*Maem* and Eleanor laughed at Mary Ann's exasperation, reveling in the return of the spirited Mary Ann they had always known. Then they stood up and reached out their hands to help her get down from the chair.

The sound of a horse and buggy approaching the cottage startled the three of them. Almost simultaneously they turned their heads to look at the clock. One fifteen.

Mary Ann frowned and hurried over to the window. "Whatever could have happened that Christian would come visiting so early? I hope nothing is wrong." She stood on her tippy toes and craned her neck to see the back of the buggy. "Oh. That's not Christian's buggy."

At this announcement, Eleanor and *Maem* joined her at the window.

"He is a creature of habit," Eleanor said. "It's far too early, so I can't imagine it would be him anyway."

"Why, I don't recognize that buggy at all," *Maem* said as she pointed to the orange reflectors on the back of the buggy. Most Amish men created their own patterns with the reflectors, just one way of identifying their buggy when it was parked among so many others that were identical in their external appearance. "I can't say I've seen that one before."

"*Mayhaps* a new client?" Mary Ann suggested.

Regardless of who it was, Eleanor began to bustle about the kitchen, picking up their sewing items and putting them back into the basket they used for storage. She swept up the scraps of fabric from the table and laid them on top of the basket. "Best tidy up, *Maem*," she said over her shoulder. "And Mary Ann, be careful taking off the dress so that you don't get stuck by the pins, *ja*?"

As Mary Ann hurried to the bedroom to slip off the dress, Eleanor picked up the last few items that remained on the counter. A quick glance of the room gave her satisfaction. Whoever had just arrived would not find their small cottage in disarray.

"Oh, help!" *Maem* whispered.

"What is it?" Eleanor joined her at the window, but before she could look out, her mother turned around and blocked her path.

"Eleanor," she said with a pale face that was drained of all color as she placed her trembling hands on her daughter's shoulders. "I want you to take a deep breath."

"Who's out there, *Maem*?" For a moment she worried that it was Willis. How would his presence impact Mary Ann, who seemed to float on air as she prepared for her wedding to Christian Bechtler? She panicked and worried how she could protect her sister.

"It's Edwin Fisher," *Maem* whispered.

"Edwin!" Nothing could have shocked Eleanor more than hearing that just outside her door was Edwin Fisher. Eleanor had not shared the contents of the letter she had mailed the previous week to Edwin at the request of her soon-to-be brother-in-law. While Edwin's appearance at the cottage surprised her, she immediately put the pieces together. Surely he was visiting with Christian, perhaps touring the farm before committing to manage it. As good manners dictated, he would stop in to visit with them along the way. While his timing most likely appeared cold and insensitive to her mother, Eleanor knew otherwise.

"Perhaps it's not so strange," Eleanor said calmly.

*Maem* didn't have time to answer, for Mary Ann rejoined them at the same moment a knock sounded against their front door.

"I'll get it," Mary Ann said, and before *Maem* could stop her, she walked to the door. When she opened it, her surprise at seeing Edwin there was more than apparent.

"Edwin Fisher! Oh!"

Eleanor felt the color drain from her face. Just hearing his name made her heart palpitate and her breath catch in her throat. If writing the letter had been hard, knowing that Edwin Fisher was walking toward their front door was even more painful. For a moment she wondered if she would have the strength to face him. But did she really have a choice? She raised her head and stared at the door, hoping to catch a glimpse of him before he saw her. But Mary Ann blocked her view.

Mary Ann looked over her shoulder at her sister, surprise still written on her face. "Eleanor! Edwin's come to visit!" Returning her attention to Edwin, Mary Ann swung the door open wider. "Come in, come in," she cried out. But as he stepped through the door, his tall, willowy frame filling the room, Mary Ann's initial expression of joy at seeing him changed. Eleanor suspected that her sister quickly understood that Edwin's visit was rather unusual. Hadn't Edwin recently married Lydia?

"I'm...I'm sure we are all rather surprised to see you here," Mary Ann managed to say.

He removed his straw hat and held it by his side rather than hang it on a peg by the door. His hands seemed to fiddle with it, playing with the brim as he held on to it. First he smiled at Mary Ann and then at *Maem*. When he finally met Eleanor's gaze, he seemed even more nervous than before. "Apparently you should get used to seeing me in the area," he said as pleasantly as he could. "I'm to take over the management of your preacher's farm."

Mary Ann gasped. "Our preacher's farm? You mean Christian Bechtler?"

Eleanor wondered why Christian would have kept this secret from his fiancée. If Edwin and his wife were to move onto the farm, Mary Ann would have to interact with them on an almost daily basis. Hearing from Edwin directly was probably not the best way for Mary Ann to have learned about the newly married Fishers living on Christian's property.

Nonplussed by her unawareness of his moving onto the farm, Edwin nodded his head. "Indeed. And I understand that, next Tuesday, you are to marry the one and the same? Congratulations to both of you."

Uncertain what to say, besides a soft "*danke*," Mary Ann lowered her eyes, averting her gaze from his face. Eleanor could see the mixture of confusion and disgust in her sister's expression, especially when he expressed his best wishes to her on her upcoming nuptials.

It was *Maem* who finally managed to offer him the same consideration. "And we offer you our congratulations as well." She seemed nervous, shifting her weight from one foot to another. "We...we were sorry to miss the wedding."

"I am sorry, too," he replied, now focused on Eleanor. "It was a fine day and the food was plentiful. The guests stayed until late in the evening. I was quite tired in the morning when I had to get up for chores."

Inwardly Eleanor cringed at his words. She didn't want to think about Edwin's wedding day, wedding night, or the morning thereafter. She could almost see Lydia in a white nightgown, still sleeping under the blankets when Edwin had to arise to help with the early morning chores. It took very little to imagine that Lydia slept while Edwin worked, but it was a vision that Eleanor did not even want to think about. She looked away, staring at a stray piece of yarn on the floor beneath a chair.

"And...and how is Lydia?" *Maem* asked, more from politeness than curiosity.

Edwin tore his eyes from Eleanor and looked at her mother. "Lydia? *Ja, vell,* I imagine she is doing quite fine."

Another moment of silence fell over them. The awkwardness of his unexpected visit created a rising tension among the Detweilers, especially with Eleanor being the only one who understood the reason for his standing before them in their cottage: her letter, and how it had paved the way for his place on Christian's farm. Certainly he had come calling on them since they were now to be neighbors. Regardless of the past relationship (or lack thereof!) Eleanor needed to get used to Edwin and Lydia living in their *g'may*. They *all* would need to get used to that idea.

"We shall look forward to having the both of you in the church district," *Maem* managed to say in a very sincere voice. She glanced at Eleanor before she added, "We were quite fond of Lydia when she visited."

At this statement Edwin frowned and followed *Maem*'s eyes, looking first at Eleanor before he returned his eyes to *Maem* as he repeated, "Both of us?"

Mary Ann had finally recovered from her shock at seeing him. "*Ja*, you and Lydia," she said pointedly.

He blinked his eyes and stared at the three women. He ran his fingers through his hair and shook his head. "How very awkward," he mumbled. He took a few steps, pacing for just a brief second before the women. "I...I thought you would have heard the news by now. Lydia will be living at the family farm in Narvon," he said. When none of them spoke, he added, "With her husband." Another pause met with silence. "My brother." When they continued to stare at him, their mouths now open in amazement, he seemed to realize they had not heard the news, so he explained in more detail. "I presume you are referring to my brother, Roy, who married Lydia last month."

Mary Ann covered her mouth with her hand. "Roy and Lydia?" she asked in disbelief. "Roy married Lydia? But we heard that..."

Her mother nudged Mary Ann with her foot to prevent any more words from escaping her mouth.

Edwin shook his head, a sheepish expression on his face. "I can only imagine what you have heard. But it appears that Lydia fancied the family farm more than the son that came with it."

It took a moment for Eleanor to digest the news that Edwin had just shared with them. As it dawned on her, something collapsed within Eleanor. She gasped when she heard his words, and she repeated them in her head, worried for just a moment that perhaps she had misheard him. If Lydia married his brother, that meant that Edwin stood before them as an unmarried man. Eleanor stared at him, her eyes fully open and the color drained from her face.

"Do you mean that you are not…" Eleanor couldn't finish the sentence; the words seemed stuck in her throat.

"Married?" He finished it for her. "Ah, I see. That is what you thought." He looked down at the floor and shook his head. "*Nee*, I am afraid not." His eyes flickered to Eleanor once more. "At least, it seems, not yet. But I do hope to change that."

Both Mary Ann and *Maem*'s eyes widened as Eleanor's legs gave out from beneath her and she fell into a nearby chair, turning her body away from all of them as her shoulders began to shake. She covered her face with her hands and began to cry, sobs wracking her back. The pent-up emotions and long-fought disappointments poured out as she wept uncontrollably.

"Come, Mary Ann," *Maem* said, motioning toward the door. "We should leave them to talk, *ja*?"

Quietly they stole out of the room, leaving Edwin alone with Eleanor. Beside herself, she continued to sob into her hands, her tears spilling through her fingers. Whether she felt joy or pain, anger or release she could not say. So much of what she had felt, would feel, and was about to feel being so intermingled. Words could not express the release of emotions, regardless of the outcome. It was almost as if she had been holding her breath, living one day at a time in order to deny her feelings and pretend that everything was all right despite the complete loss of hope. But when Edwin said that they had all been mistaken and he was not married, the floodgates opened on her emotions. Simply put, she could not hold back for one second longer.

With a brief hesitation Edwin stepped forward toward her. He reached into his front pocket and withdrew a white handkerchief. With trembling hands, he tried to hand it to her. But only after he nudged her shoulder did she accept it.

"Eleanor," he said softly. "I'm...I'm terribly sorry for giving you such a shock." He knelt before her, setting his hat on the floor by his feet. With both hands free he reached out to gently touch her wrists. "I had expected that the Amish grapevine would break the news to you before I did."

"But...how? Why?" Eleanor cried as he pulled her hands away from her face.

"I believe that my losing the family farm was the catalyst for Lydia's decision to pursue my *bruder*," Edwin said, shifting his weight as he knelt by her knees and kept ahold of her clasped hands. "Apparently Roy had formed an attachment with her while I was away working your *bruder*'s farm." He reached for the handkerchief and gently dabbed at the tears that stained her cheeks. "With no more sons to leave the farm to, my parents had no choice but to accept her once they married."

Eleanor continued to cry.

"Here, Eleanor," he said, once again placing his handkerchief into her hands.

She took it as she stood up and tried to move away from him. Her mind had a difficult time understanding what Edwin was telling her. With all that Lydia had said to her and the way she had shared her secret relationship with Edwin, Eleanor found it hard to believe that Lydia was now the wife of Roy Fisher!

"Now, I want to explain something to you," Edwin said, his voice soft and full of emotion. "While you must think me the worst of men, I need to assure you that my intentions were honorable, Eleanor." He reached out and, forcing her to turn around and face him, took her hands into his once again. "I made that promise to Lydia several years ago, before either of us knew better, and certainly before either of us was ready to marry. It happened so long ago and during our early *rumschpringe* days. I had given her a ride home from a singing, and suddenly she mentioned getting married when we were older. Perhaps it was the idea or just the novelty of the situation, but I said that sounded like a right *gut* idea. To be perfectly honest, Eleanor, I forgot about it."

Eleanor frowned. "You forget that you were engaged?"

"It was nothing more than a farce, child's play by two excited youths during our early days of *rumschpringe*, an excuse to hold hands in the buggy." He raised his hand to his forehead and rubbed his temples with his thumb and fingers. "Just before I left Narvon to help your *bruder* John, I ran into Lydia during the fellowship hour after worship. She was visiting her *aendi*, that Charlotte Peachey character. It seems Lydia had not forgotten, and she was quick to remind me of it. At first I thought she was teasing me about that promise. But when she sent me a letter while I was at your family farm, I realized she was serious. She claimed she had waited all those years for me to honor my promise."

"That's…that's horrible, Edwin," Eleanor managed to say. She couldn't imagine the cruelty of anyone, never mind a woman, preying on a man who held his personal integrity far higher than lifelong happiness.

He nodded his head. The dark circles under his eyes spoke of many sleepless nights. Eleanor could picture him in her mind, pacing the floor and worrying about how to honor a promise made in a thoughtless moment of youthful high spirits. "Short of going back on my word, I had no choice. I…I tried to tell you. I even came here with the intention of telling you, but I simply could not. I had no choice, Eleanor, unless I wanted to embarrass her by telling the bishop and her family of her deception."

"You would have sacrificed your own well-being, Edwin, to honor a promise made in a moment of frivolity? To keep Lydia from feeling humiliation?"

Edwin exhaled. "I cannot explain the torment I felt, Eleanor. My heartache over the situation was stronger than anything I could explain to you of all people, most of all because I knew that my actions would hurt you."

Another tear fell from her eye, and he reached up to wipe it away.

"But I have been freed from that promise. I have a choice now." He stared up at her, his eyes studying every feature of her tearstained face. "And I am here to tell you that my choice has been, and will always be, you, Eleanor Detweiler."

Another sob escaped her throat, and she covered her mouth once again.

He raised his hand and took hers away from her face. Forcing her to look at him, he stared deep into her eyes. "I am going to manage Christian Bechtler's farm, and there is no one I would rather have beside me than you, Eleanor.

That is, of course, if you will have me as your husband. I would like to marry you, and I make that declaration with full awareness and maturity and with every intention and desire of fulfilling it."

She tried to laugh at such a proposal and tried to cover her face so he couldn't see her blotchy cheeks. But he refused to release her hands, smiling at her as he waited for her answer.

"Is that a yes, then?" he asked.

She couldn't speak, so she merely nodded her head and let him pull her into his arms. He embraced her as tightly as he could, holding her against his chest and whispering a soothing noise in her ear. But it didn't help. Her tears continued, but this time not from shock. Instead, she cried from the joy of knowing that after weeks of pain and turmoil, of long days of enduring suffering and heartache, God's plan had played out exactly as He intended.

# ❦ *Epilogue* ❦

THE FRESH BLANKET of snow covered the field in
front of the farmhouse, making the landscape bright
and pristine. Closer to the road the bare tree limbs
looked as if God had painted the top part of them with a
broad brushstroke of white. The clouds were beginning to
break up and patches of blue broke through them, a golden
beam of light stretching from the sky to the earth like a
celestial staircase to the heavens.

Standing on the wraparound porch of the house, a heavy
black wool shawl pulled around her shoulders to keep her
warm, Eleanor gazed out into the field. Her eyes took in the
sight of what she envisioned would be their home for the
next twenty or more years. They had moved into the farmhouse shortly after the new year when the tenants had finished moving out their things and begun the long journey
to Colorado.

It was a pretty house with a warm, open floor plan. The
kitchen and gathering room took up most of the space on
the first floor, although there was a master bedroom under
the staircase. The upstairs had four bedrooms, all of them
empty until they began to expand their family. With its two
full bathrooms and a large mudroom, Eleanor could not
have asked for a better home to start a family.

She smiled when she caught sight of Edwin walking along the fence line, a brown knit cap covering his head so he didn't catch cold from the air that blew from the north. His heavy boots left a small trail in the snow, which was barely visible from where she stood. A few black-and-white cows wandered nearby, most likely wanting to head back to the small stable for the evening milking and feeding. But Edwin paid them no attention as he checked the fence along the border of the property for any breaks or weaknesses.

"Eleanor?"

At the sound of her name, she turned around and greeted her sister. "How are you feeling, Mary Ann? You shouldn't be out here. And with no coat!"

Her sister smiled and placed her hand on her protruding stomach. "The doctor recommended plenty of fresh air and outside walking. Besides, I never did hear that unborn *bopplis* could catch colds now, did you?"

Eleanor gave a soft laugh and opened up the black wool shawl to pull her sister inside. Once they were both wrapped together, she reached down and touched Mary Ann's belly. "Twins. Who would have thought?"

"I don't know who was more surprised," Mary Ann said, "me or Christian."

"Christian," Eleanor said without any hesitation. "Although the word might be *shocked*, not *surprised*."

While Mary Ann had known that she was pregnant for only six weeks, it was the previous week that they learned that she was carrying twins. She had horrific morning sickness that lasted all day and well into the evening. Out of concern for his wife as well as their baby, Christian insisted that she see a doctor. That was when the doctor shared the news that she carried not one but two babies. The news delighted both of them, while causing a few wagging tongues to cease their speculation about the rapid growth of her stomach.

"Shocked, *ja*. And not just Christian, eh? A few others thought they knew something they didn't." Mary Ann shook her head with a renewed sense of anger at how people speculated about her and her pregnancy. "I can't imagine their surprise when the bishop called on them, asking for repentance for gossiping, especially that Widow Jennings."

"The one who gossiped the most suddenly found herself being gossiped about, I reckon."

Mary Ann scoffed. "About time she got a good dose of her own medicine! And I hope it was as bitter tasting as it comes!"

At this comment they both laughed, the happy sound seeming to echo across the fields.

"I can't imagine how big I'll be in five more months!" Mary Ann leaned against Eleanor as she rubbed her stomach again.

"Five? Only that?"

Mary Ann thought for a moment. "April, May, June," she counted off, using her fingers to keep track. "July, August. *Ja*, just over five more months if they're to be born on their due date, the first of September."

They slipped into a comfortable silence, both of them watching Edwin as he approached the fence line closest to the house. He looked up, and on seeing the two women, he raised his hand and waved. Eleanor felt as if her heart expanded, her happiness so great that it filled her from head to toe with joy. After four months of marriage, his beard was beginning to fill in, and while it had taken her some time to get used to it, she thought him just as handsome with it as without.

With a sigh Mary Ann leaned her head against her sister's shoulder. "What fortunate women we are, don't you think? What amazing husbands we have to take care of us." She paused before adding, "Like God took care of us when we both were on our knees. He knew what we needed even when we did not."

Eleanor smiled to herself, overcome with the wisdom of her sister's words. Not only had God led them through the center of a storm, carrying them when they could no longer support themselves, but He had guided them through and delivered them to a better place than either of them could imagine. Not only had they been married within two weeks of each other, but they now resided on the same farm. While Edwin and Eleanor resided in the main house, Christian and Mary Ann resided in the smaller *grossdaadihaus*. Mary Ann's house, a remnant of Christian's days of living as a bachelor, was smaller than Eleanor's, but Mary Ann couldn't have been happier, for the close proximity allowed the two sisters to visit and work together every day.

During the middle of the day, Mary Ann often disappeared to the harness store, spending a few hours helping the workers so they could take their midday dinner break. Afterward, Mary Ann would walk back to the house with Christian so they, too, could sit down and eat the meal she had prepared earlier. Eleanor often saw them walking together side by side, Christian always attentive to whatever Mary Ann was saying. As she watched them, Eleanor would smile, so happy for her sister and the good fortune she had in marrying Christian Bechtler.

Every afternoon the two sisters would visit over coffee and a freshly baked cake or cut-up fruit. Not a day went by that they were not together.

It was the best of circumstances.

"Oh, I'll be so glad when winter is over," Mary Ann said. "The snow seemed nonstop this year, *ja*?"

Eleanor agreed with the last part of Mary Ann's statement but not the first. She had enjoyed the winter, the early sunsets allowing Edwin to visit with her longer in front of the wood-burning stove that heated their large gathering room. Often they sat together, Eleanor curled up by his side with his arm around her shoulders, just listening to the crackle of the wood and enjoying a moment of peace together. While she was not a big fan of the cold, she would miss those evenings, knowing all too well that during the warmer months their days would be longer, filled with more hours to work as well as chores to fill them.

Already, it being the middle of March, the days were beginning to lengthen. This last snowfall, while unexpected and undesired by most, guaranteed that Eleanor could cherish a little more time alone with her husband in the evenings. But as soon as it melted, those special moments of just enjoying each other's presence in the quiet of the house would end.

Of course she knew that she would work beside Edwin, helping to prepare the fields for the early spring planting. However, she suspected that once she told him the good news, he would be less inclined to accept her assistance with some of the harder jobs, such as baling the hay or mucking the stalls, as the summer progressed.

Edwin shut the gate behind him and began to cross the large patch of yard toward the house.

Taking a deep breath, Eleanor took a step back from her sister. "*Ja, vell,* I best get going." She paused for a moment, wanting to share her secret with her sister but knowing she couldn't. Not yet, anyway. But despite wanting to let Edwin know first, Eleanor suspected a little hint wouldn't harm her sister. "I have some *wunderbarr* news to share with my husband."

Mary Ann caught her breath, her eyes glowing and a smile playing on her lips. "I suspect I should be knitting three of everything, then?"

Eleanor gave a little shrug of her shoulder as she pulled away from her sister. "I don't know what you are talking about," Eleanor said, lowering her eyelids in a coy manner.

"Ah, I see," Mary Ann teased. "Then I best let you get over to your husband to share whatever this secretive news might be."

Waiting for her sister to disappear around the side of the porch to where she lived with Christian, Eleanor took a deep breath. All day she had been waiting for this moment, the moment when she would tell Edwin that he was going to be a father. Carefully she held the handrail as she stepped down the three stairs and shuffled through the four inches of snow toward her husband. He greeted her with open arms, glancing around to make certain no one was looking before he gently kissed her lips. When she whispered into his ear, he lifted her into his arms, swinging her around as he held her, their laughter echoing in the quiet of the snowy afternoon.

*Yes,* Eleanor thought as she walked hand-in-hand with Edwin back to the house, *God's plan was sometimes difficult to understand, but as long as a person believed, God's plan would never disappoint.*

*Coming in 2016 from Sarah Price*

# Mount Hope

# ❧ *Prologue* ❧

NOT ONCE IN her short ten years had Fanny thought
of any other place but Colorado as her home.

She loved waking up in the mornings and seeing
the white-capped Sangre de Cristo Mountains from the
small window in the room she shared with her four sisters.
Often she awoke early just so she could stare out the window,
watching the sky change from dark blue to gray to a steely
white as the sun rose to the East and cast shadows on the
mountain. She would lie in her bunk, her face turned to the
window, and wonder what, if anything, lived on top of the
mountain. *One day*, she thought, *I will climb to the top of that
mountain.*

It was a ten-year-old's dream.

Since the Amish community had settled just outside
Westcliffe, Colorado, starting with just a handful of families, they had attracted almost thirty new families to join
their community. Most of them were young couples with
small *kinner*. They made the move west in order to buy farmland that cost a quarter of the price for similar acreage in
Pennsylvania. For Fanny's *daed*, that meant he could finally
buy the larger farm of his dreams to provide for his family.

With the help of the *g'may*, he built a three-bedroom
house in the San Luis Valley at the base of those beautiful

mountains. Everyone admired the view, remarking on how the snow at the top of the mountain range contrasted sharply with the beautiful, lush green evergreen trees at its base that trickled into the green valley where Fanny's parents settled on thirty-two acres of land. Yet, as far as Fanny knew, despite the majestic beauty of those mountains, not one member of their church district had ever built farther than the tree line.

From the other room, Fanny heard her father starting to move around. Clearly it was time for morning chores. With a sigh, Fanny shut her eyes and waited until she heard the creak of her parents' bedroom door and her father's footsteps heading to the kitchen. She knew that if she waited three minutes (not two and not four), she would hear her mother's footsteps next. While the baby was still nursing, her father awoke earlier to fetch his own coffee. It would be ready by the time *Maem* joined him in the kitchen.

Usually Fanny waited until she heard her older *bruder*, William, stirring from the boys' room before she slipped down from her top bunk and, in the cold of the morning, shivered out of her nightgown in order to dress for the day. She didn't like going into the kitchen unless William was already there. His presence felt like an added layer of protection to Fanny, especially in the days following the birth of baby Ruth.

"You up, then?"

Fanny lifted her head, her long brown hair tousled and covering her face. She pushed it back and looked at the door. To her surprise, it wasn't *Maem*; it was William. "*Ja*. Are you?"

He gave her a silly look. "No, goose! I'm just standing here talking to you in my sleep!"

She giggled and slid out from under the quilt, careful not to wake her younger sister Susan who shared the bunk with her.

"You best hurry," he said. "I heard *Maem* and *Daed* talking again about Pennsylvania."

Fanny stopped herself from dropping to the floor. Her heart began to beat rapidly. "Oh, help!" she whispered. She felt frozen in place and not just from the chilly autumn air.

"Hurry!" he whispered one more time before following his own advice and scurrying back to his own bedroom to change.

For two months Fanny and William had watched their parents whispering about something. They did not know what it was, but they sensed that it involved them as well. More often than not, *Maem* and *Daed* would glance in the direction of their two oldest children when they did. Several times William heard them talking about their other family back in Lancaster County and would pinch Fanny to stop fidgeting so that she wouldn't distract him from eavesdropping.

In the barn they would speculate what their parents were talking about, and they could only come up with one thing: the family was going to move back to Pennsylvania and give up on the whole idea of farming in Colorado.

"What else could it be?" William had asked her just last week, abnegation in his voice as they mucked the small dairy shed.

The higher altitude of Westcliffe had made it next to impossible to maintain a large dairy herd. The paddock grass was not rich enough to sustain the number of cows their father needed to make enough money for sustaining the family. And the season for growing hay was too short to supply enough forage for the winters. Little by little, the herd had begun to shrink with one cow after another sold or butchered until there were only ten cows left. And then it came: the drought.

Fanny had responded with a sneeze, wiping her nose under her sleeve.

"You sick again?" William had asked, forgetting about Pennsylvania for the moment. "You need a better jacket, Fanny Price! Winter isn't even here yet! You'll catch your death from it, that's for sure and certain!"

But Fanny had ignored him, knowing only too well that she would not get a new jacket that winter. She didn't complain about it to her parents, knowing that they both had enough on their minds trying to figure out how to feed their nine children on their thirty-two acre plot of land, purchased eight years ago based on the bishop's encouragement. With such glowing reports of the slower-paced lifestyle and lack of intruding tourists, they wasted no time deciding to move from Gordonville, Pennsylvania, to join the growing community. The choice had been an easy one for their parents.

With their two children, three-year-old William and two-year-old Fanny, the Prices sold what little they had and moved out West. The money they brought with them went for a down payment on the thirty-two acres farm. After all, the Prices had reasoned, thirty-two acres of land in Colorado was an awful lot better than just barely being able to buy twelve in Gordonville. No one could live as a farmer on such a small piece of land, and larger farms were outrageously unaffordable to most young Amish couples.

Fanny knew the story well; she had heard it so often.

Her parents arrived, her mother gave birth to twins, Jerome and Peter, and her father realized that not all land is equal. Too many rocks in the soil and the higher altitude made farming almost impossible. The shorter season did not help either. For a man familiar with growing and harvesting corn and tobacco, this realization did not sit well. *Daed* was a very talented and efficient laborer when it came to the technical part of growing and harvesting, but he had given very little thought to the fact that the weather and soil conditions in Westcliffe were quite different from those in Gordonville.

While *Daed* struggled to make ends meet, *Maem* dealt with four children under the age of three. A year later another baby arrived, and two years after that another double blessing. By the time baby Ruth arrived, the ninth (and, it was hoped, final addition to the family), a hard tension seemed to linger over the Price farm and its household.

Clearly decisions had to be made and the only logical one—the only one, in fact—was for the family to cut their losses, sell the three-bedroom log house and barn, and return to Gordonville. At least they had family there who could help them start over.

Neither William nor Fanny thought there was any shame in that. In fact, they were both rather excited about the prospect. The Amish community in Westcliffe was so spread out that they usually didn't see another Amish person for days, even weeks. *Maem* homeschooled them since the schoolhouse was too far away for daily journeys, and church service was often missed since they had only one buggy. Fanny and her mother took turns missing it so the others could attend.

Yes, Lancaster County seemed like the answer to everyone's prayers.

So, when William and Fanny slipped into the kitchen, quietly joining their parents at the kitchen table where two cups of hot chocolate waited for them, their parents' announcement came as quite a surprise.

"Fanny girl, you need to pack up your things," her father said, staring at her over the top of his coffee cup.

Confused, Fanny blinked, her brown eyes looking first at her father, then at her mother. If she first thought she had misunderstood *Daed*, when she saw that her mother was avoiding her questioning gaze, Fanny knew she had not.

It was William who spoke up, breaking the silence with the one question that lingered in the air. "You mean all of us, *Daed*, ain't so?"

"*Nee*." *Daed*'s response was curt and emotionless. He too did not look at his oldest daughter. "Just Fanny."

Fanny's hands began to shake, and she spilled hot chocolate on the table. Normally her mother would snap at her, but this time she merely pushed a dirty dish cloth in Fanny's direction.

"Where's Fanny going, *Daed*?" William had always pushed the limits with their father, and for a second Fanny feared William would find himself out behind the wood pile having a man-to-man "talk" with *Daed*.

But not this time.

"Ohio."

Once again Fanny thought she did not hear her father properly. Ohio?

"Ohio?" William cried out. "What's in Ohio? Our family's in Pennsylvania!"

*Maem* took a deep breath and, without raising her head, looked at her son. "William!" She cautioned.

It surprised Fanny that her father did not reprimand William's insolence. Questioning their parents was simply not something the children did.

"Your *maem* has family in Ohio. Fanny's going to move in with *Maem*'s *schwester* for a while."

Fanny glanced at William, the color drained from her cheeks. *Maem* had a sister in Ohio?

"Naomi is married to the bishop," *Maem* contributed. "Their children are grown. And she lives on the property of my other *schwester*, Martha." For the first time, *Maem* forced a small smile at Fanny. "She has two *dochders* just about your age, Fanny. And two older stepsons from her husband's first marriage."

"You'll help them with their basket-making business."

"Baskets?" Fanny asked, more out of disbelief than as an actual question.

"They could use your help."

Fanny wasn't so certain this was true. Not once had she heard about these two sisters and their basket making. Nor did she know anything about basket making. Fanny suspected she was being sent away so her parents could provide for her other siblings.

William shook his head. "You can't send Fanny without the rest of us!"

*Maem*'s hand fluttered to the back of her neck. Fanny stared at her, silently begging her mother to say something—anything!—that would indicate that this whole discussion was a mistake. But as she looked at her mother, she saw how tired she looked. While she had only just turned thirty-two, she looked almost fifty years old. Her hair was already thinning and turning gray at the roots, barely visible beneath her soft white prayer *kapp*.

"Please, William," she said in a soft, pleading voice. "This is hard enough as it is."

"I don't want to leave," Fanny whispered, her dark eyes wide and frightened. "Don't send me away."

"You both know we are struggling," *Maem* replied, once again averting her eyes. "Just can't make do out here no more."

"But I thought we would *all* move back to Lancaster!" William cried.

"Would if we could," *Maem* said. "But we've too much money invested in this place. Fanny's going to return and help out the *aendis*. My older *schwester*, Naomi, offered to take her in, her *kinner* being all grown already and all. That will help us all."

Neither Fanny nor William remembered Naomi, but they had certainly listened to *Maem* read the sporadic letters written to her by her oldest sister. Her husband had been selected by lot to become a preacher, and within two years he was elected the bishop of his church district. Naomi seemed to see this as a sign of divine appointment rather than lot. She often wrote disparagingly of the situation that her younger sister had fallen into when the Prices moved to Colorado. It wasn't surprising to Fanny that Naomi had poked her nose into the family business. That seemed to be what she did best.

With a ten-year age difference between Martha and Naomi, it often surprised Fanny to learn from her mother that Martha and Naomi were just as inseparable as two peas in a pod. She simply could not imagine that she'd ever have *that* type of friendship with baby Ruth, especially since her sister Susie was only two years younger than her.

William put his arm protectively around Fanny's shoulders. "I won't let you send our Fanny away!"

Finally their father had had enough. He slammed his hand, open palmed, onto the top of the table and in a loud voice exclaimed, "That's enough, William!" Then, his eyes narrowing as he scowled in the direction of his son, he added, "'Sides, your turn will come next week."

William's arm stiffened, and Fanny squeezed his knee under the table.

"What's that supposed to mean, *Daed*?"

*Daed* remained emotionless. "William, you're going to have to go to your *onkle* Aaron's in Lancaster County."

At this announcement, William jumped to his feet.

"Sit down!" *Daed* commanded, his voice booming, which made Fanny shrink further into her seat. "You'll be learning the carpenter trade from my *bruder* Aaron and returning here to help me when you turn sixteen."

At their father's words, equally as surprising as what he had said earlier about her being sent to Ohio, Fanny felt William's arm drop from her shoulders. He slid his hand under the table and sought out hers. When he found it, he squeezed her fingers so tight that she thought they might start turning blue.

"When shall *I* return, *Maem*?" she asked, somehow finding the courage to speak up.

But her mother did not answer her. The baby began to cry from the cradle at the foot of their bed in the master bedroom, and she jumped up, hurrying to fetch Ruth. Her father merely gave her a look and advised her to pack and pack quickly, for the driver would be arriving within the hour and it would be best for the younger siblings if she were gone before they awoke.

Without further discussion, *Daed* stood up and gestured for William to join him outside to start on the chores. Fanny watched as her older *bruder* stood up and slowly followed his father outside, pausing at the door to cast a long look over his shoulder at Fanny. And then, after a sharp word from *Daed*, William turned and, with his head hanging down, disappeared into the lingering darkness of morning.

Alone and stunned, Fanny somehow managed to make her way into the bedroom and in a robotic fashion took her three dresses and nightgown from the hooks that hung from the wall. She folded them and placed them into a small canvas bag along with her few toiletries, undergarments, and stockings. When she finished, there was still room for more. The only problem was that she had nothing more to take.

# ❧ *Glossary* ❧

*ach vell*—an expression similar to *Oh well*

*aendi*—aunt

*boppli*—baby

*bruder*—brother

*daed*—father

*danke*—thank you

*dochder*—daughter

*Englische*—non-Amish people

*Englischer*—a non-Amish person

*esse*—eat

*fraa*—wife

*ferhoodled*—confused, mixed up

*g'may*—church district

*grossdaadi*—grandfather

*grossdaadihaus*—small house attached to the main dwelling

*grossmammi*—grandmother

*gut morgan*—good morning

*haus*—house

*ja*—yes

*kapp*—prayer cap worn by Amish girls and women

*kinner*—children

*kum*—come

*maem*—mother

*Mammi*—used as a title for grandmother

*mayhaps*—maybe

Sarah Price

*nee*—no
*onkle*—uncle
*rumschpringe*—period of "running-around" time for youths
*schwester*—sister
*vell*—well
*wunderbarr*—wonderful

# ❧ *Other Books by Sarah Price* ❧

### THE AMISH CLASSICS SERIES
*First Impressions*
*The Matchmaker*
*Second Chances*

### THE AMISH OF LANCASTER SERIES
*Fields of Corn*
*Hills of Wheat*
*Pastures of Faith*
*Valley of Hope*

### THE AMISH OF EPHRATA SERIES
*The Tomato Patch*
*The Quilting Bee*
*The Hope Chest*
*The Clothes Line*

### THE PLAIN FAME SERIES (WATERFALL PRESS)
*Plain Fame*
*Plain Change*
*Plain Again*
*Plain Return*
*Plain Choice*

### OTHER AMISH FICTION BOOKS
*Secret Sister* (Realms)
*An Amish Buggy Ride* (Waterfall Press)

*An Empty Cup* (Waterfall Press)
*An Amish Christmas Carol*
*Amish Circle Letters*
*Amish Circle Letters II*
*A Christmas Gift for Rebecca*
*Priscilla's Story*

For a complete listing of books, please visit the author's website at www.sarahpriceauthor.com.

# ❧ *About Sarah Price* ❧

T HE PREISS FAMILY emigrated from Europe in 1705, settling in Pennsylvania with the area's first wave of Mennonite families. Sarah Price has always respected and honored her ancestors through exploration and research into her family's history and their religion. At nineteen she befriended an Amish family and lived on their farm.

Twenty-five years later, Sarah Price splits her time between her home outside of New York City and Lancaster County, Pennsylvania, where she retreats to reflect, write, and reconnect with her Amish friends and Mennonite family.

Contact the author at *sarah@sarahpriceauthor.com*. Visit her weblog at http://sarahpriceauthor.com or on Facebook at www.facebook.com/fansofsarahprice.

# CONNECT WITH US!

**CHARISMA HOUSE**

( Spiritual Growth )

Facebook.com/CharismaHouse

@CharismaHouse

Instagram.com/CharismaHouseBooks

## SILOAM

( Health )

Pinterest.com/CharismaHouse

## REALMS

( Fiction )

Facebook.com/RealmsFiction